ALL
THESE
WARRIORS

ALL THESE WARRIORS

BY **AMY TINTERA**

HOUGHTON MIFFLIN HARCOURT
BOSTON NEW YORK

hmhbooks.com

The text was set in Fairfield LT Std.
Cover design by Sharismar Rodriguez
Interior design by Sharismar Rodriguez

Library of Congress Cataloging-in-Publication Data is available.
ISBN 978-0-358-01241-2

Manufactured in the United States of America
DOC 10 9 8 7 6 5 4 3 2 1
4500825705

Part One

DEAD

1

A HEAVY BODY SLAMMED INTO MY SIDE, NEARLY KNOCKING ME off balance. I spun around, quickly regained my footing, and slashed my machete through the air.

The blade bounced off the scrab's thick, gray, nearly impenetrable hide. I tried again, aiming for the softer skin under its chin. It roared as I succeeded, snapping at me with its sharp teeth. I withdrew my blade and stepped back. The scrab crumpled to the ground and went still. I jumped over its body, dodging the spreading pool of blood, and jogged out of the alley.

It was dark, the roads still damp from the light rain that had fallen earlier. The street was deserted except for the bodies of several dead scrabs. This section of north London had seen a lot of scrab attacks in recent weeks, and all the stores were deserted. One shop had a caved-in roof, the result of a scrab damaging something important structurally when it shot up from the earth. That whole side of the block was roped off with police tape, signs posted to warn people of the danger of going inside.

Grunts and a thump came from my left. I broke into a run and rounded the corner.

Maddie had two bloody blades in either hand, long blond ponytail swinging as she fought off a scrab. It was a huge one, well over six feet tall, with claws so long that two of them had broken off. An older scrab. You could often tell by the length of their claws.

She sliced her blade across its stomach and moved back as it fell. She never needed help with just one scrab, no matter how big or old. It made a *thump* sound as it hit the ground, followed by a gurgle from deep in its throat. She kicked it to make sure it was dead. No response.

She turned, spotted me, and motioned for me to follow her. We took off down the street.

"Noah?" she yelled.

"Yeah!" His voice came from somewhere nearby, but I couldn't see him. *"We're nearly clear here."*

"Laila?" Maddie yelled.

"On Weston Street!" Laila called, also out of sight. "We could use some help!"

"I've got it!" Patrick yelled. I spotted him when we turned, his tall, thin frame racing around the corner onto Weston Street. Maddie and I followed. Laila was fighting off a scrab at the end of the block, and Dorsey was a few feet away, taking on two at once. Patrick jumped in to help him.

Laila's scrab staggered back suddenly, a blade sticking out of its neck. She leapt forward, grabbing the handle of the machete and plunging it deeper.

Maddie glanced over at Patrick and Dorsey, who were also finishing off their scrabs. She sheathed her machete and walked back to me.

"Should I make spaghetti or roast chicken for dinner?" she asked. "It's my turn."

"Oh god, neither," I said. "I thought we decided to take you out of the cooking rotation."

"What? Why?"

"Because your cooking is awful, Maddie."

"It is not."

"Yes, it is," Priya said, and I turned to see her walking toward us, pulling off the leather body armor we all wore to protect our arms. She brushed some dirt off her light brown skin and adjusted her pink knit hat.

"Your chicken isn't so much roasted as blackened!" Patrick called. He was wiping blood off his ax.

Maddie flipped him off. He chuckled.

"You have other talents, but cooking is not one of them!" Noah yelled, still out of sight. "Heads up, just lost a scrab. Headed your way."

The scrab galloped around the corner, abruptly changing course when it spotted us. It ran on all fours, teeth bared as it headed for us.

"Seriously?" Priya said, making an annoyed sound. "I thought we got them all."

"I've got it," I said, stepping forward. I waited as the scrab drew closer to us, drool flying from its sharp, bared teeth. I'd had one of those teeth lodged in my skin more than once, and I could feel the memory of it every time a scrab opened its mouth.

"Dinner or the scrab?" Noah called.

"Both!"

I darted out of the way as the scrab approached, letting it pass me. It skidded to a stop, confused, and when it turned, I drove my blade in its side. It roared as it fell. I pulled my machete from its side and stuck it quickly in its neck. Some of the scrabs had learned to play dead recently, so we always made sure.

This one was definitely dead. I shook my machete, trying to get rid of some of the blood.

"We're clear here!" Noah called.

"Tell me again why we stopped wearing the earpieces," Priya said, turning in a circle like she was trying to find where Noah's voice was coming from. "It was much easier to talk when we had those."

"Because we broke them all within a month," Maddie said. "Same reason we don't wear body cameras anymore." She walked to the end of the street and peered around. "Clear here too!" She headed back to me. "I can help you, at least. With dinner, I mean."

"That's all right," I said, giving her an amused look. "I know you hate cooking."

"I really do."

"I'll help." It was Edan's voice, and I turned to see him walking around the corner with Noah and Dorsey. He'd pushed up the sleeves of his coat — probably to remove his armor — revealing the tattoos on both arms. I smiled at him.

Maddie and I headed into the street to join them. Patrick and Laila dodged dead scrabs as they made their way to us.

"A cleanup crew should already be on the way," Maddie said, glancing at her phone.

"You should maybe tell them to bring an extra truck," Dorsey said, surveying the mess. He ruffled his curly hair with one hand.

"Oh, dude, I have bad news for you," Patrick said with a laugh, his gaze on Dorsey's hair.

Dorsey looked at his bloody hand. "I have scrab guts in my hair, don't I?"

"You sure do," Patrick said.

"Every time," Dorsey grumbled, trying to shake the remaining guts off his hand.

"We don't have any people to drive an extra van," Maddie said. "It's hard enough to staff cleanup crew these days. We're going to have to start doing it ourselves soon."

Dorsey sighed. Maddie and I exchanged a look. I'd gone over the recruit list with her earlier today, and she was right—we didn't have the people.

A white van turned the corner and came to a stop, headlights catching some scrab parts in the middle of the street.

"Let's get out of here," Maddie said.

A bulky man stepped out of the van, his expression stricken as he looked from us to the dead scrabs. He was a new recruit, part of the group that had joined last month. Another recruit hopped out of the passenger's side.

Maddie turned and started walking in the direction of our van, parked at the other end of the block. The team followed her.

"Holy crap," the new recruit said from behind me. "Did you guys take on all these scrabs yourselves? Was anyone injured? Or killed?"

"Nope," I said, smiling at him over my shoulder. "Still alive."

2

WE LEFT SCRAB CLEANUP TO THE NEW RECRUITS, AND PATRICK drove the team home to central London. A few weeks after Grayson died, Maddie bought an old, deserted hostel and turned it into the official London home for the St. John teams.

It had been a tight squeeze in the hostel at first. Maddie got bunk beds and shoved as many as possible into the rooms, and she'd still had to pay for some recruits to stay in other hostels around the city.

It wasn't such a tight squeeze these days. In fact, there were a lot of empty beds. Recruits started dropping out after Grayson's death, and it had only gotten worse in the last few months. Even after Maddie brought in a new group of recruits last month, we still had plenty of space.

I shared a double room with Maddie now.

Neither of us was the decorating type, so our room looked mostly the same as when we'd first moved in — two twin beds, two dressers, a closet, and a desk with a chair. Priya and Laila's room was bright and colorful, with posters on the walls and artsy lamps on the dressers.

I'd looked at some posters in a shop a few weeks ago, but I was sort of afraid to just pick something, because I would inevitably pick the stupid art. The art that was meant for a dentist's office.

As for Maddie, she just didn't care. I asked her once if we should decorate, and she'd shrugged and said I could do whatever I wanted. *I don't need to hang my personality on a wall,* she'd said. I liked that about her. She didn't just act like she didn't care what most people thought of her, she genuinely couldn't care less.

But even with the blank beige walls, the ugly wooden furniture, and the creaky floors, it was starting to feel a little like the first home I'd ever had.

I showered and changed, pulling a sweatshirt out of my basket of clean clothes. It was late November, technically still fall, but it already felt like winter to me. It was cold and rainy most of the time. At least I didn't have to deal with the scorching hot temperatures of the Texas summer. I didn't really mind it. I preferred the cold.

I glanced at the closet. I'd bought some new clothes over the summer, but my wardrobe was still limited. I was going to need to buy some more winter clothes soon. The jacket I'd been wearing through the fall was starting to feel a little too thin.

I could spare some cash for it. Maddie had increased the stipends when we started losing recruits after Grayson's death. Then she increased them again and gave bonuses to all the original, experienced recruits who stayed. It hadn't slowed the defections, but it certainly made those of us who stayed happy. I'd actually saved up a good amount of money.

Maddie walked into the room as I was slipping my feet into my shoes. She shrugged out of her jacket and tossed it on the bed.

"You're sure you don't want my help with dinner?" She grinned.

"I may be a terrible cook, but I get dinner done faster than anyone else on the team."

"I think we're going for quality over speed," I said, returning the smile. I stood and grabbed my sweatshirt off the bed.

"Did you buy a new sports bra?" Maddie asked.

"Yes." I gave her a weird look. "Why?"

"Your boobs look great."

I bit back a laugh. "Thanks. It was really expensive, so that's actually nice to hear."

"I know your struggles to find good sports bras. I didn't want you to think I hadn't noticed."

"That's very sweet of you."

Maddie's phone rang, and she pressed Accept on the video call. "Hey, Mom."

"Hi, honey. Why is there blood on your neck?"

Maddie quickly covered the small spot of scrab blood with her hand. "Uh, it's nothing. Say hi to Clara." She turned the phone around to face me as she tried to wipe the blood off.

Nicole smiled at me. "Hi, Clara." She was a pretty blond woman who looked very much like Maddie. "Why is there blood on Maddie's neck?"

"Hey, Nicole. Don't worry, it's just scrab blood."

"You know that never makes me feel better." She gave me a look that I could only describe as a "mom look." It caused a heavy feeling in my chest.

Maddie turned the phone back around to face her. "She's just saying it's not my blood. Because I'm always careful. Not a scratch."

I rolled my eyes at the outrageous lie. Maddie, like all of us, got injured pretty frequently. She was still healing from a nasty scrab claw puncture in her side from last week.

"I'm headed out to make dinner," I said, and Maddie turned the screen around again. Nicole waved to me.

"Bye, hon."

I said goodbye and stepped into the hallway, nodding at Priya and Laila as I passed by their room. Priya and Laila had the room across from us, with Dorsey and Edan next door, and Patrick and Noah across from them.

I walked up one floor to the small kitchen. The hostel had two kitchens, a big one downstairs and this small one upstairs. Meals were provided for the recruits, but it was mostly just sandwiches and protein bars, so we occasionally cooked a real meal.

Edan was already in the kitchen, studying a bag of potatoes. He was also freshly showered, his dark hair still damp. He wore long sleeves pushed up to reveal the tree tattoo on his left forearm.

I brushed my hand to the tattoo on my left wrist. It was my first, and so far only, tattoo. All of team seven had gotten matching tattoos that Laila designed for us — an artistic version of the St. John logo that was on all our uniforms.

Edan looked up and smiled. His green eyes sparkled beneath the lights, even though I could see the exhaustion beneath the surface. Edan was nearly always tired. I hadn't noticed it about him at first, because he'd dealt with insomnia for most of his life, and he was good at hiding it. He also drank obscene amounts of coffee.

"These haven't gone bad yet," he said, holding up the potatoes. "We could make mashed potatoes to go with the chicken."

"Sure."

He pulled out his phone. "I should probably look up how to make mashed potatoes."

"Minor detail."

I grabbed a head of garlic and a cutting board. Edan found a peeler and began peeling potatoes over a bowl next to me.

"Hey, if you have time tomorrow, you want to come shopping with me? I need advice on a winter coat."

Edan looked up, amused. "You need fashion advice?"

I bumped my shoulder against his. "I need warmth advice. I don't know what to get. Back in Dallas, I just threw an old jacket over a hoodie and ran inside as fast as possible."

"Just admit that you think I have fabulous fashion sense and you're jealous." He stepped back, gesturing down to his black sweatpants—with a hole in one knee—and faded pink shirt. Or maybe it was a white shirt that had accidentally been washed with something red.

"You are truly the epitome of fashion," I said dryly. He laughed.

Though he was actually pulling that look off. I returned my attention to the cutting board. "I just need something besides my team jacket."

"Sure. I could use a new coat too." He turned and grabbed a piece of chocolate from the bag on the counter behind us, offering one to me. I took one and popped it in my mouth.

"My tía, in Mexico, always said that most American chocolate was garbage," I said. "I never really had much to compare it to, but after being here for six months, I have to admit that she's kind of right."

Edan glanced up at me. "Have you heard from her again? Your aunt?"

"Yeah, she emails pretty often. And I've talked to her a few times. She even invited me to come visit her."

He smiled. "Yeah?"

"Yeah. I told her I was probably going to be over here for the foreseeable future, but maybe one day." That was true, but I'd also felt awkward at the prospect of going to see Tía Julia. I really didn't know her that well.

But she did seem interested in having a relationship with me, which was more than I could say for my own mother. And if I stayed in touch with her, I could also stay in touch with Mom's extended family. I had cousins and some other relatives in Mexico.

"I've always wanted to go to Mexico," he said. "And South America. And not just because they've never had much of a scrab problem down there."

"That is a bonus, though."

"It is." He grabbed another potato. "You've been to Mexico once, right?"

"Yeah, Guanajuato, a few years ago, when Mom took me to visit family there. Tía Julia tried to get us to stay permanently, actually."

"Because she knew about your dad?"

"That's what I always assumed. They fought about it, but they were both speaking Spanish—and talking really fast—so I couldn't really understand. I would have agreed, if Mom had asked my opinion. I could have finally learned Spanish." I smiled at him.

"I think you'd like Guanajuato. A lot of the streets are so narrow that you can't drive down them. You have to walk a lot."

"That does sound like my kind of place."

Edan's phone buzzed, and his smile abruptly faded.

"What?" I asked. "Did something happen?"

"It's nothing, just a news alert about Julian." He rubbed at his eyes with his knuckles and put his phone on the counter. "It's the interview he did yesterday. I'll watch it later."

"Turn it on, it's fine."

He hesitated. "You sure?"

"Yeah. I've been meaning to watch that one anyway."

I used to have news alerts turned on for Julian too—hoping for a sudden arrest or news of new evidence being uncovered—but I'd had to turn them off a few months ago. Julian had acquired a small but very dedicated group of fans after Grayson's death, and they all hated me. I didn't need to read every blog and Reddit thread calling me a crazy bitch.

I'd stuck to the facts in the video we made the night Julian murdered Grayson. I told everyone exactly what he had told me—that MDG was training scrabs to build some kind of army and shipping them back to the United States. I explained that we'd stopped the shipment, but we didn't know if there were others. I told them that the bruise on my cheek was from Julian, that he'd killed two police officers and Grayson in a fit of rage, and he was directly responsible for the deaths of our teammates Archer, Zoe, and Gage.

Julian denied everything, and he and his high-powered lawyers took every opportunity to remind people that we'd dated.

The fact that I'd been in a relationship with Julian for all of three weeks made everything I said suspect, apparently.

And, as the police explained, they needed more witnesses, and no one else had seen Julian direct scrabs to kill the police officers. My word wasn't good enough, it turned out. But all of team seven believed me, and that was what was important. None of them had been there to hear Julian confess, and for all they knew, I'd made it up to get back at him or to impress everyone (*Are we sure she wasn't just trying to get attention?* one news anchor had suggested several times). But all seven members of my team had been unwavering in their support, publicly and privately.

As for Grayson, the gun Julian had used to shoot him had actually been one of Webb's, and Julian claimed he only grabbed it after Webb died, to kill a scrab. The fact that Grayson had used explosives to blow up part of a private residence had not helped matters. Julian told police that the scene was chaotic and he could understand why we'd gotten confused. In the end, prosecutors decided that a conviction was unlikely and they declined to bring charges. Julian walked free.

The law enforcement officers (British and American) we were in contact with claimed that they were still investigating Julian, as well as MDG. They just had to build a solid case based on evidence, not the word of one teenage girl. A teenage girl who had been photographed kissing Julian just days before she claimed he was a dangerous murderer.

It did not look great, admittedly.

As for training scrabs, MDG had flat out denied it for a while, before finally conceding that perhaps some of their employees had been working on programs without their knowledge. They'd vowed to cooperate with the police to get to the bottom of it. I didn't believe for a minute that the higher-ups at MDG didn't know about everything, but at least it seemed like their training program was going to fail before it ever fully got off the ground.

That's what I'd thought, anyway. Then Julian started making the rounds on cable news a couple months ago.

Edan pressed Play on the clip and propped his phone up on the counter. Julian was sitting with a blond woman, his favorite reporter, a woman who clearly found him charming and didn't ask particularly hard questions.

He always looked sharp and put together when he did these interviews — he was in a flawless pressed suit with a shiny red tie, and his brown hair was perfectly combed. He was undeniably good-looking. But I knew him well enough to see that he was fraying around the edges. He had dark circles that even makeup couldn't cover, apparently. He looked like he might have lost some weight. His cheekbones were more prominent today.

"Today we're discussing the scrab defense movement, which has been gaining serious traction in recent months. I'm here with Julian Montgomery," the anchor said. "Former second-in-command of the St. John teams, he's been employed by the Monster Defense Group since shortly after the death of Grayson St. John. Julian, you've become an advocate for scrab training since seeing trained scrabs in action in London, correct?"

"I wouldn't say I'm an advocate," he said with a smile. "But I have seen the reality of what these trained scrabs can do. I work with Roman Mitchell in the security division — I believe you had him on yesterday—and our job is to protect clients from scrabs. Protecting humans from scrabs will always be the primary goal of the security division. And we have to train our people to fight back against trained scrabs, since they may encounter them while protecting a client."

"Roman said that MDG is only focused on protecting clients from scrabs at this time, but you've spoken out in favor of MDG, and possibly other groups, embracing trained scrabs."

"I have. Listen, we can't ignore what's happening in the world right now. The trained scrabs exist, whether we like it or not. We need to get serious about protecting ourselves and our country or suffer the consequences."

"And that's what this group—the Scrab Defense League— is arguing, right? They say that trained scrabs are weapons and should be covered under Second Amendment rights."

"They do," Julian said. "I'm not a member of the Scrab Defense League, but I have been in contact with them, and they're just trying to adjust to a changing world. The right to own a gun has always been important in this country, but what do you do when you have an enemy who is nearly bulletproof? I can tell you from experience that most people aren't equipped to fight these things, regardless of the weapons at their disposal. So basically, the league is saying, what counts as the right to bear arms? If we're being attacked by scrabs, shouldn't citizens be allowed to defend themselves? And if the most effective means of protecting yourself is with a trained scrab, why shouldn't we be allowed to do that?"

"But wouldn't it make more sense to eradicate scrabs

completely? Shouldn't we be focusing our resources on killing them, not training them?"

"Oh, absolutely," Julian said. "In an ideal world, we would just kill all these things. But we're not in an ideal world. It's been ten years, and the US may have mostly gotten our scrab problem under control, but these things are still around in many parts of the world. Look at the St. John teams. They're out there in London every day, killing scrabs left and right, and there are more, not less."

Edan looked at me, brow furrowed. "Isn't that a blatant lie?"

"Yes," I said. "Our data shows a thirty percent reduction in scrab activity in the greater London area over the past two months. The London police data shows a nearly forty percent reduction. And the government recently released a report that shows a twenty-three percent drop across all of England compared to this time last year."

His lips twitched up like he was amused.

"What?"

"You just know all that off the top of your head. It's impressive."

"Oh." My cheeks warmed. "It's my job."

"You're good at it."

"Thank you."

". . . and you do have to consider the bigger picture," Julian was saying. "The people who were working on scrab training were doing it with military defense in mind. We can evolve and embrace scrab training, or we can let another country do it first and suffer the consequences."

"Same shit, different day," Edan said with a sigh, clicking his phone so the screen went black. "I've heard enough."

"Same."

I'd heard way more than enough from Julian.

3

THE NEXT MORNING, THERE WAS AN EMAIL FROM JULIAN IN MY inbox.

I moaned, dropping my phone on the bed. Maddie, who was already up (she was always up), turned away from the mirror as she finished securing her ponytail.

"What?" she asked.

I held out my phone to her. "Julian."

"Again? He just emailed you two days ago."

I moaned again, pulling the covers up over my face. She took my phone and was quiet for a moment as she read.

"Same shit," she said. I pushed the sheets away from my face, and she dropped the phone on the bed beside me. "He misses you, he's sorry, you're the best girl in the world, blah blah blah."

I sighed, picking up my phone and glancing briefly at the email before putting it in the Julian folder. A folder that was getting quite large.

He'd starting emailing me a few weeks after he left. The first time I saw his name in my inbox, I thought I'd find an angry, hateful message, but it had been an apology. A vague apology, one that didn't include confessing to murdering several people, but still, an apology.

And then there had been another. And another. Some were

long, rambling emails just telling me about his life; others were short and sad. He was clearly lonely. He'd built me up to be some kind of savior. The only girl who had ever understood him.

He kept emailing even though I never responded. He even tried contacting me through Instagram for a while, until I deleted my account. At least he didn't have my new phone number. I could only imagine the number of texts I'd get from him.

I'd thought about sending a one-line response to his emails — *Stop contacting me, asshole* — but it seemed best to just ignore him. I'd seen what happened when Julian flew into a rage. People had died. I was hoping he'd just give up one day.

I hadn't told anyone on the team except for Maddie. I was tired of talking about Julian, and everyone had still been so upset when the emails first started. I'd just wanted to stop talking about him. Maddie had agreed to keep it between us.

"I'm making the right choice by never responding, right?" I asked.

"I think so." She grabbed her coat. "But you know who could really help with that?"

"Maddie, don't."

"A therapist. Super helpful with so many things."

"You're relentless," I said. Maddie had gotten a few psychiatrists for the team after Grayson's death and had pushed me to go. I went once, talked awkwardly about my dad, and didn't feel compelled to do it again. Maddie had been pestering me to go again for months.

She smiled at me and pulled the door open. "I'll see you down there."

I climbed out of bed with a sigh. Julian sure knew how to ruin a morning. I'd considered changing my email address, but part of me was hoping he'd slip up one day and say something I could send to the police. At least the emails weren't mean. Half the time, they were just sad.

I pulled on my workout clothes and met the team in the hostel lobby to walk to the gym. We had our routine down—we started every day at the gym, then went back to the hostel for a quick breakfast before heading out to whichever area of London Maddie had assigned to us that day.

Noah fell into step beside me, typing something on his phone. The scar that ran down one side of his face, from forehead to chin, had healed but left a permanent mark. He said he didn't mind, that it made him look like a badass. It did, actually.

"Clara, I'm going to need current scrab data for London to refute a statement Julian made yesterday," he said.

"Yeah, I saw it. I'll send it to you this afternoon."

Maddie, who'd been walking with Patrick ahead of us, looked at us over her shoulder. "Do I want to know what that asshole said this time?"

"No," Noah and I said together.

"We're just going to have to work harder," Maddie said. "I want the scrab numbers so low that they can't lie about them."

I glanced back at Priya and Laila. We'd just been talking yesterday about how a lot of recruits needed a break. *We* needed a break. We hunted scrabs seven days a week. Most of the teams did, and I wasn't sure if it was an effective strategy.

If I was being honest, I wasn't sure that any of this was an effective strategy. Grayson had built these teams to help, to let people from all over the world join the scrab fight, but it was becoming clear that he'd never had a long-term plan. France had kicked us out of the country pretty quickly, and several other countries had declined our help. China had absorbed most of the recruits in Asia into their official scrab-fighting forces.

The teams had shrunk not just because of the mess with Julian, but because it became obvious that we were flailing. It wasn't Maddie's fault—she was just continuing what Grayson had planned—but she definitely got all the blame since he was gone. Which made me hesitant to even bring up any of this. She dealt with enough criticism. Everyone underestimated Maddie— many people seemed to think that an eighteen-year-old who was mostly famous for being a rich party girl wasn't equipped to lead the teams. She pretended like it didn't bother her, but I knew that it did.

"We can take a look at our strategies," I said carefully. "But the scrab numbers are down here, no matter what Julian says."

I didn't want to tell her that I didn't think that it would matter how successful we were here. We could eliminate scrabs entirely, and Julian would say that the numbers were up.

What we really needed to do was expose MDG and Julian and anyone else involved with scrab training. Once everyone knew the truth, it would be easier for us to recruit.

Maddie muttered something I couldn't understand. Patrick hooked his arm through hers and asked about the movie she'd seen last week, obviously trying to pull her mind away from Julian.

It wouldn't work. Maddie was determined to make Julian and MDG pay. She wasn't going to rest until they were in prison.

We walked into the gym, and a few recruits scattered as soon as they spotted us. Probably because of Maddie. She yelled at a lot of people in the weeks after Grayson's death, and had garnered a reputation for being scary and mean as a result. This didn't seem to bother her at all.

Laila broke off from the group when she spotted Saira, the leader of UK team thirteen, nearby. She greeted her with a kiss.

Noah looked from them to us in surprise. "When did that happen? Did we even know she was gay?"

"She's bi," Dorsey said, which was news to me. Laila was almost as secretive as I was, though I got the impression that for her, it was more that she just liked to keep things to herself. She talked to her parents and her sisters all the time, and mentioned her friends in Chicago often.

"Huh," Noah said. "Who knew?"

"Me," Dorsey said with a laugh. "Also, I found two more bisexuals the other day. I'm going to start a club."

"What do you mean, you *found* them?" Noah asked. "Were you out looking for them?"

"No, they were just drawn to me. Bisexuals, pansexuals, we can sense each other, you know. We send out a signal."

Patrick snorted.

"I don't think that's true," Noah said, squinting.

"No, it's totally not true," Dorsey said with a laugh.

We spread out to various parts of the gym, and I met Edan for sparring after a run on the treadmill. We changed up partners occasionally, but I was still the person he was most comfortable with. And I just liked having him around, always.

There was one benefit to Maddie's relentless pace—I was in great shape. While six solid months of training and scrab fighting had become a little tiresome, I couldn't deny that it had made me pretty badass. And my constant sparring with Edan had made me incredibly fast.

I thought about Dad sometimes, and how he'd take swings at me. He just used brute strength and took advantage of my fear. I had no intention of ever seeing him again, but if I did, it was nice to know that he wouldn't be able to land a single blow.

I wasn't going to see Dad *or* Mom ever again, apparently. I hadn't intended to cut off all contact with Mom, but she hadn't reached out to me once since the day of tryouts in Atlanta. Neither had Dad, though I wasn't terribly upset about that.

But Mom? She could have at least checked on me once or twice. The address of our hostel in London was public and prominent on the St. John website. It was where all letters and packages for recruits were sent. And my email address was the same one I'd had since I was ten. I was easy to contact, as my many emails from Julian so clearly demonstrated.

But I hadn't heard a word from her.

I stepped away from Edan, breathing heavily. We were in the boxing ring, surrounded by recruits working out. He wiped the back of his arm across his brow. I noticed some recruits nearby staring at us, clearly impressed.

"Done for the day?" I asked.

"Yes," I heard someone groan from behind me. I turned to see

Priya leaned dramatically over the ropes of the ring, arms hanging down toward the ground.

"Yeah, I think we're done," Edan said, looking at Priya in amusement.

Dorsey walked up beside Priya, using his shirt to wipe sweat from his face.

"Did you do that?" I asked him, pointing to her.

"I just suggested that we race around the building a few times," he said.

"I hate running," Priya moaned.

"I won," Dorsey said. Priya punched him in the side.

Behind them, I spotted two of the new recruits sparring in the corner. I winced as one took a hit directly to the face and then promptly fell on his butt. This new group needed some work.

Patrick, who was at the punching bags with Maddie, pulled his earbuds out and said something to her. He frowned as he pointed at the new recruits. I edged closer to them as Maddie also pulled out her earbuds.

"Jayden was needed on assignment today," she said. "They're fine."

Patrick made an exasperated noise. "They are not fine. They need good trainers, not whoever happens to be around today."

Maddie shrugged. "Noah's in charge of training, take it up with him."

"Noah assigned Jayden to them!"

"Oh, right." Maddie glanced around the gym. "Naomi!"

Naomi, one of the more experienced UK recruits, hopped off the rowing machine and walked over to them.

"Work with the new recruits today, will ya?" Maddie asked. "They need some help."

"Yeah, all right," Naomi said, a little wearily. I watched as she trudged over to the new recruits.

"Happy?" Maddie asked Patrick.

"You can't keep pulling the trainers for assignments," Patrick said. "At least talk to Noah about it first so he can send someone else."

"It's fine. We figure it out. See?" She gestured to where Naomi was working with the recruits. Patrick turned away, rolling his eyes.

"Guys!" I heard Noah call, his voice urgent. I turned to see him standing in front of the television mounted on the wall. He turned around, eyes wide. "Julian's parents are dead."

"What?" Priya said. Everyone rushed to the television.

The TV was tuned to a news channel, and someone increased the volume as I approached. Two familiar faces filled the screen. It was a picture of Richard and Faye Montgomery, Julian's parents. They were dressed in fancy clothes — most likely a picture from some rich people event — smiling for the camera.

". . . suffered extensive injuries. Again, if you're just joining us, Richard Montgomery, founder and chairman of Montgomery Properties, and his wife, Faye Montgomery, died today in London following a scrab attack outside their hotel. Their son, Julian Montgomery, was reportedly not with them. We've been told that he's safely in New York, where he's been since leaving the St. John fight squads earlier this year."

"Why were those assholes in London?" Maddie said quietly, almost to herself.

"Same thing they were doing in Brussels last month," Noah said. "Picking up scrabs."

"I'm surprised they came back here, though," Maddie said. "I figured they were in Belgium because we're not allowed to go there."

"Wait, we're not allowed into Belgium?" Dorsey asked.

"Not while you're a part of the teams. They have antimercenary laws, which they are enforcing very strictly these days."

"Do you think they would still be trying to ship scrabs out of the country?" Edan asked. "With the security these days? The police here have really cracked down."

"They can't possibly search every shipping container that comes into and out of the UK," Maddie said. "And I wouldn't put it past the Montgomerys to bribe the police into looking the other way. I'm almost certain they were doing it before." A few recruits looked at each other, clearly alarmed. I winced. We probably shouldn't have been having this conversation in front of them.

"Maybe this is way too optimistic, but do you think it's possible that Julian will step back from MDG now?" Patrick asked.

Maddie frowned. "Why would he?"

"To grieve. And to . . . I don't know. Go to college? He's only twenty years old. I felt like he was just doing all the MDG stuff to make his parents happy." He looked at me. "You said that he mostly seemed motivated to keep his dad happy."

"He did," I said. "Maybe . . . ?" I looked at Maddie, unsure.

"I really don't know. He could, I guess. He'll have a lot on his plate, since he was their only child." She looked down at her phone, and then turned away, pressing it to her ear. "Hey, Mom." She walked toward the exit.

I really wanted to believe Patrick's optimism. Was it naïve to hope that Julian would find a tiny shred of humanity and just walk away from it all? He'd just inherited an enormous amount of wealth, and the Montgomerys were deeply invested in MDG. Maybe he'd decide to abandon his father's stupid, dangerous ideas and pull his funding. Maybe MDG would go under without it.

Maybe.

~

That evening, after our assignment, I walked into the lounge to see Maddie sitting at the large round table in the center of the room, laptop in front of her. The room was empty except for three recruits talking quietly on the couch on the back wall.

"Got it," Maddie said to the screen, and then typed something into her phone. She looked up and smiled at me. "Hey, Clara."

"Hi, Clara!" came a voice from the laptop.

I walked around the table and smiled at the dark-haired girl on the screen. "Hey, Hannah."

Hannah was a freelance writer and journalism student at NYU. She'd contacted me after my video went up, and became so engrossed in the mystery of the MDG Dust Storm facility that Maddie had ended up hiring her to do research.

Beside her was Victor, one of Grayson's friends and the guy I'd talked to when I signed up for the squads. He ran various aspects of the operation from New York—uniform and weapons orders, meal planning, and general assistant work. He still did all that, but these days he mostly researched MDG with Hannah. We didn't have much time to devote to MDG when we were out fighting scrabs and training new recruits every day.

"Clara!" Victor exclaimed, waving at me. Victor greeted everyone like he'd never been so excited to see them in his life.

"Hey, guys," I said, sliding into the chair beside Maddie.

"Tell me about Arizona," Maddie said to her.

"Right." Hannah riffled through her notes. "Arizona . . . Arizona . . ."

"Is it that one?" Victor asked, pointing to a corner of the room off screen. "I'll get it." He pushed away from the table. Victor used a wheelchair, and he rolled behind Hannah, disappearing for a moment before reappearing with a notebook in his lap.

"Thanks," Hannah said, pushing her hair back with a sigh. "I'm scattered today."

Maddie pressed her lips together like she was trying not to smile. Hannah was always scattered. She was super smart—she'd graduated from high school a year early and was already a senior in college at the age of twenty. But she seemed like one of those smart people who couldn't handle everyday life. Like she had so much information stuffed into her brain that she couldn't remember things like eating meals or where she put her notebook.

"I thought I was on to something in Arizona, but it was a dead end," she said. "Oh! Right. This is where they found a nest of dead scrabs. But they'd been dead a long time. Years. I'll send you the pictures. It's super gross, though."

"OK," Maddie said with a disappointed sigh.

"I'm trying to find some people to check out a tip in New Mexico," Hannah said. "But it's been a struggle to find someone trustworthy. The former recruits I had investigating in Arizona won't go."

"Offer to pay them double," Maddie said.

"I did. They said they're done. But!" she said, perking up. "I did get a tip from one of my Reddit bro friends."

"Your Reddit bro friends?" I repeated.

"Yeah, the guys on the scrab conspiracy threads are very familiar with me. They think I'm a dude named Hank, but they love me." She waved her hand. "Anyway, they haven't announced it yet, but the Scrab Defense League is having a big get-together in early January. Their first annual conference. They've reserved a hotel for it."

"Where?" Maddie asked.

"Dallas."

I groaned. "Why *Dallas*?"

"Aren't you *from* Dallas?" Hannah looked confused.

"Yep. I sure am."

She squinted at me, obviously expecting more. "Huh. OK. Anyway, it's apparently going to be a big thing. Facebook has exploded with various chapters of the league in the last couple months, and the Texas branches are especially active. I imagine that's why they chose Dallas."

"Any idea what they're going to do?" Maddie asked.

"Sit around and talk about how much they like guns and trained scrabs?" Victor guessed.

"That is literally our best guess right now," Hannah said. "But it'll be announced publicly soon. The chapters are all aware and pumped up."

"Great," Maddie muttered, running her hands through her hair.

"Is there anything you need me to do with this news about the Montgomerys?" Hannah asked.

"Yeah, can you find out which hotel they were staying at and if they were using a car service? I might be able to bribe someone into telling me where they went while they were here."

"You got it. Oh! Hold on." Hannah jumped up, disappearing from the screen.

"Sorry, our Chinese food is here," Victor said.

Edan walked in, changed from his uniform into jeans and a gray T-shirt, a sweatshirt slung over his shoulder. He strolled over to us and leaned down to see the screen. "Hey, Victor."

"Edan! A pleasure to see you, as always."

Hannah zoomed back into the frame, almost knocking into Victor as she sat down. "Hey, Edan," she said breathlessly.

"Hey," Edan said, and Hannah beamed. She so obviously had a crush on him. And maybe the feeling was mutual. Hannah was really cute, with her wide, dark eyes and pale skin and sleek hair cut into a bob. Plus, she was smart and quirky and only two years older than him. I wouldn't have blamed him for returning the feelings.

He'd taken the job of compiling all of Hannah's research and tips into a spreadsheet and then a report for Maddie, which required him to talk to Hannah at least once a week. It made me wonder if maybe he also liked her. Or enjoyed that she liked him, at the very least.

I tried not to obsess over it. It wasn't like I was dating Edan. He was free to do what he wanted.

I'd thought about the possibility of dating Edan, of course. Back when we first became friends, Maddie had said she thought he liked me, and maybe he had. But then Grayson and several of our team members had died and everything was different. Dating hadn't seemed like a priority.

Not to mention that I still wasn't sure I could be trusted with romantic decisions. When left to my own devices, my dumb ass had gone straight for the first rage-filled overprotective jerk I could find. I'd been away from home *two days* when I started swooning over Julian. I wouldn't date again until I was sure I could be trusted to make smart decisions.

Which would maybe be never.

Edan glanced back at me, tossing a piece of dark hair out of his eyes with a smile. I quickly looked away.

I was, maybe, just a tiny bit pleased that Hannah was thousands of miles away, though.

"OK, I'll let you pass along the rest to Edan," Maddie said, getting to her feet. I stood as well, and Edan took my chair, putting his laptop on the table.

I followed Maddie down the hall and to our room. She flopped down on her bed with a sigh, and I perched on the edge of mine.

"Is it too early to go to bed?" she asked. "I feel like I need to sleep for at least twenty-four hours."

"You know that you could take the day off tomorrow, if you wanted. I'm sure we can manage without you."

"No, I can't. I want to set a good example."

I didn't think that running herself ragged was a good example. I slowly sat down on my bed, considering my next words carefully.

"Have you thought about what you want to do with the teams long term?" I asked.

"What do you mean?"

"Do you have any . . . changes in mind? This was Grayson's initial vision for the teams, but maybe . . ." I didn't want to say *maybe he was wrong*. It seemed ridiculous for me, noted idiot, to question Grayson's plan. He'd been a genius. Literally. Whatever the official requirements were for being labeled *a genius*, Grayson had them.

But I also couldn't help but wonder if he'd thought everything through. How long had he expected mercenary teams to last?

She was staring at me, waiting for me to finish.

"We're just spread pretty thin right now," I said. "I feel like we should be devoting more time to figuring out what's going on with MDG and Julian and the Scrab Defense League. We'll have an easier time recruiting for the teams once they're gone. But we also have new recruits, and we're out on assignments every day . . ."

"I mean, we can't lighten up on assignments. MDG or no, there are still scrabs out there."

"I know, but it just seems like the league is getting bigger every week. And I'm not even sure I trust the police or the FBI to do anything about it, because I think half of them are on their side. It's frustrating."

"It is. But we've got Hannah and Victor on it, and I've given up sleep for the next five or so years, so we'll be fine."

I raised a judgmental eyebrow. "You're sleeping tonight, even if I have to drag you into bed."

"We'll see," she said, waving a hand dismissively.

"Maybe we can look at pulling back on some of the assignments?" I asked cautiously.

"Clara, we're fine. There's only so much we can do from here anyway."

"Yeah. I guess you're right." I wanted to push further, but Maddie never listened when I suggested slowing down. It was not her strong suit, and it certainly hadn't been Grayson's. Part of me was annoyed that she didn't seem interested in my opinion, but the other part of me wasn't sure my opinion was worth anything. Maybe Maddie was right, and pushing ahead was the best strategy. Changing things up would take time and money, and she was right that the scrab threat was still there.

"We'll get someone to go to that conference in Dallas and report back," she said. "And we'll look for more people to help search for Dust Storm. Don't worry. We've got this."

I forced a smile. I genuinely hoped that she was right.

4

I STUCK MY HEAD OUT OF THE WEAPONS CLOSET AND LOOKED left and then right. Laila was standing a few feet away, organizing her weapons pack.

"I think that's it," she said, standing and slinging her pack over her shoulder. I noticed a flash of color on her dark skin—a colorful bird inked onto her right forearm.

"Did you get a new tattoo?" I asked, cocking my head to look at it.

"No," she said, looking down at the bird with a laugh. "That would be a bit much for me. Saira was just messing around. It'll wash off."

"I didn't know she was an artist too. It's beautiful."

"I'll tell her you said so," she said, smiling at me before heading for the stairwell.

I retreated back into the closet and closed the machete trunk. I'd been one of the recruits in charge of weapons security since a few weeks after Grayson's death. At first, Maddie let everyone have unlimited access to weapons, but that had led to a lot of them disappearing as recruits dropped out. Then there was the time a recruit nearly cut off another recruit's fingers during a drunken brawl. Now everyone had to check most of their weapons in and out. And we'd gotten rid of guns completely.

Most of our remaining recruits weren't cleared to use them anyway.

I stepped out of the closet, locking the door behind me, and headed up to my room. I pushed open the door.

I stopped abruptly.

Noah quickly finished pulling up his pants. Maddie tugged her shirt over her head.

"Sorry." I whirled around.

"No, it's my fault," Maddie said. "I thought I locked the door."

"I'll just, uh—" I took a step out of the room.

"It's fine, I was just about to head downstairs," Noah said, walking past me with pink cheeks and a sheepish expression.

I pushed the door closed behind him and turned to Maddie. "I'm still amused by this pairing."

"What do you mean?"

"You and Noah."

She sat on her bed to put her shoes on. "We're not together or anything. We're just messing around."

"You've said. I'm still kind of confused."

"Why do you say it like that? What's wrong with Noah?"

"Nothing! He's just . . . not your type, I guess?"

"I don't have a type. I'm an equal opportunity slut."

"Is *slut* the word we want to use here?"

"Yes. I enjoy reclaiming the word *slut*."

"Fair enough. But this has been going on for what, five, six months? It's really not a relationship?"

She tied her shoe. "Yes. I mean, we're friends. I like him. But I'm not interested in anything more."

"Is he?"

"Not that he's said. He seems perfectly happy with the arrangement."

"You are super hot, so who can blame him?"

"Why, thank you."

"And it's still a secret?" I asked.

"Yeah. It's just less awkward that way."

"You should probably remember to lock the door next time if you're going for secrecy. Also, I'd rather not see Noah in his underwear again."

"You should see him naked, though." She grinned at me.

"I did not need that image in my brain."

~

Maddie and I met the rest of the team downstairs, and we walked to the tube, several other teams trailing behind us. Noah glanced at me as we boarded the train and turned red when I gave him an amused look.

"You sure you're all right?" I heard Dorsey say quietly as I took a seat.

I looked up to see that he was talking to Edan, who was rubbing a hand across his eyes. He had dark circles, which wasn't unusual for him, but they did seem worse today.

"I'm fine, just a little tired." He leaned against the rail.

"You can sit this one out if you want," Maddie said to him.

"I don't need to."

Dorsey looked like he was going to say something, but Edan smiled at him and bumped shoulders with him.

"I'm fine, Andrew. Lay off."

Dorsey rolled his eyes, but his lips turned up in a smile. He and Edan exchanged a look I couldn't quite read. They'd become good friends since they started rooming together, surprisingly. Dorsey's main activities seemed to be drinking and partying, neither of which interested Edan. And Dorsey had been Gage's friend, which gave me pause.

But Edan liked him, and for some reason called him by his first name, instead of his last, like everyone else did. I wasn't sure why. Maybe Edan just did it to annoy him. Guys loved giving each other shit, which had always baffled me.

Dorsey caught me watching him and smiled. I returned it and then quickly lowered my gaze, pretending to look at something on my phone. I never knew what to say to Dorsey. Compared to the rest of the team, I barely knew him. I wasn't really sure I wanted to know him, if I was being honest. He seemed like the sort of friend you called when you needed someone to party with, and I didn't really need that kind of friend in my life.

"The movement has been really heavy in this area yesterday and today," Maddie said, standing so she could address all the recruits on the train. "Just FYI. You probably need to prepare for a shit day. I've got a bunch of teams already there."

A woman sitting nearby looked up from her phone, an alarmed look on her face. The few other civilians on the train wore matching expressions.

"Yeah, I wouldn't get off when we get off," Maddie said to them. She looked up at the map. "I'd ride for at least three more stops, actually."

None of the civilians got off at the next stop, as we piled out. Priya waved to them as the train began moving again.

"You're welcome!" she called.

"Come on," I said with a laugh.

We walked up the steps to the street. The area was full of trendy, overpriced shops, but it was pretty empty today, many of the shops closed. The police did a good job of getting possible scrab attack locations out to the public.

Maddie directed a few teams to spread out, and then joined us on the sidewalk. It was a cloudy day, but not too cold, and a lot of the recruits seemed in good spirits. I watched two guys from an Australian team laugh as they took a selfie.

The scrab attacks had begun to slow in recent weeks, especially since the army had taken out several nests near the city recently. The scrab tracking technology Grayson helped develop was being used widely, even by police and military, and it got better with each update. I hadn't seen Maddie assign so many teams to one place in a while. It seemed like a bad sign.

I sat down on the curb next to Priya. Her gaze was on the teams across the street. She lifted her hand to greet Saira and Thomas, standing not far away with the rest of UK team thirteen. They waved back.

"Archer would say he had a bad feeling," she said quietly.

"He would. And his bad feelings were always right, unfortunately."

One side of her mouth lifted in a half smile. "They were. But probably because bad things are always happening."

Her gaze was still across the street, and I followed it. Thomas was giving her a small smile.

"Are you and Thomas . . ." I trailed off, worried that she might not want me to pry.

She sighed. "I don't know. Maybe. Part of me doesn't want to do it again, you know?"

"What? Date?"

"Yeah. Or get attached to someone. He'll probably just die again. Or I'll die. Or we'll all die."

"Jesus, Priya," I said, giving her a horrified look.

"What? It's true." She put her chin on her knee with a sigh. "Look at how many teams are out here. At least one recruit will die today if this scrab attack is as big as we're expecting."

"I guess," I said softly.

"My mom reminds me of that every time I talk to her," she said. "She treats every phone call like it's our last."

"You ever think about going home?" I asked. "Just for a visit. Or for the holidays. Maddie is paying for recruits who have been here the longest to go back to the States for vacations."

"I know. But I hate to leave you guys."

"We'd be OK."

"You might, but I'd be sad." She met my gaze. "You're not going home for the holidays." It wasn't a question.

"No."

"Does that . . . Is that OK?" she asked carefully. Everyone on the team knew what I'd left at home, but a lot of them didn't seem to know how to talk about it.

"It really is," I said, smiling at her. "I'm looking forward to holidays without screaming."

"Recruits!" Maddie called suddenly. "Significant movement nearby! Be ready!"

Priya sighed as we got to our feet. "No screaming, but plenty of scrabs."

I pulled out my machete as the ground began rumbling and secured my leather arm coverings.

I caught a flash of movement across the street, a familiar black coat and dark hair standing outside a restaurant. Julian.

No. It couldn't be Julian. He was in New York, planning his parents' funeral. I squinted, but the man was turned away from me, looking down the street.

A scrab burst up from the concrete only a few yards away from me, shielding my view. I leapt forward, machete poised.

It couldn't be Julian. I was imagining things.

I focused on the scrab in front of me. Fighting them had become routine now. Scary—always—but still routine.

The scrab tried to dodge my weapon, but it was too slow. I slid the blade into its neck and then stepped back as it fell. It tried to grab for me as it went down, and out of the corner of my eye, I saw another scrab galloping my way.

I stepped out of reach of the scrab on the ground and stuck my blade into its soft belly. Then I quickly turned, slashing the blade across the neck of the scrab that had almost reached me. It toppled over onto its dead buddy.

I finished off another scrab and turned at the sound of a yell from behind me. It was Laila, warning me about an approaching scrab. It was a small one, not quite fully grown, but its sharp teeth looked plenty big enough to do some damage. Noah took it out before it reached me, and I waved my thanks.

There were more scrabs at the end of the block, and I broke into a run. I skidded to a stop as I caught sight of a scrab tunneling up in an alley. It burst through concrete and dirt, claws first.

I waited until it was completely out, making sure there were no more behind it. Fighting one scrab alone in an alley was fine. Several was a disaster.

But nothing followed it out of the hole as it shook dirt from its hide. It caught sight of me and roared. It lowered its head and bared its teeth.

I took a step back, waiting as it galloped toward me. My foot hit something uneven, and I stumbled, falling headfirst and losing my grip on the machete. It skidded into the alley.

I scrambled for it, barely reaching it in time. I lifted it to the scrab's throat.

It screamed suddenly and reared back. Blood dripped onto the ground. It whirled around and then collapsed. A knife stuck out of its side.

Julian stood on the other side of the scrab. His hand was still extended, even though his knife was now lodged in the scrab. He slowly lowered his arm.

He was thinner than last time I'd seen him, his cheeks sunken and his eyes dull. He wore the same black coat I'd often seen him in back in May, the one with the high collar. I used to think he looked so handsome in it.

He had on fancy leather shoes, and his clothes looked

meticulous, despite the blood pooling at his feet. He wasn't dressed to fight scrabs, but he'd still been carrying a weapon, apparently. He wasn't dumb enough to walk the streets of London without a weapon.

"Hello, Clara."

The familiar voice sent a flash of fear down my spine. I gripped my machete tighter.

I looked past him, at the road. I saw dead scrabs, but no recruits. I could hear them in the distance, though.

Still, he had me cornered in this alley. I would need to edge around the scrab and him to get out.

"Would you mind putting that down?" he asked, nodding at my machete. "I'm unarmed now." He pointed at his blade, still in the scrab's neck.

"You don't put away your weapon until you're sure all the scrabs are dead," I said, repeating a line he had told the team during training. In fact, the one at our feet wasn't quite dead. I quickly stuck my blade in its throat and then edged around it.

"Are you scared of me?" he asked, cocking his head. "You know I would never hurt you."

I faced him, taking several slow steps back until I was closer to the street. There. Now he was the one who was cornered. I could easily turn and bolt.

"Why are you here, Julian?" I asked. "Shouldn't you be in New York?"

"I came to collect my parents' remains. Not much left, unfortunately." He said it bitterly. "Thought I'd drop in on the St. John teams, see how you're doing. Those of you who stuck around, anyway. I heard you've been bleeding recruits lately."

I took a step back, and then another, until I was almost in the street. I could hear recruits laughing nearby, but no roars. They must have gotten all the scrabs. Julian moved forward with me.

"I wish you wouldn't look so scared. I just saved you," he said, gesturing to the scrab. "Why would I save you if I wanted to hurt you?"

"I didn't need your help," I said. "I had that under control."

He gave me a deeply condescending look, like he didn't believe that for a minute. Julian never had believed I could take care of myself.

"Did you get my emails?" he asked.

"Yes."

He paused, rubbing his lower lip with his thumb for a moment. When he spoke again, it was soft, and a little shaky. "You never replied."

"I don't have anything to say to you."

"But . . ." He took a deep breath. "You said all those things about me, and you didn't even give me a chance to explain. Do you have any idea what it was like for me after that night? I couldn't sleep. I couldn't *think*, and I just needed to talk to you."

"You lost the right to talk to me when you punched me in the face."

He flushed. "That was an accident. Things got out of control. I will *never* do that again. *Never*."

I rolled my eyes.

He reeled back, like he was actually shocked by this response. "I, um . . . OK." He let out a long breath. "I guess I can understand that you don't really trust that, given your history. But you have to know that I care about you, Clara. So much. And I know you care about me too."

I just stared at him. I *had* cared about Julian. Until I found out who he really was.

I glanced over my shoulder and took another step back.

"Wait, wait." He held out his hand to stop me. "Just give me one minute, OK? I want to ask you a question."

I considered turning and bolting, maybe flipping him off as I went, but I had to admit that I was curious what he wanted to ask me. I crossed my arms over my chest and raised my eyebrows expectantly.

"Why did I only get one chance?" He said the words slowly. "Why didn't you give me the opportunity to do the right thing? You hated Edan when you first met him. He tried to rob your friend. He's robbed tons of people. He made mistakes, but you saw past that and gave him another chance. Why is he worthy of redemption, and I'm not?"

"Edan never hurt me. He never spied on me and exploded with jealousy and tried to control who I was friends with. He never got together with his rich buddies and developed an idea to use scrabs against people."

"And I'm not saying that I didn't make mistakes!" he said. "I definitely did. It was so wrong to spy on your phone. I never should have done that. I know that I get carried away with the jealousy sometimes. It just gets away from me, and I don't know what to do about that. I don't know how to fix it. It's honestly really disappointing that you can't be more understanding about that."

"About your irrational jealousy? It's disappointing that I can't be understanding about that?"

"Yes! I don't *want* to be this way. I just have all these demons, and I don't know how to control them sometimes. I feel like you could have helped me with it if you'd been willing to try."

"Hard pass," I said dryly.

"Not to mention that you and I never even had a real discussion about MDG and the scrabs and everything," he continued, like he hadn't heard me. "I would have given all that up in a heartbeat for you."

"You should have given it up because it was the right thing to do, Julian. Instead you're in deeper."

"You have to understand, my dad . . ." His voice shook, and tears filled his eyes. "You met my dad. You saw what he was like. And that was him on *good* behavior. He left no room for argument on MDG, or on anything, really. It always had to be his way. I didn't know how . . . how to say no, I guess."

I said nothing, because I didn't think Julian would appreciate me telling him that he could have made his own choices. I could sympathize with having a father who was controlling and abusive, but I didn't use it as an excuse to turn around and do the same thing to other people.

"I just wish that you would *talk* to me," he pleaded. "You're the only person who has ever understood me. And I know that I'm the only person who has ever really understood you."

I cocked an eyebrow and thought of Maddie and Edan,

who understood me just fine. Certainly better than Julian ever had.

"You and I were meant to be together," he said. "I know it. There's a reason that I'm the one who got that email from your dad. I was supposed to help you. And I know I screwed it up, but I'm going to make it up to you, I promise."

"I don't want you to make it up to me."

"I'm sorry, but I don't believe that."

"What?" I asked, exasperated. "Why not?"

"You didn't call the police."

"I've talked to the police about you on numerous occasions, Julian. British and American."

"I don't mean about the stuff with MDG, I mean about you and me, personally. You told the whole world about how terrible I was, how mean I was to you, but you never filed a restraining order."

"You went back to New York," I said.

"It's just odd, I think. To act like you're so scared of me, but then not do anything about it. Makes me think that maybe you don't really want me to stay away."

I didn't reply.

"Listen, we both know that we got a little heated that night at the farm," he continued, after I said nothing. I realized too late that my silence might be interpreted as agreement. "I definitely said some things I regret, and I apologize for that. But I feel like your version of events was really unfair to me. You hit me too."

"I defended myself after you hit me." I was familiar with this tactic—I'd heard Dad use it on Mom more than once. *Well, we were both pretty out of control, remember?*

"I just think that's a really simplified version of events," he said. "It was way more complicated than that, which I bet you knew. You knew it, and you still put out a video that's going to be up for the rest of my life." His words took on a hard edge. My pulse quickened, and I had to take a look around, remind myself how many people were in the area.

"I just told the truth."

"You told your version of the truth, which is the only thing that some people care about. I try to explain, and no one will even listen to me. Your truth matters more than mine, apparently."

I rolled my eyes. "Plenty of people listened to you. In fact, I'm pretty sure that the accepted narrative at this point is that I was the jealous girlfriend and you were just trying to calm me down."

I heard the sound of running footsteps, and I turned to see Maddie jogging down the street. Julian was shielded from her view by the wall. I took in a sharp breath.

"Oh, there you are, I was worri—" She came to an abrupt stop beside me. Her entire body went still.

I grabbed her hand. I couldn't be sure that she wouldn't start taking swings at Julian.

"What are you doing here?" Maddie's voice shook.

"Well, you may have heard that my parents were killed by the scrabs that you continue to fail at eliminating." He glared at her.

"Maddie, let's go," I said quietly, tugging on her hand. Julian's eyes flicked to the movement, annoyance crossing his face. It was a weird thing to be annoyed by, our holding hands, but I supposed he liked it better when Maddie and I were fighting over him.

He moved forward suddenly, taking long strides until he was right in front of us. I took in a sharp breath, squeezing Maddie's hand tighter.

"Spare me, Madison. Stop looking at me like I killed your puppy."

"You killed *Grayson*, you unbelievable son of a—"

"Grayson signed his death certificate the minute he started these stupid squads," he hissed. "The fact that he caught a stray bullet meant for a scrab is not my fault."

I gawked at him. He said that like he actually believed it. Julian had never been a great liar, but that lie had slid easily, and believably, from his mouth. Maybe because he'd repeated it so many times.

"You should be careful, Maddie," he said, eyes flashing as he stared at her. "This scrab-hunting business is dangerous. Clara almost died in this alley just now. And look what happened to Grayson. You should stop before you get everyone killed."

Maddie's lips parted. No sound came out.

Julian stepped around me, pausing at my shoulder to speak softly. "For the record, Clara, I forgive you. And I know this isn't how our story ends." He lifted his hand like he was going to touch me. I shrank away. He dropped his hand and turned to leave.

Maddie and I stood there in stunned silence for several seconds, listening to his retreating footsteps.

"Did you really almost just die?" she asked.

I rolled my eyes. "No. I had it handled; he just thinks I'm help-less." I tugged on her hand. "Come on." I led her around the corner to where the other recruits were.

I spotted Edan right away, standing with Noah, a stricken look on both their faces. I followed their gazes. They were watching Julian climb into a cab. Noah put a hand on Edan's arm.

"Has anyone seen Clara? Or Maddie?" Edan yelled.

"Edan," I called. I saw him blow out a relieved breath when his eyes landed on me and Maddie.

We walked to him and Noah. Edan's hands were shaking as he slid his foldable ax into his weapons pack, and I was struck by the sudden urge to lace my fingers through his.

"You saw Julian?" Noah asked.

"Yeah. I talked to him in the alley," I said.

"You *talked* to him?" Priya repeated, as she joined us with Laila. Dorsey and Patrick were right behind them.

"He threatened us," Maddie said bitterly. "Or just me, I guess. Said I was going to get everyone killed."

"And he claimed that Grayson was hit by a stray bullet meant for a scrab. Said he wasn't trying to kill him," I said.

"Seriously?" Laila said, clearly baffled.

"He was trying to kill *me*," Edan said. "So yes, if you want to get technical about it, Grayson's death was an accident. He was hit by a stray bullet meant for *me*."

I put a hand lightly on Edan's back. Of all the things Edan and I discussed on the balcony every night, we didn't often touch on Grayson's death. I'd only broached the topic once and quickly realized just how much guilt Edan was carrying about his friend jumping in front of a bullet for him. I knew that telling him that it wasn't his fault wouldn't help, but I'd done it anyway.

"I don't want to hear any fucking technicalities from that shithead," Maddie said. "He was aiming his gun at a person, not a scrab." She hesitated, her eyes flicking to mine. "Right?"

"What?" I asked, startled.

"There wasn't a scrab behind Edan, was there?"

I shook my head emphatically. "No, Maddie. Don't let him do that. He aimed the gun at Edan. More than once."

"Right." She blew out a shaky breath. "Right. I know that."

"So, what do we do?" Priya asked. "Why would he even come see us? His parents just died two days ago. He really has time to come find us and threaten you?"

"I think you underestimate Julian's level of pettiness." Maddie looked at me. "What did he say to you before I got there?"

"He just apologized. He wants me back."

Priya gave me a truly horrified look. "Ew."

"Let's get out of here," Maddie said. "I want to let the police know that Julian's back in town."

5

Maddie called an all-team meeting that evening. Word of Julian's return to London had spread quickly among the recruits, and there was definitely a hint of panic in the air.

I stood against the back wall of the lounge with Priya on one side, Edan on the other. The rest of team seven and UK team thirteen were nearby. The room was crowded, recruits milling about, though I remembered how only a few months ago, it had been tough to fit everyone in here. We'd been shoulder to shoulder. Not so much anymore.

People kept looking at me and whispering. It had been so many months since our brief relationship, but everyone still associated me with Julian. Maybe even blamed me. It was enough to make me never want to date again.

I wanted the recruits to look at me like they did when they saw Edan and me sparring at the gym. Like I was strong and capable. Not like I was someone's sad ex-girlfriend.

"Do you know what Maddie's going to say?" Connor asked. He glanced at Patrick. "She's not pulling teams out of the UK, is she?"

"No way," Patrick said with a frown. "Julian won't be here for long, and the UK is still the worst. The worst in terms of scrabs, I mean."

"And proud of it," Connor said.

Patrick slipped his hand into Connor's, his expression softening. "It's nice you're so worried I might be leaving."

"Actually, I was hoping to get rid of you." He smiled up at Patrick and then pressed a quick kiss to his lips.

"Never," Patrick said. "We're finally starting to make some progress here."

"And I'm here." Connor poked him in the ribs, and Patrick laughed.

My email dinged, and my stomach dropped to my feet at the sound. I braced myself as I unlocked my phone.

It wasn't Julian. It was actually Adriana, one of the girls I'd been friends with in middle school. Maybe we were friends again, actually. She'd emailed me after seeing the video I made about Julian, and we'd kept in touch since. Apparently, everyone at school thought I was a badass for joining the teams. Or that was what Adriana told me, anyway.

Maddie walked to the front of the room, and everyone quieted. She was wearing workout clothes, hair in a messy ponytail. I slipped my phone back into my pocket.

"Hey, guys," she said. "Just a few updates for you. First, a heads-up that our new recruits will be joining us on assignment starting day after tomorrow. I'm pairing them with more experienced teams, so if you see them out there, give them some support."

I raised my eyebrows. I'd seen the new recruits, and they were not ready to be out on assignment. Most of them had never had combat class in high school, and a few of them had even been rejected during the first round of recruitment. Our standards were lower these days. Still, I would have given them at least a couple more weeks of training before throwing them into the fire.

"As I'm sure you've heard by now, Julian Montgomery is back in London," Maddie continued. "I don't know for how long. He said he was in town to claim his parents' bodies, and then he should be going back to New York. It's true that he showed up at a scrab site today and talked briefly to me and Clara. He did not share anything of note with us." Her eyes flicked to mine. "If anyone sees Julian while they are out on assignment, please text me immediately."

One of the team leaders, Jayden, stepped away from the wall. "Maddie, do you know what this means for MDG? Were the Montgomerys doing work for them here and in Brussels?"

"I don't know. I'm looking into it, and all my law enforcement contacts are looking into it. They are aware that Julian is back in the UK. I will definitely pass on anything they tell me."

"MDG started using trained scrabs against us last spring," Jayden said. "I think we need to talk about what we're going to do if that happens again."

"We're going to fight them, like always," she said. "A trained scrab is still a scrab. It dies the same way. But, yes, if anyone sees anything that even looks like a trained scrab, please let me know. And try to take a picture, if it's safe to do so."

Jayden looked like he had more to say, but he just leaned back against the wall and crossed his arms over his chest. He glanced at the team leader next to him, a disapproving look on his face. We'd lost a lot of team leaders after Julian left. We couldn't afford to lose more.

I glanced around the room at the other recruits. Their faces were tight and nervous. They probably needed reassurance, something that Maddie was not very good at.

And I wasn't even sure what she would say to them if she were good at it. We didn't know if Julian was doing something here besides collecting his parents' remains, and we didn't know what MDG had planned.

Maybe she could have said something about how we valued their lives, and their safety was our first priority. I might have said something like that.

"As always, I'm all ears if you have information about MDG," Maddie said. "Or about Julian, or anything. We're not letting these assholes get away with this, I promise."

She walked away from the front of the room, and a murmur went through the crowd. Recruits began to filter out.

"I've got to get to the weapons closet," I said. "I'll see you guys later."

I walked out of the lounge and down the hall to the weapons closet. I unlocked the door and grabbed the tablet that I used to mark everything in and out.

Naomi appeared at the door, weapons pack in hand.

"Hey, Naomi," I said, glancing down at the schedule. "You're cleared for whatever you want since you're headed up to north London."

She shook her head, extending the weapons pack to me. "I'm turning this in. I just quit."

I slowly took the pack. "Why?"

"I'm tired. And my mates were supposed to join me in the next round of recruits, but they ended up changing their minds . . ." She shrugged. "They wanted to help, but they're not the athletic type. They wouldn't have been good at fighting."

"You sure you don't want to just take a break? Maddie's fine with recruits taking a few weeks off."

She shook her head. "No. Sorry, but no. I just don't want to do this anymore. Especially with Julian suddenly showing up, and the possibility that MDG may be around again. I don't know what's going on with them, but I signed up to fight scrabs. I don't want any part of all that other stuff."

"I understand," I said quietly.

"Good luck though, OK? Be careful now that Julian's back. That guy is the worst."

I made a noise of agreement. "I will. Thanks." She waved at me, her expression a little sad, and then turned to walk away. I watched her go. UK recruits dropped off less frequently than recruits from other countries. We'd be in real trouble if we started losing them too.

My phone rang as I was locking up the closet, and I looked down to see it was a video call from Laurence. I'd forgotten he was calling today.

I slid my keys into my pocket and pressed Accept. Laurence's face filled the screen.

"Hey," he said with a smile. He'd let his dark hair grow out so it curled softly above his ears. It made him look less morose. Or maybe that was just because I actually knew a little about Laurence now. It was weird that I'd lived in the same house with him for seventeen years and had barely gotten to know him at all.

I headed down the hallway and then started up the stairs. "Hey."

He was sitting in a kitchen. I could see a microwave behind him and an open cardboard box on the countertop.

"Is this your new place?"

He glanced over his shoulder. "Yeah. It's small, but at least I don't have a roommate. And it's just a sublease, so I'm not stuck here," he added quickly.

Laurence moved back to Dallas last week. Mom had called him crying a month ago, during one of Dad's rages. And then she called again two weeks ago, because it was always the same story.

He broke down and went back. His job in Tulsa had ended, and he said he didn't like Oklahoma anyway. Which was probably true—Oklahoma wasn't known for being exciting—but we both knew that wasn't why he went back.

We both just stared at each other for a moment. Long stretches of silence were not uncommon in my calls with my brother. I looked away for a moment as I walked down the hallway and opened the door to Maddie's and my room. It was empty.

"Did you go see them?" I finally asked, sitting down on my bed. "Mom and Dad?"

"Yeah. I went over for dinner two nights ago." He let out a long sigh and went quiet for several seconds. I waited for him to find the words. "They asked if I'd heard from you lately. I lied and said no."

My eyebrows shot up. "Why?"

"It caught me off-guard. I don't know why. Of course they were going to ask about you. But we hadn't talked about what I was going to say to them, and I didn't want to tell them something that you didn't want them to know."

"I . . ." I didn't know what I wanted them to know. There was a lot of information out there about me, some of it untrue, and I wasn't sure I cared if they knew the truth. If they would even accept what was true. *Truth* had always been a nebulous concept in our house.

"I don't mind lying." Laurence shrugged. "I prefer it, actually."

"Yeah?"

"When I said no, that was the end of the conversation."

"I know how you enjoy ending conversations."

"Or never starting them at all, in the case of Mom and Dad." He smiled.

I laughed. "Yeah, just keep lying for now. It's not like they couldn't get in contact with me if they wanted." The words came out bitter. "Was dinner OK otherwise?"

He rubbed his forehead. "It was terrible. I regretted my decision to stop smoking."

"I didn't know you quit smoking."

"A couple months ago. Almost stopped on the way home for some cigarettes after that dinner, though."

"What happened?"

"Nothing. They were in one of their overly cheerful moods. It freaks me out when they do that, you know?"

"I really do."

"It's like . . ." He shrugged. "I don't know."

"Like you can feel the tension simmering just below the surface, but everyone is pretending it's not there, which makes you even *more* nervous, and then when Dad inevitably blows up, it's even worse, because you've been dreading it for an hour."

He looked amused. "Yes. He didn't blow up, though. He was on good behavior."

"Probably because now he knows you can successfully tackle him if you want."

"Probably." He shifted in his chair. "I saw that you guys are actually making a dent in the London scrabs."

"Yeah, we are, despite what Julian says."

"That guy just blatantly lies all the time. I don't understand why people keep going along with it. Dad was talking about how Julian had a point about Second Amendment rights and scrabs."

"Of course he was," I deadpanned.

"I told him exactly how stupid I thought that was, but I'm not sure it made a dent. I feel like everyone has lost their minds."

"They're scared," I said with a sigh. "They're being told that other countries are going to invade us with scrab armies."

"Are . . . Are they?" Laurence asked hesitantly.

"I mean, I hope not, but who knows? Every time I talk to Interpol or the FBI about that, they look at me like I'm an idiot."

"*Every time* you talk to the FBI and Interpol? *Every time?*" He laughed. "Your life is weird, Clara."

"Yes, it is."

There was another long stretch of silence, and I saw him shift in his chair.

"Uh, I should probably let you go," he said. "I'll talk to you soon?"

"Yeah. Bye, Laurence."

"Bye."

I ended the call. That had actually been one of the better ones. Maybe a good sign for the future. We just needed to find more things to talk about.

I pulled my sweatshirt on and walked down to a room we used for storage on the third floor. I edged around the boxes and stepped outside onto the small balcony. I sat down, crossing my legs and leaning back against the wall.

It was too cold to be out here, but I'd gotten in the habit over the summer. I liked looking out at the city, listening to the sounds of car horns and watching people pass by. I never considered whether I wanted to live in a city or the country or the suburbs when I got older, but I thought that the city was probably my choice. It seemed safer, to be surrounded by so many people. London was huge, but it didn't feel like it when I was on the street or the subway. It felt tiny, almost claustrophobic. But in a nice way. It was so easy to disappear among all those people.

The door behind me opened. I turned to look, even though I already knew who it was. Edan stepped onto the balcony, holding a blanket.

"You really do need that coat," he said, draping the blanket over my shoulders.

"Thank you," I said, pulling it tight around me.

He sat down next to me, zipping up his hoodie. We met out here often. Edan's insomnia kept him up later than most, and I'd needed a quiet place to think back when we were all in big group rooms.

Edan found me out here the first week we moved in, and it

became a routine. But I really did need to buy that coat. I didn't want these chats to end just because of the weather.

"How is Maddie doing with Julian being back?" he asked.

"She seems OK. She's talked to her mom, like, three times today, though."

"That's good, at least. Maddie and her mom have always seemed close."

"Yeah, they are." I glanced at him. "You've met her, haven't you? Nicole?"

"I have, a few times. She's very nice."

"She was friends with the Montgomerys, wasn't she? I mean, not anymore, obviously. But before."

"Yeah, before. They were close." He leaned back against the door. "I'm surprised Maddie didn't stay in New York longer, back when she went home for Grayson's funeral. First her dad, and then her brother . . ."

"Yeah," I said quietly. I'd thought the same thing when she returned only a few days after the funeral. But she'd been determined to keep the teams together. "I think she wanted to come back and take out all her aggression on scrabs."

He let out a short laugh. "I can relate."

"Me too. Some days I suddenly remember that Julian got away with murdering Grayson and Archer and Zoe and Gage, and I'm just . . ."

"A huge ball of rage?" Edan guessed.

"Exactly."

"I'm familiar with the feeling."

"Are you?" I gave him a skeptical look. Edan was the most even-keeled person I'd ever met. The word *rage* didn't suit him.

"Oh god yes. Remember how I had a headache for, like, all of July?"

I nodded.

"My therapist said it's because I keep all my feelings inside. Also, I started to worry I had a brain tumor, which made the stress even worse." He laughed softly.

"You still talk to that therapist Maddie got for us?" I asked. I knew that a lot of people kept up with sessions via Skype, but I hadn't known that Edan was one of them.

"Yeah. I like talking to her. It was especially helpful after my mom started trying to contact me. I didn't want to dump all of that on you."

"You can dump anything you want on me," I said with a smile. He returned it. "Does she have advice? About your mom?"

"She's not really the 'give advice' type. But she didn't try to change my mind and push me to respond to Mom. I would have stopped seeing her if she did."

"That's good." Of the two of us, it was ironic that Edan was the one who'd suddenly heard from his mom. I actually wanted to hear from mine, so, of course, not a peep.

"You didn't feel like you needed to go?" Edan asked, after a brief silence. "To see one of the therapists Maddie brought in?"

"I went once," I said. "She was nice enough, but no, I didn't really feel like going again. Maddie's been bugging me about it, but I don't know. It wasn't really for me."

He studied me, clearly waiting for more, but I didn't have more for him. I'd found the hour with the therapist to be uncomfortable and not particularly helpful. I was supposed to pour my heart out to a total stranger? I wasn't even good at telling my friends what I was feeling.

"What?" I asked, when he kept looking at me. "Do I seem like I need therapy?"

"Oh god, one hundred percent yes," he said with a hint of a smile.

I laughed. "You sound like Maddie."

"Maddie says everyone needs therapy. And she's right, by the way."

"Maddie's right about everything," I said with a grin. "Just ask her."

My phone dinged with an email alert, and I looked down at it. I felt my smile vanish at the sight of his name on my screen.

Julian Montgomery
Subject: Please

"What?" Edan asked. "Hey." His tone softened, his hand landing gently on mine. "What is it?"

I started to say it was nothing, but I could tell that it was too late. His eyebrows were drawn together in concern. He could see something was wrong.

I hadn't said it to Maddie, but the reason I hadn't told rest of the team about Julian emailing me was because of Edan.

He'd been in bad shape after Grayson's death, and I couldn't bring myself to make it worse.

And, honestly, I'd wanted to talk about something—anything—other than Julian with Edan. The beginning of our friendship revolved around him, and I could always feel the weight of Julian hanging over our heads. I took a deep breath.

"It's an email from Julian," I said softly. "He's been sending me a lot of emails."

He reeled back, clearly startled, and pulled his hand from mine. "He's been sending you a lot of emails." He repeated the words slowly.

"Since not long after he left. I'm sorry I didn't tell you. I didn't tell anyone but Maddie."

"What has he been emailing you about?"

"Apologies, mostly. Sometimes he just updates me on his life. Tells me he'll always be there for me." I made a face. "That he doesn't hold a grudge, and he hopes we see each other again one day. I've never responded," I added quickly, and turned my phone for him to see. "Do you want to see my inbox? I can show you that I never responded. I just—"

"Clara." He put his hand over mine again, gently pushing the phone down. "I don't need proof. I believe you."

"Right." His hand was warm on my mine, and I almost reached for it when he pulled it away. I would have liked to hold his hand right now.

"I did sort of want to respond, a couple times, to be honest. Especially at first. I still had all these leftover romantic feelings for him mixed in with fear and sadness back then, and I hated how it made me feel."

"And now?" he asked.

"Definitely no more romantic feelings." My short relationship with Julian felt like a memory of someone else's life. Some other girl had been that sad, crying mess who fell for him. "Fear and anger still, sure. Especially after seeing him today."

"Sure." He stared out at the city, his expression unreadable. "Why didn't you tell anyone but Maddie?"

I could hear the actual question—*why didn't you tell* me?—and I lowered my gaze. I should have told him. It was a glaring omission, considering how many hours we'd spent on this balcony, talking about everything else.

"It just . . . seemed like it would upset everyone," I finally said.

He nodded, his gaze still anywhere but on me.

"I'm sorry," I said. "I should have told you."

"It's OK." He finally looked at me with a smile that didn't seem genuine. I wasn't sure if it actually was OK. When Edan got mad or upset, he just retreated into himself or ran away. We had that in common.

"Uh, I could read it to you," I offered, trying to smooth things over. "The email he just sent. Do you want to hear what he has to say?"

"If you don't mind, yeah."

I glanced at him with a wry smile. "I think it would actually infuriate Julian if he knew that I was reading you his email."

"It really would," he said with a laugh. Some of the tightness in my chest loosened.

I opened the email. It wasn't very long. He'd sent me a few rambling ones, but this one was only a few lines. "Clara," I began, reading his words aloud. "Please talk to me. I honestly don't know what to do now that my parents are gone. They were all I had left. I know that I made mistakes in the past—we both have—but I really wish we could at least talk. We only got a few minutes today, and I have so much more to say. I miss you and I really need you right now. I know that our relationship was brief, but I can't help thinking that we were destined to meet, and I honestly never fell as hard for a girl as I did for you. I know that you felt our connection too, and I know that I ruined it, but I really wish you could find it in your heart to forgive me. Please send me an email or a text or anything. I really need you right now."

I lowered the phone. Edan's expression was pained.

"Christ, that almost made me feel bad for him," he said.

"I know. There are a couple more emails that are like this, actually. Where he tells me he doesn't have anyone, and he desperately needs to talk to me. His parents' death is just an excuse, as terrible as that sounds." I paused. "I really am sorry I didn't tell you sooner."

"You don't have to apologize. I'm glad you told Maddie, at least. I wouldn't want you to have to deal with that alone."

I smiled at him, but he was already standing, his gaze on the door.

"I think I'm going to try and get some sleep."

"Oh. OK."

"I'll see you tomorrow, Clara."

6

EDAN LOOKED MORE TIRED THAN EVER THE NEXT DAY. HE skipped our morning workout, and when he emerged from his room for our assignment that afternoon, he had dark circles beneath his eyes. His steps were sluggish as he shrugged on his weapons pack.

I was standing outside my door, and he caught me watching him. "I'm fine," he said wearily.

"I didn't say anything!"

"You're looking at me weird."

Dorsey emerged from their room, pulling the door shut behind him. "Her expression is because you look like someone hit you with a car, backed up, hit you again, and then leaned out the window and punched you in the face."

"Thanks," Edan said dryly. I tried not to laugh.

"I'd tell you to get back in bed, but apparently no one wants my opinion." Dorsey gave Edan a meaningful look and then turned to me. "He won't take his sleeping pills."

"It's dangerous!" Edan said. "I can't be all groggy and disoriented if scrabs start attacking in the middle of the night. Or worse, not wake up at all."

"I think you could still fight off scrabs half asleep," I said. He smiled. "But we'll come get you and, like, shove you in a closet or something if you don't wake up during a scrab attack."

"That's what I said!" Dorsey exclaimed. "I offered to throw him over my shoulder, though."

"You do not have the strength to throw me over your shoulder," Edan said.

"Rude," Dorsey said.

"I'll think about it," Edan said. "I just don't like the idea of you guys having to take care of me if something happens."

"Yes, heaven forbid we ask for help with anything," Dorsey said, rolling his eyes before walking away.

I watched Dorsey disappear into the stairwell and then turned back to Edan. "That was a slight exaggeration, if it makes you feel better. You only look like they hit you with the car once."

"Hilarious."

"I was talking to Laila and Priya recently about how we all need a break. And I think that especially applies to you."

"Probably." He ran a hand down his face.

"No one wants to desert the team, so maybe we can all take a break together?"

The door next to me opened, and Patrick stepped out of his room, giving me a concerned look. Maybe he'd heard our conversation. Noah followed him out, smiling at us before they both headed toward the stairs.

"Maddie will never go for it," Edan said as they walked away.

"I can try. I mean, even Dorsey is worried about you. Don't you think that there might be something wrong if even that guy is concerned?"

He looked amused. "You clearly don't know Andrew at all. He

is constantly hounding me about whether I've taken my meds and talked to my therapist and how much I slept last night."

"Seriously?"

"He's like the parent I never had. Which I told him to try and get him to back off, but I think it just encouraged him."

I laughed. "Take the sleeping pills, OK? If Dorsey can't carry you by himself, I'll help him."

He smiled. "OK."

I pushed open the stairwell door. The rest of the team was already waiting in the lobby, and we walked out and headed toward the tube station. Patrick and Noah appeared on either side of me.

"Hey, what did you mean about us all taking a break together?" Noah asked. "We heard you say that to Edan."

"He's just been pretty run-down lately. We all are. A break might be a good idea."

"Edan can certainly take a break if he wants, but we can't all go together," Patrick said.

"Why not?" I asked.

"We don't have enough people as it is," Patrick said. "We're one of the best teams, and we've got the new recruits out there now too."

"And I have several of our team members lined up to start training people," Noah said.

"One person can go," Patrick said. "All eight of us is out of the question."

"You guys know we can't keep this up forever, right?" Exasperation crept into my voice. "Everyone is overworked and overtired."

"We're just in a rough patch," Patrick said.

"Things will get better once we up recruitment," Noah said. "I have some ideas."

Patrick slung an arm around my shoulder. "In the meantime, what about massage therapists? I was thinking of asking Maddie to spring for a few."

I sighed. I didn't think a few massages were going to help, but I supposed it couldn't hurt. "I'm sure she'd be fine with that."

~

We took the train to north London. There were already several teams milling around the sidewalks, about fifty recruits total in the area.

"You detected big movement today?" I asked Maddie as we crossed the street.

"Eh, medium, probably," she said, eyes on her tablet. "The army took out a bunch of this pack earlier this morning, so we're just getting the leftovers. But I've got the new recruits out here, so I wanted plenty of backup."

I spotted a few of the new recruits right away, laughing and joking around outside a Starbucks. One of them didn't have his leather armor already strapped to his arms, which was a mistake. There often wasn't time to put it on once the scrabs started tunneling up. Especially when you were still getting used to wearing it.

"Are you sure they're ready?" I asked.

"No less ready than our team was when we started," she said with a shrug.

That was what worried me. Grayson hadn't provided nearly enough time for training. It was part of the reason we'd had so many causalities that first assignment in Paris. We'd managed to squeak by after that just because of the sheer number of recruits, but we didn't have even half as many these days.

"They'll be fine," Maddie said, clearly reading my expression. "I'll go check on them, OK?" She walked toward them, yelling at the one without his armor to put it on.

I moved to an empty corner with Laila, stealing a glance at Edan. He was across the street with Dorsey, gaze distant, holding a cup of coffee. I wished I'd pushed harder for him to stay at the hostel. It couldn't be safe for him to be fighting scrabs when he was so obviously exhausted.

On the other hand, Edan was one of the best members of the team. One of the best recruits, period. Edan at half speed was probably still better than half of the people out here.

"Movement!" Maddie yelled suddenly.

I pulled out my machete. Laila did the same with a sigh.

"You all right?" I asked.

"I was kind of hoping they'd change course today, honestly." She gave me a half smile.

I glanced past her to where Priya and Patrick were pulling their weapons out. Priya noticed my gaze and widened her eyes in an expression I could only describe as *this shit again, huh?*

A block away, the first scrab popped up, followed by several more. There were only a few, and I waited until one popped up closer to me to take a swing.

I drove my blade into the scrab's side and Priya jumped forward to swipe hers across its neck. We moved back as it fell. Priya bumped her fist against mine before taking off down the street.

I turned and spotted Saira a few yards away. The ground behind her was starting to break open, but she was turned away, focused on the scrab in front of her.

I sprinted toward her. Out of the corner of my eye, I saw something flying toward me, and I barely ducked in time before it hit my head. It clattered to the ground. An ax. I cast a baffled glance over my shoulder.

"Sorry!" a recruit yelled, flying past me. He scooped up the ax and kept running.

I skidded to a stop behind Saira, catching the scrab behind her before it was fully out of the ground. I sliced my machete across its throat. It gurgled and slid back into its hole.

Saira turned, catching a glimpse of the scrab as it disappeared into the ground. "Thanks," she panted.

I nodded, and then spun around, searching for the best place to help. Laila was nearby, but she had just killed a scrab. Priya and Patrick were at the end of the street, taking down two more.

I heard a scream from behind me, and I turned to find one of the new recruits wildly swinging his machete at a scrab. Behind him, two civilians were trying to sneak into the Starbucks to escape the chaos, and I gasped as his blade barely missed them.

I ran to them, whistling to try and get the scrab's attention. It whirled around to face me.

"Move away from the building!" I yelled at the recruit, who was still wildly swinging his machete. "Watch out for civilians!"

The scrab turned back to him, and the recruit swung again. His blade caught the woman behind him, ripping across her arm. She screamed.

The recruit froze, horror dawning on his face as he saw the blood. The scrab lunged at him. I dove forward, but I was too late; the recruit was already dead in between the scrab's teeth. I drove my blade into its neck, and it dropped the recruit and toppled to the ground. The sobbing woman ran into Starbucks.

I looked down at the dead recruit and then quickly away, letting out a soft curse. A familiar face was watching me from not far away. Julian.

He stood half a block away, weapons in both hands. Our eyes met, and he lifted the hand with the machete in greeting. I spread my arms, silently asking him what he was doing here. He actually laughed in response, and then lifted both weapons to indicate that he was fighting scrabs. I rolled my eyes and turned away.

Edan and Dorsey were on the other end of the street. Edan had just killed a scrab, and he was shaking blood off his machete. As I watched, another scrab barreled out of the hole a few yards behind him. Edan didn't turn.

"Edan!" I yelled.

He whirled around just in time, barely missing scrab claws. He stumbled back, losing his footing and tumbling to the ground.

I broke into a run. The scrab lunged, and Edan wasn't on his feet again yet. He scrambled across the concrete, swinging his machete. His back hit a wall. He was cornered.

The scrab snapped its teeth, barely missing taking off a chunk of his leg. It reared back, preparing to swing a giant claw at Edan. My heart stopped.

Dorsey dove for the scrab, aiming his machete at the claw headed for Edan. The scrab noticed just in time, turning and whacking Dorsey instead. He gasped, stumbling back but managing to stay on his feet.

Edan jumped up and killed the scrab with one swipe across its neck. He grabbed Dorsey's arm as I skidded to a stop beside them.

"Are you OK?" Edan asked, eyes wide as he looked Dorsey up and down. There was no blood.

"Yeah," Dorsey wheezed. "It was backhand. Just took the air out of me."

Edan dropped Dorsey's arm, letting out a relieved sigh. "Good." He turned to survey the area. We'd cleared the immediate area of scrabs, but there were some down the block. Edan pointed at them. "I'm going to go—"

"No, you're not," Dorsey interrupted. "Go back to the van."

Edan blinked. "What?"

"Go back to the van. You're barely awake, and you're going to get yourself killed."

"No, I—"

"Edan!" Dorsey raised his voice sharply. "We've got this. Go back to the van."

Edan looked startled, but he nodded, then turned and practically bolted away from us. He was headed for the scrabs, not the van.

"Dammit, Edan!" Dorsey called. He made an exasperated noise. "He always does that."

"What?" I asked, my eyes following Edan. He stopped to help Noah, which made me feel a little better. Noah would protect him.

"Whatever he wants. He won't even fight with me about it, he just nods and then carries on being an idiot." He rolled his eyes.

"I feel like it's ruder to do that, you know? I'd rather he just stayed and yelled at—"

A loud crashing noise cut him off. I turned to see a scrab busting out from the window of a store across the street. I could see another behind it, climbing from the hole they'd created in the middle of the shop.

I caught Maddie's eye and gestured at the scrabs to indicate we would take care of them. Dorsey was already on his way. She nodded.

I remembered Julian suddenly, whom Maddie certainly hadn't spotted yet, considering she didn't look ready to murder anyone. I glanced over either shoulder as I broke into a run behind Dorsey. I spotted him in a crowd of recruits, watching me.

Dorsey took care of a scrab that had just climbed out of the shop, and I edged around him and stepped through the now-destroyed window. Another scrab had just pulled itself out of the giant hole in the middle of what looked like a clothing store. There were two more holes in the floor, one on either side of the room. A lot of scrabs had come up from here. At least it looked like the store had been closed or abandoned. There were no dead bodies.

The scrab didn't lunge at me. It stood near the hole, drool pouring out of its mouth and pooling on the floor. No, it wasn't drool. It was some sort of thick brown mucus. Same with its eyes. It could probably barely see with that gunk in them.

"Shit, Clara, this is an MDG scrab," Dorsey said from behind me.

I glanced back at the scrab he'd just killed. Sure enough, it had sensors all across its forehead. MDG put those on their scrabs to help control them.

I turned back to the motionless scrab. It didn't have any sensors on its head, but I did spot a small silver circle on its neck. Also an MDG scrab.

"This one is sick or something," I said, making a face as I stepped forward. I killed it quickly. It didn't even put up a fight. Dorsey stepped up next to me, looking down at the scrab.

"Oh, that's disgusting. Is there a scrab flu?"

"I really hope so. That thing didn't even try to fight back."

I glanced over my shoulder, looking for Julian again. We'd come across MDG scrabs only once or twice in the last six months. Was it a coincidence that they popped up again as soon as Julian reappeared?

I spotted him not far away, still staring at me.

"Is that Julian?" Dorsey asked.

"Yes," I said with a sigh.

Julian turned at a rumbling noise, and I followed his gaze to see the earth splitting open and at least twenty scrabs climbing out. *Oh, shit.* This was definitely more scrabs than Maddie had been expecting today. We didn't have enough people for that many.

Dorsey cursed. "We should get over there."

I took a step toward the broken window. I heard a loud *crack* from above my head. I looked up.

"Oh god," I heard Dorsey say. He grabbed me as the building collapsed around us.

7

ROCKS AND DEBRIS POUNDED AGAINST MY BODY, AND I GRIPPED
the arm Dorsey had around me. It felt like forever until the sky
stopped falling, but when it did, all I could hear was the ringing in
my ears. I realized I'd squeezed my eyes shut, and I opened them,
slowly. It was very dark, and for a moment, I couldn't tell what was
right in front of me.

Rocks, I realized suddenly. Concrete. The whole building had
caved in. It wasn't uncommon in scrab-heavy areas like London.

Dorsey was still wrapped around me, and I realized with horror that he wasn't moving.

"Dorsey?" I grabbed the arm he still had wrapped around my
stomach.

"Ow," he said. I let out a huge whoosh of air. "Are you OK?"

"Uh . . . yes? You?"

"Yes? Yes. I can feel all my limbs. That seems like a good sign."

I was trying to figure out why it was so dark. The building had
fallen on top of us, but still, I should have been able to glimpse
sunlight.

But Dorsey had yanked me with him just as the building
started to fall. Toward the scrab tunnel. I took in a sharp breath.

"Dorsey, that was really smart," I said.

"What?"

"Getting us into the scrab tunnel."

"Seemed like the safest option."

I wriggled away from him and tried to turn, but there wasn't enough room. I looked up at where the exit hole for the tunnel would have been, but it was now covered in debris.

I looked down. A few slivers of light poked through the rocks, but my eyes were starting to adjust. We were wedged at the top of the tunnel, and I looked down to see a tiny hint of sun at the other end.

"However, I did not consider how we would get out," Dorsey said, and then took a sharp breath.

"What?"

"Nothing. I think . . . I think I scraped up my back. It's fine."

I pushed my hands against a large rock above us, and several smaller ones rained down on us. I coughed and lowered my arms.

"I don't think we're getting out that way." I looked back down at the tunnel.

"Maybe we should wait for them to dig us out. Maddie saw us come in here."

"Yeah, but who knows how long that will be." I wriggled against him until I was free and dropped onto my hands and knees. The tunnel wasn't too tight of a squeeze—the scrab was bigger than us—but I still felt uneasy in the dark, enclosed space. "Let's try the other end of the tunnel."

"We have no idea how long that tunnel is. We could be crawling for miles."

I shook my head, pointing. "There's light, see?"

"Oh yeah."

"You OK to move? I could go by myself and come back to dig you out."

"No, I'm fine."

I could only barely make out his features in the dim light, but he nodded at me reassuringly. I scooted around so I was facing the other end of the tunnel, and began crawling.

From above, I heard a scream, and then a roar. I winced.

"Jesus, it sounds bad out there," Dorsey murmured.

"Yeah." Something skittered across my hand, and I shivered and moved a little faster. "Thank you," I said, trying to distract myself from the bugs and the darkness around me. "For pulling me into the hole. I think I would have been crushed if it weren't for you."

"Oh." He sounded embarrassed. "Nah, don't thank me for that. I wasn't even really thinking."

"You weren't thinking, but your instinct was to grab me and try to save me, even though I . . ." I trailed off, not wanting to be rude.

"Even though you don't like me?" he guessed.

"No," I said quickly. I almost turned my head to look at him, but it had gotten darker as we made our way through the tunnel. The light at the end was farther than I'd thought. "I was going to say even though I never talk to you."

"Because you don't like me." He didn't say it as a question this time, but he didn't sound particularly upset about it.

"I don't dislike you," I said. "I don't really even know you, I guess."

"It's all right. I know Gage was a dick to you, and we were sort of friends, so I can't really blame you. I have bad taste in guys, I admit it." He paused. "I don't have great taste in girls either, actually."

I bit back a laugh. "Were you and Gage more than friends?"

"No. Sadly."

I made a face. "You really do have terrible taste in guys."

He laughed, and then moaned. "Ow. Don't make me laugh."

"Sorry. Do you think it's serious?"

"No, I think some of my skin is just . . . not there anymore."

"You OK to keep going?"

"Too late to turn back now."

"Good point." I dug my fingers into the dirt as I crawled a little faster. "Was this a terrible idea?"

"Me pulling us in here? Probably."

"No, crawling to the other side."

The light at the end of the tunnel flickered. A large body slithered into the hole and disappeared in the darkness.

I froze.

"I don't think we had any good—" Dorsey cut himself off as he bumped into me.

I heard a scratching noise from ahead.

"Dorsey," I whispered. "There's a scrab."

I heard him take in a breath.

I fumbled for my weapons pack and quietly pulled out my machete. "Don't move," I whispered. "If we surprise it, I can—"

"Clara!"

Julian's voice rang out from behind me, loud and insistent. Ahead, I heard the scrab snarl.

"*Clara!*" Julian yelled again. I looked over my shoulder to see rocks tumbling into the hole. Light filtered into the tunnel.

"Do we go back?" Dorsey whispered.

I heard another snarl, followed by a rustling noise.

It was getting closer. I gripped my machete tightly.

I smelled the scrab before I saw it—its putrid breath against my skin. Then I could see its teeth, bared and aimed at my face.

I dropped my arm and drove my machete into its neck.

It screamed, and I pulled my blade out and stabbed it again. It shrank back and then collapsed in the dirt.

Behind it, I saw another scrab slither into the hole.

"Go back," I said urgently. I kept my machete in hand as I turned and started crawling back the way we came. Dorsey moved quickly, and I picked up the pace, my knees aching in protest.

I stole a glance over my shoulder. I could see the outline of the scrab as it approached the dead one. It was stuck, trying to maneuver around it. I heard scratching noises as it tried to widen the hole.

Julian's face appeared at the entrance of the tunnel. "Come on!"

We crawled even faster, and Julian's face disappeared as he extended his hand.

"Come on, Gage!" he yelled.

"I'm *Dorsey*, you dick," he growled. "You killed Ga—"

"Just take my hand!"

Dorsey scrambled forward, finally reaching the tunnel entrance. He braced his foot against a rock to propel himself up and Julian grabbed his arms, yanking him out of the hole.

The scrab had made it around the dead one, and it moved through the tunnel with alarming speed, its beady eyes fixed on me. It lunged.

I used my machete as a shield, narrowly missing getting a claw in the face. I slashed my blade across its face, and it screamed.

"Heads up!" Julian yelled.

I glanced up and then leaned back as he thrust his machete down and into the scrab's ear. A second scrab was right behind it, and it stumbled as its buddy fell backwards.

"Give me your hands," Julian said, dropping his machete and holding his arms out.

I grabbed them, letting him help me climb out of the rubble. The scrab was right on my heels, and Dorsey leaned around us to sink his blade into its neck. He sighed, sitting back on his heels as the scrab fell back into the tunnel.

"Are you OK?" Julian panted. He still had a grip on my arms, and I quickly pulled them free. I ignored the question and turned to Dorsey, who was still on the ground. I stood and extended my hand to him.

"Thanks." He winced as he stood. I leaned around to see his back. His shirt was torn, his skin bloody and raw.

"You all right?" I asked.

He nodded. His gaze shifted to Julian.

I turned to look at him. He was dirty and sweaty, and behind him I spotted a pile of rocks that he'd had to move to dig us out. He stared at me for a moment.

"I should go see if they need help elsewhere," he finally said. "It's bad out there."

"Those are MDG scrabs," Dorsey said, pointing to the one I'd killed earlier. Only its foot stuck out from the rubble.

"Did you send those?" I asked, my voice shaking.

He gave me a baffled look. "Why would I send scrabs to attack you? I followed you here to protect you. I knew you needed the help."

Dorsey looked so deeply confused by my needing help that I felt a burst of affection for him.

"There are a lot of injured recruits out there," Julian said. "I'm going to go see what I can do." He turned to go, hopping over rubble. The entire building had cratered in, including the shops on either side of the clothing store.

On the street, recruits were everywhere, some of them dirty and bloody. The ground was littered with dead scrabs and humans.

Maddie was running across the street, her expression frantic until she spotted me. I climbed out of the broken window, and she crashed into me, throwing her arms around my waist.

"Oh my god, I saw that building go down, and I thought you guys were dead. I was trying to get over here but—" She cut herself off as she pulled away, and I saw that she was crying.

"Is everyone OK?" I asked, and then realized how stupid that question was. I could see three dead recruits from here. I swallowed down a wave of terror. "Is the team OK?"

"I—I think so. Priya and Laila are . . ." She trailed off, turning to the street and pointing. "There they are. With Patrick." They were helping to pull an injured recruit out from under a dead scrab.

"Please no hugs," Dorsey said, and I looked over to see Noah pulling his arms back as he approached him.

He peered at Dorsey's back and winced. "Come on, you need to get to the hospital."

I looked at each team member in turn. "Where is . . ." My throat closed as I turned left and then right. "Where is Edan?"

Maddie grabbed my hand. "Edan! He's fine. I saw him." She used her hand to shield her eyes from the sun. "He's there."

I turned to see him in the middle of the street, staring at us. I waved, but he didn't respond.

"I have to . . ." Maddie swallowed. "I don't know. Help somewhere." She started to take off, but I grabbed her arm.

"Julian's here," I said.

She froze. "What?"

"Don't make a scene, OK? But he's here, and we saw some MDG scrabs, so we're going to need to tell the police about that."

She stared at me, understanding my meaning. She slowly nodded.

I let go of her arm and ducked around a few recruits as I headed toward Edan. He was still standing motionless in the middle of the street. His chest was heaving up and down too quickly, like he'd just been sprinting.

I walked quickly toward him. He didn't move.

He pressed a hand to his forehead, his shoulders curving forward, and when he looked back up at me, I could see that he was crying.

Edan and I didn't really hug—we hadn't since the night Julian killed Grayson and we lost three team members. But I pulled him into a hug as soon as I was close enough to touch him.

He wrapped his arms around my waist and held me so tightly

that it was a little hard to breathe. I curled my fingers around his shoulders. Breathing was overrated anyway.

"Is Dorsey . . ." He pulled away, wiping both eyes quickly.

"He's fine," I said. "He scraped up his back, so he's going to the hospital, but it's not serious."

"Jesus." He blew out a slow breath. "I thought you both were . . ." He didn't finish the thought.

"Hey! Can I get some help over here?" a voice called. "We've got a recruit under some rocks!"

I looked in the direction of the voice, but several recruits were already running to help one of the UK team leaders. I realized suddenly that there were bodies in the street — dead bodies. Recruits. At least five that I could see right in front of me. Another three when I turned slightly.

Edan ran a shaky hand through his hair. "I'm going to go help over there." He pointed to where recruits were helping civilians out of an overturned bus. I spotted a flash of black coat.

"No." I grabbed his hand. "Not there."

He gave me a confused look, and I pulled him in the opposite direction. "Let's go help over there." I pointed across the street to where Priya and Laila were helping injured recruits.

"O-OK?" He held my hand tightly as I steered him away.

"Julian's over there," I explained quietly.

"What?" he whipped his head around to look over his shoulder. "Why is he . . . Do you think he had something to do with this?"

"I really don't know."

8

The final tally showed that fifteen recruits died and over thirty were seriously injured.

I kept thinking about Grayson. Maybe because we hadn't suffered such a massive loss since that day in Paris. I kept thinking about him sitting on the ground of the cafeteria in the Paris training facility the next day. The sad set of his shoulders. The smile he'd given me when I tried to cheer him up.

I knew better than to try to cheer up Maddie. She returned to the hostel briefly to shower and then left to go to the hospital. I'd offered to go with her, but she said I should stay in case anyone needed anything.

No one needed anything. Everyone had shut themselves away in their rooms. The halls were quiet and deserted.

Edan's door was open, and I stopped, peering inside. He sat on his bed, phone in hand, freshly showered and dressed in loose black pants and a white T-shirt. The lamp on his bedside table was the only light in the room, casting a warm glow over his bed. Dorsey's bed was unmade and empty.

"Hey," I said softly.

He looked up from his phone, one side of his mouth lifting slightly. "Hey."

"Heard anything about Dorsey?"

"Yeah, he's still waiting. The hospital is really backed up."

"I'll bet."

He touched his phone, making the screen come to life. "It's late. What are you doing up?"

"What are *you* doing up?"

"I'm always up."

I leaned my head against the door frame. "I can't sleep. Every time I close my eyes . . ." I saw a dead recruit on the ground. Heard the sound of scrab claws digging their way through a tunnel. Saw Julian's worried face.

"I know," Edan said. He held my gaze for a moment, and then another moment that felt heavier than the first. My stomach clenched in a way that wasn't at all painful.

He scooted over on his bed, putting a hand in the empty spot beside him. "You could . . . Do you want to stay? I was going to try to sleep, if you want to stay."

"Yes," I said immediately. He smiled and then quickly lowered his gaze, pink spots appearing on his cheeks. I didn't think I'd ever seen Edan blush before.

I stepped inside the room, shutting the door behind me. He pushed down the blankets, and I walked across the room and slipped underneath them. I pulled off my sweatshirt and dropped it on the ground next to the bed, revealing the T-shirt underneath.

Edan reached up and switched the light off, and he disappeared in the darkness. I felt the bed shift as he moved, smelled his soap and shampoo in the air.

It was quiet for a moment, and then I felt his hand very lightly on my waist.

"Do you mind?" he asked quietly, his fingers curling there.

"No," I whispered. An understatement.

His arm circled my waist, pulling me closer to him. Our legs intertwined, and I closed my eyes briefly as I let my forehead rest against his chest.

I *really* didn't mind.

"Edan," I said softly. I was feeling brave in the dark.

"Yeah?"

"Were you mad that I didn't tell you about Julian emailing me?"

"No." When he spoke, I could feel his breath on my hair. "I wasn't mad at you. I was kind of mad at *myself*, honestly."

"Mad at yourself? Why?"

"Because I've been such a mess lately that I figured you didn't feel like you could tell me. Between the not sleeping and all the stuff I've told you about the drama with my mom . . . I just felt like I'd failed you or I should have been stronger or . . . something. I don't know."

"It's not that I didn't think you could handle it," I said. "I actually just really hate talking about Julian with you. I mean, I hate talking about him in general, but especially with you."

"Why?" His hand lightly brushed my hair back.

"Because . . ." Because Julian tried to kill him, and Grayson took a bullet for him. Because Edan and Julian had always hated each other. Both things were true, and I could have said them. But they weren't actually the reason.

"Because I don't like reminding you that I dated Julian.

Because it was a stupid choice, and I could have—" I cut myself off before I said, *I could have chosen you instead.*

But I thought about it a lot. What would have happened if I'd been in a seat next to him on the flight over to Paris. He definitely wouldn't have slept, and maybe we would have talked and I wouldn't have been able to resist that smile. Or those eyes. Maybe we wouldn't have hated each other when we started training, and I would have stopped lusting over Julian.

"You're not stupid," he said. "I've never thought you were stupid for dating Julian. I know how kind he was to you at first."

"I just feel like everything about me has become defined by Julian. Before, it was my dad, and now it's him, and I just wanted to be me. Especially with you."

"I've never thought of you as being defined by Julian." He held me a little tighter. "But I know what you mean."

We were both quiet for several minutes, our chests rising and falling together.

"Do me a favor?" he asked.

"What?"

"Don't go crawling into any more scrab tunnels. My anxiety can't handle it."

I laughed softly. "No promises, but I'll try." My hands were clenched into fists, and I slowly unfurled one, letting it rest against his chest. "I should have said something about the new recruits. I knew they weren't ready, and so many of them died today."

"Are they ever *really* ready?"

"No. But it was worse this time."

"This wasn't your fault, Clara."

"I know, I just . . ." I sighed. "More people are going to quit, and we're already stretched thin."

"Do you ever think about quitting?"

"No," I said, surprised. "Do you?"

"I did, after Grayson died. Thought about hopping on a train and going back to France and on to Italy or wherever."

"Why didn't you?"

"I didn't want to leave the team. Or give up trying to take out MDG."

"You . . . aren't thinking about it again, are you?"

"No." His hand pressed into my back, warm and firm. "I wouldn't leave you. Any of you."

"I'm thinking of asking Maddie to take a break, maybe see if she'll go back to New York for a while so we can regroup. Would you come with us, if I can get her to agree?"

"Yeah, I'd come with you." His breath was warm against my forehead. "I would go anywhere with you."

I let out a slow breath, my heart thumping against his. "I don't want to go anywhere without you, so that works out."

He chuckled softly, his arms tightening around me. I smiled as I closed my eyes.

~

I woke to the sun streaming in through a crack in the curtains, and the sound of Edan's deep breathing. I rolled over to see him curled into a ball, head tucked into his chest. Dorsey's bed was still empty.

I silently slid out of bed and grabbed my sweatshirt, pulling it over my head. I shouldn't wake Edan, not when he had so much trouble sleeping. That was what I was going to tell myself as I snuck out of his room, anyway.

I crept across the floor and out the door, shutting it quietly behind me.

I should not have gotten in Edan's bed last night. And cuddled with him. And said that I didn't want to go anywhere without him, even though it was true. There must have been thirty empty beds in this place, and I had to go climb into his.

I wanted to do it again, if I was being honest. I wished I were still there.

But I'd avoided any possibility of romance with Edan for a reason. For several reasons. I'd needed some time after Julian, but I also didn't want to always be defined by who I was dating. After I made that video all anyone on social media could talk about was my relationship with Julian and whether I was with Edan now. I wanted to be known as more than just the girl in between Julian and Edan.

I shook the thoughts away. I needed to find Maddie and check to see if there were updates on the recruits. I had more important things to worry about than whether I'd just complicated my friendship with Edan by cuddling him all night.

I grabbed my phone from my room, scrolling through the texts as I walked to the lounge. Maddie was on the couch, phone pressed to her ear and two laptops open in front of her. The look she gave me clearly said she didn't want to be disturbed. She was probably making calls to families.

I trudged through the empty halls to the kitchen. Dorsey was there, spreading peanut butter on a piece of bread.

He looked up and gave me a tired smile. "Hey."

"Hey." I walked in and leaned against the other side of the island. "How are you feeling?"

"Pretty good, actually. They gave me some nice pain meds. I think the doctor felt sorry for us. It was a pretty bad scene at the hospital."

"I'm sure," I said softly.

He held out the bag of bread to me. "Do you want some?"

"I'm fine, thanks."

Patrick appeared in the doorway of the kitchen. "Have you guys seen Maddie?"

"She was in the lounge a minute ago," I said.

"I just checked, and she wasn't there."

"She might be hiding somewhere to make family calls. I wouldn't go looking for her, honestly."

"Do you think she'll care if I take off with Connor for a few hours? I just need to get out of here," Patrick said. "I figured we probably weren't going on an assignment today."

"I'm sure it's fine," I said. "I'll let her know when I see her."

"Thanks." He started to walk away, then gripped the edge of the door frame, sticking his head back in and smiling at Dorsey. "I heard you heroically saved Clara's life, by the way. Nice work."

"What?" Dorsey gave me an exasperated look. "I did not."

Patrick was already gone, and I laughed. "Yes you did. And I told everyone."

He let out a dramatic sigh. "I just acted on instinct and—"

"Dorsey, take the compliment."

"I will not." His phone buzzed, and he glanced down at it. "Rude."

"What?"

"Hazel dumped me."

My lips parted. "Your girlfriend? Just now?"

"*Girlfriend* is probably overstating our relationship." He typed something into his phone. "But yes, just now. She says she's thinking about quitting the teams and can't handle the added stress."

"That really is rude." The quitting part was unsurprising, though. We were already looking at a wave of dropouts, and this was definitely going to make it worse. In fact, I really couldn't blame them.

"I told you I have terrible taste in romantic partners." He finished typing on his phone and set it aside. "I did hit on Patrick once, though. That was a good choice, in my opinion. But he either didn't notice or very nicely ignored it."

"Patrick gets hit on a lot, so I'm sure he's used to it."

"True."

"Did you get any sleep?" I asked carefully.

"You mean, did I stop by my room and see you in Edan's bed? I sure did." He grinned.

I felt my cheeks go hot. "It was just . . ." Just what? I didn't know what explanation I was going for.

"Hey, I wasn't judging. I've often wondered why there aren't more girls in Edan's bed. He's an excellent choice."

"We're not . . ." I cleared my throat, trying to think of a way to change the subject. "You and Edan became really good friends, huh?"

"Why do you say it all surprised like that? I'm likable. I have friends."

"Come on, I didn't mean it like that. It's nice that you became such good friends. He even calls you Andrew, though I always wondered if that was just to annoy you."

His lips twitched. "I don't think he's trying to annoy me. Maybe he doesn't like my last name? I don't know. He just asked me one day if he could call me by my first time. I said sure, you can call me whatever except Drew."

"Why not Drew?"

"It's what my parents call me."

"And you don't want him to call you that because it's special to them or because it reminds you of bad things?"

"Uhhh . . ." He looked taken aback. "Wow. No one's ever asked me that. Both, I guess."

"Ah."

Edan walked into the kitchen then, hair still rumpled from sleep. My cheeks went hot again.

"Hey," Dorsey said. "We were just talking about you. Finally get some sleep?"

"Uh, yeah. Some." Our eyes met briefly, and he quickly looked down at his phone. "Are you feeling OK?"

"Yeah, I'm fine. And I did not save Clara's life, by the way."

One side of Edan's mouth lifted. "That's not what I heard."

Dorsey gave me an exasperated look. "Dammit, Pratt, I have a reputation as a selfish asshole to protect, and you are not helping me out at all here."

I laughed, and a smile spread across Edan's face. Maybe we

could just pretend last night didn't happen. Carry on being friends without ruining it by becoming more.

My phone buzzed, and I looked down to see a call from Laurence, which was weird. It was like one in the morning in Dallas.

"I should take this," I said, and then pointed at Dorsey. "You should be resting, by the way." I looked at Edan. "Make him rest. His girlfriend just dumped him, so he has nowhere to go anyway."

"Hey!" Dorsey called as I walked out of the kitchen. I heard Edan laugh.

I pressed the phone to my ear as I walked down the hall. "Hey, Laurence."

"Hey." He said the word slowly, almost like he was uncertain.

"Are you OK? It's late there."

"I know. Did I wake you up? I was waiting until I thought you'd be up."

"No, I was up. What's going on?"

"Julian called me a few hours ago."

I stopped. "What?"

"He called me a bunch of times, actually. I kept having all these missed calls from a New York number, and when it rang at like ten o'clock at night, I figured I should find out what the hell this person wanted. So I answered it."

"What did he say?"

"He . . . It was weird. He told me how much he loves you, and he's just trying to protect you. He said that I'd probably heard some really bad things about him, but he was trying to make it up to you and he wanted my help."

"Your *help*?"

"Yeah."

"Did he say with what?"

"He said that you were in danger. That the teams were a mess, and you were going to get killed. And he said that you were hanging around a bunch of bad people and I needed to step in."

I rolled my eyes. "That's insulting."

"Do you know who he's talking about?"

"Maddie, probably. Maybe Edan too. Neither of them is bad, by the way."

"Are you and Edan . . . I'm sorry, that's probably none of my business, is it?"

"I'm not dating Edan."

"I wasn't—"

"Or anyone. I'm not dating anyone."

"I wasn't judging you. Or Edan."

"Sure. Just, for the record, I'm not dating anyone." I closed my eyes, letting out a breath. This was even more awkward than usual. *Thanks, Julian.*

"How did you respond?" I asked. "When he asked for your help?"

"I told him to go to hell. And I asked how he got my number."

"What did he say?"

"He just said, 'I did a little digging.' I guess it isn't that hard to find someone's number, if you really want it, but . . ."

"He might still have access to the forms I filled out when I first joined," I said with a sigh. "I put your number as my emergency contact."

"What is wrong with this guy? Have you talked to him lately?"

"Yes. He's here, in London. I've seen him a couple times. I'm sorry that he called you. I really suggest you block his number."

"It's not your fault." He paused. "You don't think he's tried to call Mom or Dad, do you?"

"I can't imagine. He knew my relationship with them. He and Dad might get along, though."

Laurence let out a humorless laugh. "Sounds like it."

"Block Julian's number and let me know if you hear that he tried to contact Mom or Dad, OK? And maybe save a screenshot of all the times he tried to call you."

"Got it."

"I'll talk to you later, OK?"

"Yeah."

I slipped my phone back into my pocket, an uneasy feeling growing in my chest. It seemed that there was no escaping Julian.

9

I FOUND MADDIE IN THE THIRD-FLOOR STORAGE ROOM, SITTING on a bare mattress with her laptop in front of her. She was staring out at the balcony, and it took a moment for her face to clear when she turned to me. I'd seen that expression a lot a few months ago. I was pretty sure it was the face she made when she was thinking about Grayson.

I edged around the boxes and a bed frame and walked to her.

"Hey," I said, easing down onto the floor next to the mattress. "You OK?"

"I've been better," she muttered, without looking at me.

"Did you make all the calls to the family members?"

She nodded.

"I'm sorry. That must have been tough."

She sighed, running a hand through her hair. "Half the new recruits died. And several civilians were injured. By our recruits, not the scrabs."

"I heard."

"It's just . . ." She closed her eyes for a few seconds. "It's just a setback. We had one in Paris, and we were fine. A few people have quit today, but I'm thinking of calling an all-teams meeting tonight. Try to reassure people and keep their spirits up."

"Are you sure that's the best idea?" I asked quietly.

She turned to face me. I didn't think she'd slept at all. Her eyes were glassy, and she looked ready to pass out. "What do you mean?"

"I think we should suspend the teams, Maddie."

She stared at me. "What?"

"Just temporarily," I said quickly. "We lost a lot of people, and there were MDG scrabs there."

"So you just want to give up?" She looked at me incredulously. "If anything, we need to work harder! Can you imagine how scared people must be, hearing that the trained scrabs are still out there?"

"You're right," I said, and some of the anger left her face. "I'm not saying we should give up. I'm saying we should let everyone else think that we have."

"What do you mean?"

"Let's pretend like we're scared. Let MDG think that they've won. And while they're celebrating, we'll go back to the US and finally find Dust Storm."

"But . . . I'll have to actually disband the teams to do that. I can't tell everyone that plan. It would definitely leak."

"It would. I don't think we could tell anyone except team seven."

She blew out a long breath. "I don't know."

"You could say it's temporary. The holidays are coming up any-way—just send everyone home and say we'll be regrouping in the new year. We need to take some time to recruit and develop new training methods anyway. Put some people on that, so everyone knows that we're actually coming back soon, and let team seven deal with MDG."

She was quiet for a long time, her face pensive. "Well, shit."

"What?"

A tiny smile crossed her face. "That's a really good idea."

I returned the smile. "Thank you."

"You'll come stay with me in New York?"

"Of course. I think we should let the rest of the team visit their families, if they want, but I'm sure as hell not going to Texas. Not until that conference, anyway."

Her eyes widened. "The conference. It's in January."

"It sure is. And I bet Hannah could get us some passes."

"I take it back; this is a *brilliant* plan."

~

Maddie called a team meeting that afternoon. The eight of us squeezed into Maddie's and my room, and I could see from everyone's faces that they knew something was up. We usually met in the lounge, or just out in the hallway.

I perched on the edge of my bed with Edan on one side and Priya on the other. Edan's shoulder kept lightly brushing against mine, which was intensely distracting.

We hadn't discussed our sleepover, and I'd slept in my own bed last night. So far, my plan of pretending it had never happened was working out well.

Priya leaned past me to peer at Edan. "You look better."

"I know. I'm quite dashing, aren't I?" He grinned, and Priya rolled her eyes.

"I meant you look like you slept more than an hour last night," she said.

"I did. And no scrab attacks so far, so Andrew hasn't had to carry me out over his shoulder."

"Dorsey does not have the upper body strength for that," Priya said.

"Excuse you," Dorsey said, looking up at us from where he was sitting on the floor and flexing his right biceps. "Why does everyone keeping saying that? I totally have muscles. They're just . . ."

"Small?" Priya guessed.

"I was going to say subtle."

"OK, sorry," Maddie said, putting her phone aside. She was sitting cross-legged on her bed. "Just had to finish that email." She took a breath. "I wanted to let you guys know first that I'm about to go downstairs and suspend all the teams."

Silence fell over the room. Patrick, who was leaning against the door, stared at her in shock.

"Seriously?" Noah asked.

"Just temporarily," she said.

"It was my idea," I added quickly. Everyone's attention turned to me. "The teams need time to regroup, and we need time to figure out what's going on with MDG. Maddie and I are going to New York to work with Hannah and Victor, and then we're planning to attend the Scrab Defense League conference in January."

"You're all welcome to come with us to New York, or you can go home for the holidays," Maddie said.

"We're just going to leave?" Patrick asked. "What about all the UK teams?"

"I'm suspending all St. John teams, but they're welcome to stay in the hostel for now."

"We can't just leave them here." Patrick looked from me to Maddie with a frown. "We've been killing scrabs out there nearly every day. We're saving people. We can't just pack up and desert everyone."

"We're not deserting them," Maddie said. "I plan to be back very soon. But for now, I agree with Clara that we should focus on MDG. Once we expose them, it will be easier to recruit."

"You could still leave some teams in place here," Patrick argued.

"It's too dangerous," I said. "We lost so many recruits yesterday."

"It's a miracle that Clara and I didn't die too," Dorsey said quietly.

Patrick looked like he wanted to protest further, but he just crossed his arms over his chest and leaned against the door.

"So what do you guys think?" Maddie asked. "Would you want to go back to the US?"

"I wouldn't mind going home for the holidays," Priya said.

"Me neither," Laila said. Noah nodded in agreement, but took a quick glance at Patrick. They exchanged a look that I suspected meant that neither of them were happy with this plan.

"Ugh, I guess," Dorsey said with a sigh. "I actually wouldn't mind seeing my friends."

"Edan?" Maddie asked. "You want to go back to New York for a while? You can stay with me and Clara."

"Sure," he said. "You know how I enjoy making fun of your fancy-ass house."

"I do," she said dryly.

I'd forgotten that Edan would have been to Grayson and Maddie's house. In fact, Edan had a lot of history in New York. He didn't have a home in terms of an actual building, but he had friends. People who cared about him.

I glanced at Dorsey and Laila, who were talking about going to Chicago. *Everyone* had friends or family or something to go back to. Everyone but me.

Edan caught my eye and smiled in a way that made me think my feelings had been splashed across my face. I blushed and looked away.

"This is just temporary, guys," Maddie said. "I promise. We'll be back before you know it."

~

We walked with Maddie to the lounge for the all-teams meeting. It was already packed, and the room quieted as she stepped onto a chair to address everyone. Her expression was tight, and I saw her swallow hard as she waited for a few more recruits to trickle in. The rest of team seven circled around us.

"OK, guys," she said, her voice so soft it barely carried to the back of the room. Everyone went still.

"I've notified all the families of the recruits who were killed, so you can feel free to post your tributes. We—" She stopped abruptly, and when she spoke again, her voice was shaking. "We'll be having a memorial tonight." She took in a deep breath. "And I'm suspending all teams temporarily."

A shocked ripple went through the room.

"We suffered extensive causalities, and there were some

civilian injuries as well. I think it's best if we take some time to regroup. Some of the trainers will be working from here to develop new recruitment and training strategies, and I'll be touch in the new year about next steps. The hostel will remain open, if you'd like to stay."

"Can we keep fighting scrabs if we want?" a recruit called.

"What you do in your free time is up to you, but I'm going to need everyone to turn over their St. John uniforms and all weapons."

Grumbles went through the crowd.

"If you want to return home, please just put the details in an email and send it to me by the end of the day. Team seven will be handling all travel plans, so come to one of us with any questions."

She paused, taking in a shaky breath. "I didn't want to do this. My brother gave his life for these teams, and I believe in them just as much as he did. He wanted to create a huge, global alliance of warriors to fight these things, and I know you guys want to be out there doing exactly that. But we can't continue right now if it means sacrificing huge numbers of recruits. I know he wouldn't have wanted that."

I saw a few people nod in agreement.

"I'm sorry, guys." Her voice cracked. "I'm so sorry."

I blinked back tears of my own. I knew we were making the right choice, but my throat tightened as I looked around at all the disappointed faces in the room. Even though we had every intention of coming back, I couldn't help but feel like this was the end of something great.

Part Two

THE MOST DEPRESSING CLUB IN THE WORLD

10

MADDIE, EDAN, AND I ARRIVED IN NEW YORK IN THE LATE afternoon. We'd spent a week in London before leaving for New York. A good number of recruits went home, others decided to travel around Europe, and some just kind of disappeared. Maddie found someone to manage the hostel for the recruits who were staying. All of team seven had elected to go home for the holidays, and they'd left earlier in the week.

Maddie's mom was waiting for us in baggage claim, and Maddie broke into a run when she spotted her and threw her arms around Nicole's neck.

Maddie wiped away tears when they pulled apart, and her mom wrapped an arm around her as she turned to face us. If I'd seen my mom again right then, I definitely wouldn't have cried. She probably wouldn't either. The whole interaction would have been awkward and uncomfortable, with a hefty amount of guilty thrown in for good measure.

Nicole's eyes lit up when she spotted Edan, and she stepped away from Maddie, holding her arms out. "Edan."

He stepped forward and hugged her briefly. She patted his cheek and said something I couldn't hear. When she pulled away, she smiled at me.

"It's so nice to finally meet you in person, Clara," she said.

"It's nice to meet you too." I sounded as nervous as I was, and I quickly lowered my gaze to the floor. Maddie's mom seemed kind and calm and completely different than either of my parents, but I was still apprehensive about spending several weeks with her. I hadn't had to deal with any parents — mine or other people's — for more than six months. I wasn't sure what to expect.

We followed Nicole to the baggage carousel, and I spotted the words *St. John Teams* on a television playing the news as we walked. A lot of the news outlets were reporting that teams were done for good.

Nicole led us outside after we got our bags, to a waiting car. A driver helped us load our luggage.

"Edan, why don't you sit up front?" Nicole said, putting a hand on his back as she pointed to the passenger's seat.

"Thank you," he said, smiling at her.

I climbed into the car and took a seat next to Maddie, who sat in the middle. We rode for over an hour through stop-and-go traffic.

Part of me already missed London. I'd found some time to take long walks before we left — sometimes alone and sometimes with Edan. I'd grown attached to the city, despite the constant drizzle and relentless scrab attacks. I knew it was for the best that we take a break, but I was still sad to say goodbye to the first city that had ever felt like home.

Edan never brought up the night in his bed on our walks, so I didn't either. The air between us felt different now, but I was probably just imagining it. Maybe it hadn't even been a big deal to him.

That thought wasn't all that comforting, actually.

We turned onto a narrow tree-lined street. New York reminded me of London a little, except without all the scrab destruction. I hadn't realized how accustomed I'd grown to all the scrab warning signs until I was in a city without them.

"You've never been to New York, right, Clara?" Nicole asked as the driver hauled our bags out of the car.

I shook my head. "No."

Maddie and her mom headed to the door, and Edan and I followed.

"This is a weird way to see New York for the first time," he whispered, amused, and I didn't have to ask what he meant. I was pretty sure that if I'd come to New York alone, I never would have ended up in this part of the city.

I stepped inside, my eyes going wide. The floors were shiny white marble, a curved staircase to my left led up to the second level.

Nicole led us through a dining room with an impressive chandelier and a colorful flower arrangement on the center of the table.

"You're free to wander wherever you'd like," she said, walking through the dining room and into a very large, very clean kitchen. "Except the sixth floor. That's the master suite."

The sixth floor? *Sixth?*

"I had a couple rooms made up for you guys," Nicole said. "Why don't you show them, Maddie?"

"Come on," Maddie said, heading to the stairs. "I'll give you guys the tour."

She led us past the second floor, where there was a living

room and a "formal" dining room. It seemed weird to have a dining room so far away from the kitchen, but I guess you could get wild when you had more than one dining room in your house.

The third floor had a media room and two bedrooms, and Maddie opened one door, and then the other. They were right next to each other.

"These are your rooms," she said. "They both have their own bathroom, so you guys are free to pick whichever you like."

Edan and I looked at each other. "Whichever one you don't want," he said.

"This one is fine," I said, patting the door frame of the closest room.

We dropped our bags, and Maddie led us to the fourth floor, which was a giant library. Plush burgundy chairs and a couch sat below tall bookshelves, and lamps on the end tables cast a soft glow over the room. "And this is where we lose Edan," she said with smile. He was gazing up at the books.

"I've always loved this room," he said softly.

"I don't think Mom wants us to go into Gray's room, OK?" Maddie said to him.

He nodded, glancing at her. "OK."

"Where is that?" I asked, because I didn't want to wander into Grayson's room by mistake and make Nicole angry.

"Next floor up, with my room. Come on, I'll show you." Maddie gestured for me to follow her.

We walked upstairs, and she pointed to a closed door. "That's Grayson's room." She walked to the room opposite and led me into a massive bedroom. It was pristine, with cream-colored carpet that I surely would have ruined. She had a four-poster bed with sheer white drapes, the kind I'd only seen in movies. There was a large vanity, a desk, and a dresser with a small speaker atop it.

Unlike our room back in London, she'd actually decorated this one. There was a framed poster of a movie called *Jennifer's Body,* which I'd never even heard of, much less seen. There was a bulletin board with lots of stuff tacked to it—invitations to school dances, a flyer for a fundraiser, some concert tickets. There was a digital photo frame on the desk, which was playing a parade of photos with people I didn't recognize.

I felt out of place suddenly. I'd known that I wouldn't feel entirely comfortable in Maddie's world, a world marked by massive wealth and a kind, supportive family, but I hadn't thought about everything else. She'd had friends here. She didn't talk to most of them regularly outside of social media, but perhaps she would reconnect with them now that they were in the same city again. I felt weirdly jealous about it.

"Your house is amazing," I said, not quite meeting her gaze.

"We're selling it," she said, sitting down on her bed. "Next year sometime."

"Why?"

"Because it's just the two of us now, and I'm not even here anymore, so, you know, it's kind of ridiculous. Plus, it's always been too much for Mom. It was my grandparents' originally, on my dad's side. My mom never would have chosen this."

"What do you mean?"

"It's just . . ." She cocked an eyebrow. "I know it must seem ridiculous to you. You don't have to pretend."

"It's not *ridiculous*. It's just big." It was actually kind of ridiculous. The St. Johns only had two children. Only four people had lived in this giant house, in a city that was known for having limited space. And I couldn't imagine what it was like now for Maddie's mom, alone in this quiet mansion. No wonder she wanted to sell it.

I sat down next to her on the bed. "It's really nice of your mom to let us stay here. I've always thought your mom seems pretty great in general, actually."

She avoided my gaze. "Uh . . . yeah, she is."

"Why do you say it like that? She's not great?" I felt a sudden familiar tightness in my chest.

"No, she really is. It's just seemed kind of rude to advertise that. Like I was bragging." She fiddled with the edge of her comforter. "I'm sorry, but your mom sounds like the worst, and I didn't want to be all, like, 'Guess what, my mom is super great and we get along so well!'"

I laughed, some of the tension in my chest loosening.

"Sorry I said your mom's the worst."

"That's all right."

"It's true, though."

"I think it's nice that you get along with your mom. Especially since you lost your dad and your brother."

She smiled at me. "Thanks. So you don't think I'm a horrible rich asshole?"

"Why would I think that?"

She gestured at nothing in particular. "The ridiculous house."

"No. I think you're a lovely rich asshole."

"I'll take it." She hopped up. "Do you want to see the pool?"

"Jesus Christ, you have a *pool?*"

~

I found Nicole in the kitchen later that afternoon, inspecting the contents of her pantry. Edan was in the library reading a book, and Maddie had disappeared into Grayson's old bedroom. I was trying to stay awake long enough to get on New York time.

I lingered awkwardly in the doorway for a moment, waiting for her to notice me, but her gaze stayed fixed on the pantry. I considered fleeing back to the safety of my room.

No. I was going to be nice to Maddie's mom, because Maddie loved her and I could learn how to interact with my friends' parents.

"Do you need help?" I finally asked. I sounded nervous again. "Maddie said you were making dinner."

She turned and smiled at me. "Yes, actually. Do you want to chop some vegetables?"

"Sure." I walked to the sink to wash my hands, and she pulled out a cutting board and knife for me. She put several carrots, bell peppers, and potatoes on the counter.

"Maddie tells me that you're a much better cook than she is."

"That's a really low bar," I said.

"It is," she said with a laugh. She pointed at the vegetables. "Just chop them into one-inch chunks. I'm going to roast them."

"OK."

"Did your mom teach you?" she asked. "To cook?"

"Yeah, I helped her sometimes." I'd take the knife from Mom, alarmed by her frantic chopping pace, and she'd smile and thank me for helping. *I can always count on you, mija,* she'd say. It wasn't true then, and it wasn't true now.

I cleared my throat. "She taught me to make a few things — tamales, mole, her mom's version of arroz con pollo. I think she wanted me to know at least a little of her culture, since she didn't teach me Spanish and I've only been to Mexico once."

"She's from Mexico?"

"Yes. She came to the US when she was a kid."

"Why didn't she teach you Spanish?"

"My dad doesn't speak it."

"Ah." The brief glance up at me and the lack of further questions told me that Maddie had shared a few things about my parents with her.

"Do you have grandparents who are still alive?" she asked, eyes on the garlic she was mincing.

"No. Well, my dad's mom is still alive, I think, but they haven't spoken in years. My mom's parents died before I was born."

"That's too bad," she said softly. "Maddie knows her grandparents — my parents — well. We're going to go see them day after tomorrow."

"That's great," I said.

"Gregor's parents are both gone, unfortunately. Though . . ." Her lips twitched.

"What?"

"They didn't like me at all. It made holidays very uncomfortable."

"Why didn't they like you?"

"They thought I was a gold digger. I didn't come from money like him."

I looked up at her in surprise. I'd assumed she'd grown up like Maddie—filthy rich parents, private schools, some fancy college where she'd met Maddie's dad.

"My parents weren't poor," she said. "We were solidly middle class, but that might as well have been dirt-poor to the St. Johns. They were old school—they had a few girls in mind that they'd decided were appropriate, and they thought they'd be able to control Greg and make him marry one of them."

"I guess that didn't work out so well for them."

She laughed. "No one controlled Greg. Gray and Maddie inherited that trait, unfortunately." Her smile faded, and she closed her eyes, taking in a long, shaky breath.

"I'm sorry," I said, my voice nearly a whisper. "About Grayson."

She opened her eyes, but didn't say anything.

"I really liked him," I continued. "And I feel . . ."

"Responsible?" she guessed, wiping her eyes with the back of her hand.

"Yes." I gulped, alarmed that she'd guessed correctly. Maybe she blamed me too.

"So does Maddie. So does Edan. So do I. Julian . . ." She trailed off, gaze distant. "That little shithead. I should have put my foot down about him years ago."

I almost laughed, and she smiled a little at my expression.

"I never liked Julian. He was an entitled little shit, but so were most of Maddie and Gray's friends. Greg said that I didn't understand what it was like to grow up with"—she gestured around the kitchen—"all of this. He said they'd grow out of it, be nicer adults. But Gray and Maddie weren't like that." She laughed. "Most of the time, anyway." She picked up her knife. "But Julian was horrible. He was so angry all the time, and always taking it out on whoever was closest. I blame myself for not pushing harder to get him out of Gray and Maddie's life."

"You couldn't have known that he would . . ." I couldn't finish the sentence. The image of Maddie sitting over Grayson's dead body flashed through my brain.

"In my experience, men who can't control their anger in small situations tend to be the most dangerous when the big situation comes," she said, holding my gaze.

"Yes," I said.

"But that's not something you should blame yourself for, OK? You were not responsible for Julian's anger, even if you were the one he was mad at."

"I know, but . . ." Tears pricked my eyes. "Keeping an angry guy calm is what I'm supposed to be good at. I've done it my whole life. I went back to Julian because I thought I could handle him, and I couldn't. As soon as he got mad at me, I froze and I got scared, and I should have been able to handle it. I should have." I had to put the knife down because I couldn't see through my tears.

"Clara, honey, no one could have handled Julian. It was not your responsibility to stop him or to calm him down. You did what Grayson wanted you to do—stop the shipments. He'd be proud of you."

"Thanks," I said, wiping my eyes.

"I've asked Maddie to let the police handle Julian, but she doesn't seem too keen on that idea."

"I'm not sure that any of us have faith in the police after Julian got off scot-free."

"Just because they haven't charged anyone yet doesn't mean they're not building a case." She sounded as if she was trying to convince herself as much as me.

"Maybe," I said skeptically.

"But I know that Maddie will do what she wants. She isn't the most forgiving girl in the best of circumstances, much less now. If I force her to let this go and Julian never pays for what he did, I think it might eat her alive."

"I think so too," I said softly.

"Just be careful, OK?" she asked. "Take care of each other."

I smiled at her, realizing suddenly that my nerves had passed at some point during our conversation. "We will. I promise."

~

I fell asleep quickly that night in my giant, plush bed, and woke at three a.m., groggy and disoriented. I tossed and turned for a while, until I heard the sound of footsteps outside my room. I sat up, listening as they faded. Edan.

I slid out of bed, grabbing a sweatshirt and pulling my hair into a ponytail. I opened the door to find the media room dark and deserted. I quietly walked up the stairs to the next floor.

The library was dark except for the lamp next to one of the couches. Edan sat on the end, absentmindedly tugging the zipper of his hoodie up and down with one hand, and holding a book with the other.

He looked up and smiled as I drew closer. "Hey. Can't sleep?"

I shook my head and lowered onto the other end of the couch. "It's morning in London."

He put his book face-down on the cushion next to him. "And it's too quiet."

I cocked my head in question.

"You don't think so?" He leaned his head back, looking up at the ceiling. "I've never slept in a place this quiet. There isn't even any street noise. No snoring roommate."

"Does Dorsey snore?"

"A little. Plus, there was always someone in the hall or honking outside or something noisy. Here it's, like . . . unnaturally quiet."

It was, now that I thought about it. It hadn't been this quiet at night since I left home.

Actually, it hadn't been this quiet *ever* since I left home, night or day. I realized suddenly that I'd never been this alone with Edan, unless you counted the time we were kidnapped and locked in a room together. Even our nights on the balcony weren't really private—recruits would often spot us and wave from the street. A drunk guy did a dance for us once.

Even that night I'd spent in his bed, I knew Dorsey would return at any time. Or a recruit would come looking for us.

Here, we could have all the privacy we wanted. My bedroom door locked. And suddenly my excuses for keeping Edan at a distance felt like just that—excuses. I could have scooted over on the couch and leaned into him just to see how he reacted. The thought was terrifying.

I pulled my knees up to my chest and pressed myself harder into the armrest instead.

"Did you let your friends know you're in town?" I asked, after a silence that had stretched out for too long. I didn't know if I was imagining it, but it seemed like those types of silences were becoming more common between us.

"Yeah. I'm going to meet up with them day after tomorrow, I think." He looked down at his phone, on the cushion beside him. "And I realized too late that I maybe shouldn't have posted that picture to Instagram."

"Which one? The one from today?" He'd posted a picture of the skyline from the roof of the house, with just the caption NYC.

"My mom messaged me as soon as I posted it, asking to meet up. She said she was staying with a boyfriend in the Bronx and would be happy to come to me."

"What did you say?"

"Nothing. I didn't respond."

"Did you change your mind? Do you want to see her?"

He leaned back with a sigh. "No. I'm positive that she just wants something from me. Money, probably. She's mentioned Maddie in a few of her messages. Asked me if I was dating her." He scrunched up his face in an expression that was either thoughtful or grossed out.

"What is that look?" I asked with a laugh. "Don't pretend to be disgusted at the prospect of dating Maddie. I have eyes."

He chuckled. "No, of course not. Not disgusted. Terrified, maybe."

I bit back a laugh.

"No, I was thinking about Grayson," he said quietly, his lips turning up as he spoke. "He actually tried to set the two of us up once. Did Maddie tell you that?"

I nodded. Maddie had told me early in our friendship, back when she kept telling me that Edan liked me. There had still been a bit of awkwardness to our relationship because of Julian, and I was pretty sure she'd wanted me to know that it wouldn't happen again with Edan. I couldn't imagine any guy coming between us now.

"Yes," I said. "She didn't tell me the whole story, she just said Grayson was the worst matchmaker of all time."

"God, he really was. He told me that he thought I was a good guy because I'd never hit on Maddie the three brief times I'd met her. I was like, 'Low bar, Grayson.' But I guess all his friends hit on her and he was good friends with Julian, so . . .".

We both winced.

"Anyway, he invites me to his birthday party, and Maddie's there, of course," Edan continued. "He corners us both, says something about how great I am, and then practically runs away. It's so obviously a setup, and we both just stand there, staring at each other awkwardly. She tries to be polite—actually, now that I know her, she was making a huge effort to be nice. I'm kind of surprised she didn't just roll her eyes and walk away. But it all immediately goes downhill. She asks how I know Grayson, and then looks like a deer in headlights when I tell her I was staying at the homeless shelter where he volunteers. It's so obvious that she has no idea what to say to that." He laughed. "She sort of recovers and asks where I go to school, and I'm like, well, I dropped out. And she gets this expression on her face, like she thinks someone is playing a joke on her. We're surrounded by all these people who go to fancy private schools and attend Ivy League colleges, and her brother just set her up with the high school dropout who is crashing on friends' couches."

I cover my face with my hands. "Oh no."

"At that point, there's no way for it to get more awkward, so I say I'm going to find the restroom, and I just leave the party. But I guess she sees me ducking out, because she follows me onto the street."

I drop my hands from my face. "She did?"

"Yeah. She apologizes and says she didn't mean to be an asshole and tells me to come back inside. She says to give her my number and we can go out sometime. And I'm like, 'Uh . . . I'm actually seeing someone.' Grayson had neglected to ask me about that."

I threw my head back with a laugh.

"At that point, the polite version of Maddie totally fades away and she's like, 'Oh for fuck's sake, I'm going to kill Grayson.' She grabs my hand, drags me back inside, and makes me come with her while she yells at Grayson about never setting her up with his friends. He sheepishly agrees, Maddie apologizes to me again, and the rest of the party was incredibly awkward."

"Wow."

"Yeah. Later I found out that she'd just broken up with Julian and Grayson thought that I was the exact opposite of Julian, and therefore a good choice. Which, honestly, I've always taken as a compliment."

"It certainly is."

"But Maddie always avoided me after that. In fact, we didn't interact much until we were put on the team together. Grayson really was the worst matchmaker of all time. He made it so we both felt too awkward to speak to each other again for, like, a year." His smile faded, and he looked down at his hands. He cleared his throat. "Anyway, I think my mom thinks that I've hooked up with a rich family, and that's the only reason she's contacting me. I considered going to stay with my friends in Queens instead just because I didn't want her thinking I was mooching off the St. Johns."

"No," I said quickly. Too quickly. He looked up at me, clearly surprised. "You can't leave me alone with the rich people." I smiled to try and sell the lie. I wouldn't have minded being there with just Maddie and her mom at all. I just didn't want him to go.

He returned the smile.

I held his gaze for a beat too long, and silence settled between us again. I quickly looked away, clearing my throat.

"Uh, I should try to go to sleep." I stood, glancing at him.

He reached for his book, his gaze downcast. "Yeah, I probably should soon too."

But he didn't get up, and part of me wished that he would. Part of me wanted to go upstairs together and climb into one of our beds. I wanted to feel his arms around me and bury my head in his chest and listen to his heartbeat.

Of course, things were this awkward between us because we'd done that once. I couldn't imagine what would happen if we slept in the same bed a second time. We'd probably never look at each other again.

Or sleeping in the same bed would turn into kissing in the same bed and then I would surely ruin our friendship entirely.

I turned and headed to the stairs, not looking back at him as I went. "Good night, Edan."

11

The next day, Hannah and Victor made plans to come over. I tried to pretend I was excited about it.

I *was* excited about it. I wanted to meet Victor and Hannah in person. I was *not* disappointed that Edan and Hannah were now going to be in the same room. Edan and I weren't together. He was allowed to date whoever he wanted.

I kept telling myself this.

Maddie's mom made us breakfast—eggs, toast, potatoes, and fruit, and we all ate together in the dining room off the kitchen. My breakfast for the past six months had been a protein bar eaten on the way to the gym, and at home I usually tried to leave before Dad got up, so the family meal felt a little strange. In a nice way.

"So where is Priya from again?" Nicole asked Maddie as we ate.

"Birmingham, Alabama."

"Right. And Dorsey? Where did he go?"

"He's from Indiana, but he went to Chicago to see friends," Edan said. "Laila's there too, actually. She's from Chicago."

Nicole looked at me. "Your brother is in Dallas, isn't he? You didn't want to go see him over the holidays?"

I hadn't even considered that. Laurence and I were closer

these days, but I couldn't imagine going to Dallas just to see him. Would I stay at his apartment? That would be so awkward. We would run out of things to talk about in about ten minutes.

"I think that would be weird," I said.

"Why?" Maddie asked.

"We're just . . . not very close," I said, uncomfortable.

"You could change that, if you wanted," Maddie said. "Do you want to invite him here? Mom wouldn't mind." She looked at Nicole for confirmation.

"I wouldn't mind at all," Nicole said with a smile. "But it's up to you, Clara."

"No, it's fine," I said. "We're going to Dallas next month anyway. I can see him then." If he even wanted to see me. Laurence and I never hung out when we lived together. Maybe awkward phone conversations were the extent of our relationship.

"What about you, Edan?" Nicole asked. "Are you going to see any of your old friends?"

"Yeah, we're going to meet up tomorrow," he said.

"I guess you'll have the house to yourself tomorrow," Nicole said to me with a smile. "Maddie and I are going to Long Island to visit her grandparents."

I smiled like I enjoyed being the only loser without friends or family to visit.

After breakfast, I took my laptop into the media room and sat on one of the huge sectional couches. The room was like a mini movie theater, complete with a giant screen and a bunch of remotes that looked like far too much work to figure out.

I opened my messages and clicked on Laurence's name. I'd told him I was going to New York, but I hadn't updated him since we arrived. I figured I could do that, at least.

Hey, made it to New York. I think we'll be here through the holidays.

I'd asked Noah to send me all our training plans, and I clicked over to my inbox to see an email from him. He'd sent everything—the original plans Grayson and Julian had created, some of the tweaks they'd implemented after the program got off the ground, and what Noah and the other trainers had been working with lately. The current program was pretty much exactly how I'd been trained—a couple weeks of intense work, and then throwing the trainees right into the fire.

Noah had also sent the numbers on our dropouts, going all the way back to people who'd left in Paris. We hadn't kept very thorough records of why people dropped out, but Grayson had, and the most common reason was *recruit doesn't feel strong enough in hand-to-hand combat to stay.*

I wondered if more training would have changed that. I suspected that for some, it would not have. Fighting scrabs wasn't for everyone, regardless of how much training you had.

A note that Grayson had scrawled across the top of a recruit's exit paperwork caught my eye—*inquired about a noncombat option. Follow up in the future if we have teams that don't engage directly with scrabs.*

Teams that didn't engage directly with scrabs? I hadn't heard anything about noncombat teams. I wrote a quick email to Noah, asking if he'd seen anything else in Grayson's notes about that.

The elevator opened, bringing laughter with it (I still wasn't over the fact that they had an elevator *in their house*). I pressed Send on the email and closed my laptop.

Maddie stepped out of the elevator, Victor behind her. He stopped his chair when he spotted me, his face breaking into a grin. His dark hair was cut shorter than last time I'd seen him on Maddie's laptop screen.

"Clara!" He opened his arms, and then abruptly dropped them. "Oh. Are you a hugger?"

I smiled, walking over and leaning down to embrace him briefly. "For you, I definitely am." I looked at the empty elevator as the doors closed. "Wasn't Hannah coming too?"

"I'm here!" a breathless voice called. I heard running footsteps on the stairs, and Hannah appeared a moment later, bracing her hands against her thighs. "Oh god. So many stairs."

"I told you we'd all fit in the elevator," Maddie said, amused.

"I know but . . ." She gasped for air. "It seemed like a good idea . . . to get the full experience. But . . . so . . . many stairs." She sucked in a breath, her eyes landing on me. She was prettier in person. She had pale, lightly freckled skin, and she wore a pink sweater dress with an oversized gray scarf, tights, and knee-high black boots. I'd never been able to clearly see Hannah's clothes over Skype, or maybe I just hadn't been paying attention. But she was clearly the sort of person who cared about fashion, and it looked good on her.

She strode over to me and gave me a quick hug. "It's nice to meet you in person, finally," she said.

"You too."

She pulled her backpack off, set it on the table, and unzipped it. "I made cookies. Chocolate chip."

"Seriously?" Maddie asked.

"Why do you say it like that? What's wrong with cookies?" she asked, pulling out a giant plastic bag full of them. Her eyes lit up suddenly as she spotted something behind me.

I didn't need to look to know it was Edan. That was how she always looked when he appeared on screen.

"Hey, Hannah," he said, walking across the room and giving her a quick hug. I watched as they pulled away and her eyes flicked up and down his body. Edan must have seemed really different in person to her. There was just no way for the camera to capture Edan—the subtle way he took in a room, his eyes finding each person and then an exit, because he was always totally aware of his surroundings. The way he leaned slightly away from some people and slightly toward others. The way he touched the scar in the tree tattoo on his left arm, rubbing his fingers over it absentmindedly. Hannah wouldn't have seen any of that through the lens of a camera, and part of me was desperately sad that she knew all of it now.

And I couldn't help but notice how Hannah's eyes kept sliding back to Edan as she offered cookies to Maddie and Victor. Edan was pretending not to notice. I'd wondered once, before I knew him well, if he really didn't notice when people stared at him. Now I was sure—he was pretending. Edan always knew who was around him, where their attention was directed, and which pocket their wallet was in.

He'd confessed that last thing to me sheepishly one night. He said it was a habit he couldn't kick; he just immediately looked for a sign of a wallet or other valuables. So, right now he knew two things about Hannah: She probably had her wallet in her backpack, because her dress didn't have pockets, and she kept glancing his way.

Maddie sat down at the end of the one of the couches, and Victor wheeled over to sit next to her. I took my spot on the other side of the couch.

Hannah grabbed her bag of cookies, opening it and offering it to Edan, who sat next to her.

"Thanks," he said, taking one with a smile.

I took one when she passed the bag to me. They were soft and delicious.

"Wow, these are good," Edan said. Hannah beamed.

"She bakes all the time," Victor said. "My girlfriend loves her because every time Hannah comes over, she brings us something. She's still talking about those brownies you made last week."

"I'm a stress baker," Hannah said. "And I'm stressed, like—"

"Always," Victor finished.

Hannah laughed. "Yeah. Always." She glanced at her watch. "Speaking of, I should hurry this up, because I have to be in class in an hour." She pulled her laptop out of her bag and opened it. "I managed to get you four tickets to the conference in Dallas. It sounds pretty disorganized, but they're all pretty pumped about it. Might be helpful." She punched a few keys. "I just forwarded the tickets to you. Just a heads-up that you're going to stick out if you go. It's going to be, like, ninety-nine percent dudes, from what I can tell."

"I am *definitely* going," Maddie said.

"You always stick out, anyway," I said.

"And you're coming with me," Maddie said.

"Of course."

Hannah frowned at her laptop. "I think the Arizona leads on Dust Storm are a dead end, so there's no need to go down there right now. But I was thinking I could organize all the other places I've heard about recently into, like, a kind of road trip? So you can hit them all up?"

"Sounds good," Maddie said.

"When do you think you'll go?" Hannah asked.

"We can go now," Maddie said, reaching for her phone. "I'll look up flights."

"Maddie, she hasn't even made the list yet," I said, my exasperation coming through in my voice. "Let's just regroup here in New York for a bit, OK?"

She frowned at me. "I don't want the teams suspended for too long. The faster we do this, the faster we could get back."

I bit back a sigh. Trying to get Maddie to slow down and listen to me was an incredibly annoying task at times. "Christmas is just around the corner, and your mom was just telling me how excited she was that we would all be here for it and New Year's."

Maddie blew out an annoyed breath.

"Plus, I think you should go to this fundraiser that's here in town in a couple days," Hannah said quickly, clearly noticing the tension between us. "If you can get tickets."

"What fundraiser?" Maddie asked.

"The Lexington Foundation's annual gala."

"Oh yeah, I know them. That's Howard and Jill's foundation.

I've actually been to one of those fundraisers. With my parents, a few years ago."

"It looks like they go way back with Roman Mitchell, and on the foundation's website —"

"Wait, who is Roman Mitchell again?" Edan cut in. "I know that name from somewhere."

"He's the head of security training at MDG," Hannah said. "He coordinates all their training programs. He's Julian's boss. Way up the chain of command, probably fully in the know about all the shit they've been doing. Anyway, there's a section on the Lexington Foundation website where they say they donate to 'new technologies.' It's super vague, but it says they invest in bioengineering projects. And something about emerging technologies and artificial intelligence. Which could be nothing or could be code for 'we're sending lots of money to MDG because we're besties with Roman.' Might be worth going, seeing who shows up and seems chummy with the MDG crowd."

"Absolutely," Maddie said. "I'll get some tickets. It shouldn't be a problem. Edan, do you own a tux?"

He gave her a look like that was the stupidest question he'd ever heard. I bit back a laugh.

"Do you seriously want me to go to that? Do you remember what happened, like, every time Grayson made me hang out with your rich friends?"

"That's a good point."

"What happened?" Hannah asked.

"I'm not great at pretending I'm not horrified by the amount of money these people spend on stupid shit," Edan said.

"It's kind of hilarious to watch, actually," Maddie said. "One of Grayson's friends would be talking about buying a second boat, and Edan would just make this weird face and walk away. It really wasn't subtle." She paused, considering. "Maybe I'll just take Clara."

"I should point out that I definitely don't have a dress for that kind of event," I said.

She waved her hand. "We'll get you one."

"And we'll stay in New York through the holidays?"

"Yes, we'll stay," she said with a sigh.

Hannah and Victor caught us up on a few more things, and when it was time for them to leave, Edan offered to walk Hannah to the subway. I watched as the three of them piled into the elevator. Part of me wondered if he just wanted to spend some time alone with Hannah.

Maddie stopped beside me as the elevator doors closed.

"You know that Hannah is going to make a move on Edan," she said. "Soon, probably."

I nodded, swallowing. "She's nice."

Maddie turned to me with an exasperated expression. "Yes, she is. She's nice and pretty and smart, and she fucking bakes. And unless you tell Edan that you have feelings for him, he might very likely take her up on her offer."

"I don't have feelings for Edan," I said.

Maddie rolled her eyes. "Clara, please."

Heat crawled up my neck. It was a lie, and we both knew it. "I mean, I guess I *could* have feelings for Edan. But I'm not letting that happen."

"Seriously? You think you can just turn it off like that?"

"I . . . Yes?"

"You're seriously going to keep punishing yourself for one mistake? You're never going to date again just because you made one very brief mistake with Julian?"

"It's not that I'm *never* going to date, it's just that . . . it's complicated. And I don't know if I should date my friends."

"No, so much better to date your enemies," she said dryly.

"You know what I mean. You know it was hard for me to make friends, and now that I have, I don't want to ruin it."

"I think it says a lot about your state of mind that you think becoming romantic with someone means *ruining* your relationship."

"That's . . . I don't think that's exactly what I meant." Though she had a point.

"What did you mean, then?"

"I don't know. It's complicated."

"You know who could really help you sort this out? A therapist."

"I just need time."

"Or a therapist."

"Maddie," I said, exasperated.

"Sorry."

"I told you I'm good."

"OK." She paused. "But just for the record, I vote for Edan. And the therapist."

12

ANOTHER EMAIL FROM JULIAN LANDED IN MY INBOX EARLY THE
next day. He really did know how to ruin a morning.

> I just heard you're in New York.
> Do you want to meet for dinner soon?

I rolled my eyes as I climbed out of bed. Why in the world did
he think I would want to meet him for dinner? I didn't feel like
I'd left any room for interpretation in our interactions, but apparently he thought there was still hope. If I weren't worried about
the police calling my parents, I'd go ahead and get that restraining
order.

Maddie and Nicole left after breakfast to go to Long Island
to see Maddie's grandparents, and I decided to wait to tell them
about Julian's new email. No use ruining Maddie's day.

Edan was going to visit his friends today, which would leave
me all alone in the biggest house I'd ever seen. Now that we were
back in the States, it was more obvious than ever that I'd had no
friends and no life before. Everyone else had people to catch up
with, shared histories, and a life they could go back to, if they
wanted.

All I had was the teams, but at least that was something. I took my laptop into the media room and opened an email from Noah, responding to my question about Grayson's note regarding noncombat teams.

I didn't find anything, Noah wrote. *Worth exploring, though. You may want to talk to Laila. She mentioned something about that once. She might have some ideas.*

I grabbed my phone and called Laila. She picked up right away.

"Hey, Clara."

"Hey."

"How's New York?"

"It's good. You should see Maddie's house."

She snorted. "I can imagine."

"How's Chicago?"

"Really good, actually. It's nice to have a break."

"Listen, I've been going through some of Grayson's old notes about recruit dropouts, and he mentions noncombat teams at one point. Noah said you'd had ideas about that?"

"Not really ideas, but I did talk to Grayson about it once."

"Yeah? What'd you say?"

"I asked him if he had plans to help in other ways—like with scrab destruction or homelessness caused by scrabs. He said he'd like to, but there was only so much he could do at once."

"That's true," I murmured.

"Why?"

"I'm working on putting together new training and recruitment plans, and I just came across that note, and it made me wonder. Naomi said the same thing to me when she quit—her friends wanted to join, but they weren't the fighting type."

"You think there should be another option?"

"I don't know. Grayson could have been right about focusing on one thing at a time. I just wonder if we could recruit more people if we had other options. Or maybe even bring back some of the ones who quit."

"Maybe," Laila said. "I'd be in favor of it. What we do is flashy and exciting, and people love it, but I feel like it could be even more important to address some of the shit that happens after the scrab leaves."

"Yeah, I think so too. Let me know if you have any ideas, OK? I'm going to start looking into some of those organizations that do rebuilding after scrab attacks."

"You got it."

"Thanks. I'll talk to you later."

My email notification dinged as I hung up the phone, and I looked to see Julian's name again.

I clicked on the email with a sigh.

I know that it's not a coincidence that you're in New York. You never would have come here unless you were hoping to see me. If we need to be discreet about meeting up so that Madison doesn't find out, just let me know.

"Oh my god," I exclaimed, pushing my laptop onto the couch beside me.

"Are you OK?" a laughing voice asked. I looked up to see Edan standing at the door of the media room, an amused expression on his face. I muted the television.

"Yeah, I'm fine. Just new emails from Julian."

He walked into the room and sat down on the couch, sliding my laptop back to me. "What does he want now?"

"To have dinner. He said that I never would have come here unless I wanted to see him. To New York, I mean."

"Sure. Logical. Everything you do is about him."

"Apparently." I sighed. "Are you on your way out?"

"No, we're not meeting up until later. I was actually wondering if you wanted to come with me."

Yes. I really did. I didn't want to be here alone, like a friendless loser. And I always wanted to be wherever Edan was.

But I didn't want a pity invite. I hated the idea that Edan felt sorry for me. I opened my mouth to decline the invitation.

"I'd really like to introduce you to my friends," he said, almost shyly. "I've told them a lot about you."

Heat bloomed across my cheeks. I didn't know why it hadn't occurred to me that he was asking because he actually wanted me to come. Because he wanted me to meet his friends.

"I would really like that," I said.

"Great." He smiled. "Meet downstairs at five."

~

Edan and I took the subway into Queens. It was rush hour, and we didn't talk much on the crowded trains. We had to squish together as people piled into the subway car, and I tried not to notice how close we were, but it was hard when I kept bumping against his chest. The girl next to me had circled her arm around her boyfriend's waist and leaned into him, and I couldn't stop thinking about how nice that looked. I turned to look at the guy muttering to himself near the door instead.

We didn't talk as we walked out of the subway station and a few blocks to a red-brick apartment building. We climbed the stairs to the fourth floor, and a bearded man threw open the door with a grin.

"You crazy bastard," he said, grabbing Edan and pulling him into a massive hug.

Edan laughed, returning the hug and then stepping away to gesture at me.

"This is Clara."

He held his hand out to me. "Tucker."

"It's nice to meet you," I said, shaking it. He looked older than us, maybe in his early twenties. And he had more tattoos — they covered every inch of his arms and part of his neck.

We stepped into the apartment, and three people rushed forward, nearly tackling Edan. There was another guy who looked a bit younger than Tucker, and two girls. They were all talking at once, telling him he was crazy, asking how long he was in New York. The pretty pale-skinned girl with long black hair moved in for a second hug, lingering for several seconds, and I knew immediately who this was — Andrea.

"Clara, this is Pedro and Kim and Andrea," Edan said after Andrea released him.

"It's so nice to meet you in person!" Kim exclaimed, throwing her arms around me.

"Oh," I said, startled. "You too."

"Sorry." She laughed as she pulled away. "Between Edan's Insta stories and Noah's videos, I feel like I know you already."

"Sit down," Tucker said, gesturing to the living room. It was a tiny one-bedroom apartment, and the living room consisted of a worn gray couch and a wooden chair in the corner. Kim dragged a couple more chairs away from the round table off the kitchen.

Edan sat on the couch, and I lowered down next to him. Andrea's eyes followed me, and I smiled at her.

She was Edan's ex-girlfriend. He'd told me about her — they'd dated for about six months, and then were on and off again for another six months after that. He said that they were just friends now, but I knew that she was the girlfriend that he'd been most serious about. And the way Andrea looked at him made my stomach tighten. There was such open affection in her gaze.

Edan had so many experiences that I didn't have. He'd lived away from home for three years. He'd had several different jobs. He had an ex-girlfriend. *Girlfriends*, actually. Plural. I'd kissed three guys in my entire life, and all of the relationships had been so short that they barely qualified as *boyfriends*.

"Clara, do you want something to drink?" Tucker asked. "We have beer, wine . . . Kim, we still have some vodka too, right?"

"No thank you," I said. "I'm fine." I'd still never tried alcohol, and I didn't feel much desire to with Edan around. He never drank, and it was nice to have a friend who was sober when all our friends were getting tipsy.

"How long are you in town for?" Tucker asked, sitting down on the ground and resting his elbows on the coffee table. "It's just the three of you here, right? You guys and Madison?"

"Yeah, the rest of our team is visiting their families," Edan said. "I'm not sure how long we're staying. Not permanently, but the plans are . . . in flux, for now."

"Is this your first time in New York?" Pedro asked me. "Where are you from, again?"

"Dallas. Yeah, first time. I like it. It's like London, without the scrabs."

"I can't believe you've been in London for six months," Kim said, sitting down next to Tucker and looping an arm around his waist.

"I can," Pedro said with a laugh. "Edan is the craziest bastard I ever met."

Everyone laughed, and I cocked my head, confused by that description of Edan. He'd been a thief and a pickpocket while living here, but "craziest bastard I ever met," was not the Edan I knew.

His eyes flicked to me and then quickly away, pink splotches appearing on his cheeks.

"Edan's not crazy," Andrea said. "He's just fearless."

"Fearless, crazy, same thing," Pedro said with a wave of his hand.

Fearless was a more apt description of Edan. Or it had been, before. Not so much these days, and I wasn't sure that was a bad thing.

"Do you think you'll live here after all this is over?" Andrea asked me.

"Oh. Uh, I don't know."

"Isn't it sort of already over?" Kim asked, her tone apologetic. "The teams?"

"We're just regrouping," Edan said.

"Regrouping?" Tucker repeated.

"Maddie just suspended the teams for a while," I said. "The media is reporting that they're dead, but she is definitely planning to keep them alive."

"But you think you'll come back to New York, when the time comes?" Andrea pressed. "You won't want to go back to Dallas?"

"Oh god no," I said, too quickly. Tucker laughed, and Edan brushed a hand across his lips, like he was trying not to smile.

They were all looking at me expectantly, and I realized they wanted more.

"I hadn't really thought about where I'd go after," I said. "But Maddie is a good friend of mine, and she lives here, and . . ." I trailed off, stealing a glance at Edan. It seemed weird to say I'd stay in New York because he was here too.

But I would. The thought of being in a separate city, miles or even an entire ocean between us, made my chest hurt.

"Is *Maddie* Madison St. John?" Kim asked with a laugh. "You call her Maddie?"

"Everyone calls her Maddie," Edan said.

Kim rolled her eyes. "I seriously can't believe you're friends with the St. Johns. Are you staying at their place? Is it as ridiculous as it looks in the photos?"

"Hadn't you been there before?" Tucker asked.

"Yeah, I went there with Grayson a few times," Edan said. "It is absolutely as ridiculous as it looks in photos."

"There's an elevator," I said. "And a pool."

"Jesus." Tucker bumped Edan's knee. "I was going to ask if you needed a place to stay tonight, but clearly you're fine."

"I'm good. But thank you." Edan smiled at him. "What have you guys been up to?"

Tucker told us about work—he was a tattoo artist. The artist who had done all of Edan's tattoos, except the most recent one. He told us he'd moved studios, and business had really picked up.

Tucker moved forward to see Edan's new tattoo, his eyes flicking to my wrist. "You have the same one."

"We all do," I said, turning my wrist over so he could see. "The team, I mean. All eight of us got this."

"Your first?" Kim asked me. I wore long sleeves and jeans, so I wondered how she knew that. Apparently, I looked like the sort of person who didn't have tattoos.

"Yes," I said.

"Do you want more yet? It's impossible to stop with just one."

"I do, actually." I glanced at the tree on Edan's arm, and then at Tucker. "I love Edan's tattoos. I will definitely come to see you when I decide on my next one."

Tucker looked pleased by the compliment, and Edan smiled at me.

~

We stayed for a couple hours, sharing stories of scrab fighting in London, telling them about the team, and confirming that yes, Patrick really was that good-looking in person.

We took the trains back and walked side by side down the street toward Maddie's house. It was colder in New York than it had been in London, but it was a nice night, the air crisp and still. We weren't far from the house, but I wished we were. I would have liked to stay out all night with Edan.

I glanced over at him as we walked. He was looking up at the hazy black sky, and it took him a moment to notice my gaze.

"What?" he asked.

"Andrea seemed kind of worried about you. I saw her talking to you right before we left. And Tucker kept looking at you in this surprised way. Right? Or was I imagining it?"

"No, you're right. I think I seem really different to them. Andrea wanted to know why I was so quiet."

I guess the difference in Edan would seem jarring to them. For me, I'd watched it happen slowly, over the course of months. But when I thought back to the Edan I'd talked to on the bus during tryouts, I could see the difference. He was less quick with a snappy comeback these days, and perhaps a bit quieter, but I couldn't really know about that one. My relationship with Edan had always been marked by quiet — in the closet hiding from scrabs, in the room MDG had locked us in, in the days after Grayson's death, when we took long walks just to get out of the hotel room for a while, and barely spoke. Quiet used to be easy with Edan. It felt heavier these days.

"They were very nice," I said.

"Yeah," he said softly. "It felt a little weird, though. The three of them are some of my closest friends. I've known them for, like . . . three or four years? But it sort of felt like I had lived this whole other life that I couldn't quite describe to them. Do you know what I mean?"

"Not really," I said to the ground. "I don't have anyone from before. The only person I ever try to explain things to is Laurence, and things have always been weird between us."

"Did you tell him we'll be in Dallas next month?"

"Not yet."

"Why not?"

"I don't know. It's still a couple weeks away. And part of me thinks he isn't going to want to hang out in person. We almost never did before."

"I'm sure he's going to want to, even if only for a few hours."

"I guess."

He was quiet for a moment. "I got the impression that you wanted him in your life?"

"I do! It's just weird, you know?"

He tilted his head and said nothing, which I took to mean he didn't know.

"Sorry," I said. "I sound like an asshole, don't I? You don't even have any siblings, and Maddie just lost hers. I shouldn't be complaining about this."

"You weren't complaining; I asked. But you can complain to me anytime, if you want. I don't mind."

He smiled at me, a shy smile that made me feel like I was melting into a giant puddle on the sidewalk. I quickly looked away before he noticed my reddening cheeks.

"I was just curious," he continued. "I don't want my mom in

my life, and I wouldn't like it if people pushed me to reconcile with her just because she's family. It should be your choice. I'm not going to judge you if you decide not to call him when we go to Dallas, for the record."

"Thank you," I said. I hadn't really thought about it as a choice. It just seemed too rude to be within a few miles of my brother and not call him.

Two women walked down the street toward us, and I moved a little closer to Edan, making room on the sidewalk for them to pass. Edan's fingers brushed against mine, sending a jolt of electricity up my arm. My hand moved, almost on its own, until I felt his skin against mine again. I felt one of his fingers barely hook onto mine.

I quickly shoved both my hands in my pockets, my heart pounding. I didn't know whether he'd just tried to hold my hand or if we were just so close it couldn't be helped. I put a tiny bit of distance between us after the women walked past.

Edan's phone dinged as we approached the house, and he pulled it out of his pocket and read the message with a smile. He stopped, typing out a reply.

"I'm going to go meet up with Hannah. She's loaning me some books." He slid his phone back into his pocket. "I shouldn't be too long. Unless you want to come with?"

I couldn't help but think that Hannah would have sent me the message too if she wanted me to come. She had my number, and she knew Edan and I were alone together at the house tonight.

And I couldn't help but think that Edan didn't really want

me to come either. It wasn't a real invitation, like the one he'd extended to come meet his friends. This was a polite invitation, because he felt like he had to.

"No, that's OK," I said, my voice too quiet. I cleared my throat. "I'm kind of tired, actually. I think I'll just go in."

"OK."

He walked with me the short distance to the house, and then waited while I unlocked the door. I turned around and waved as I pushed the door open. He lifted his hand with a smile, and then turned to go.

I stepped inside, closed the door behind me, and leaned against it. I felt like crying, which was stupid, because this was the choice I'd made.

I'd thought it was a good choice. But tonight, it mostly just felt awful.

13

Maddie got us tickets to the Lexington Foundation's gala. Her mom insisted on going with us once she realized what we were up to, and bought me a dress that I suspected was wildly overpriced. It was blue lace with a sweetheart neckline and cap sleeves, and I had to hold it up so I wouldn't trip as I descended the stairs.

"What do you even do at a gala?" I asked Maddie as we stepped into the foyer. She wore a long deep purple dress with a back that was open but for a few strings of crisscrossed fabric.

"Eat mediocre food, bid on stuff you don't want, make small talk with people you don't like." She opened the closet and pulled out our coats, handing me mine. I'd finally gotten a good winter coat before we left London. "We're not bidding this year, though. It's bad enough that I bought the tickets."

"But there's a chance that they really are just saving orphans and curing cancer, right?"

"Clara, I admire your positivity," Nicole said, buttoning her red coat as she walked into the room. She wore a long glittery black dress, her hair pulled into an elegant updo.

"That means no," Maddie said.

"It does not," her mom said, giving her an amused look.

She paused. "Though it does seem unlikely, given their circle of friends."

"You don't think Julian will be there, do you?" I asked.

"He won't be, I checked," Nicole said.

I blew out a relieved breath. "Good."

"Edan, we're leaving!" Maddie yelled.

"He left like half an hour ago," I said as Nicole opened the door and led us outside. A black car waited at the curb. The driver hopped out to open the back door for us.

"Oh. Where'd he go?" Maddie asked.

"To dinner with Hannah and Victor."

Maddie raised an eyebrow, which I ignored.

We piled into the car, and the driver took us to a hotel about fifteen minutes away. I followed Maddie and her mom through the incredibly fancy lobby, tilting my head up to look at the massive chandelier and nearly bumping into a passing woman in the process.

"Sorry," I said. She just frowned at me, adjusting her pale pink coat like I'd sullied it with my touch.

I wished Edan had come with us. I was out of place with all these rich people, and they could see it. He'd offered to rent a tux and come with us, but I'd told him there was no need. I regretted that choice now. And I was willing to bet he looked really great in a tux.

We dropped off our jackets with a harried man at coat check and walked through the doors into a ballroom. It was already crowded with people. Round tables with white tablecloths and extravagant flower arrangements led to a small stage with large screens hung on either side. Two more elaborate chandeliers hung from the ceilings. Waiters with trays of drinks milled in between the guests. Several people turned and stared as we walked in.

Maddie slipped her arm through mine. Her face was impassive, but I saw her take in a long, slightly shaky breath. She was nervous.

"Were these people your friends?" I asked quietly. A woman in a long ivory dress was shooting a disdainful look in our direction.

"Some of them." She pointed at two women who rushed over to give Nicole a hug. "Look, a few people still like us."

We found our seats, and Maddie grabbed a glass of champagne from a passing tray. A waiter offered me a sparkling water when I declined the champagne, and I accepted it and took a sip.

"What's the plan?" I asked, setting the water down on the table.

She took out her phone. "Well, I'm going to be on my phone all night, because that's what teenagers do."

"And that's helpful because . . ."

She turned in a circle, eyes on her phone. "Because I'm taking pictures of all these assholes so they can't try to lie about their involvement later." She lifted her phone slightly. "Oh look, there's Roman Mitchell right there. Smile, assholes."

I stifled a laugh.

"I see an old friend of Grayson's," Maddie said, still taking pictures. She finally returned her attention to me. "I'm going to go talk to him. Want to come?"

"No, go ahead. Do you know where the restroom is?"

She pointed to the corner, and I stood and weaved through

the crowd. An older man glanced at me, his eyes lingering for several seconds on my boobs. He finally found my eyes and smiled. I moved a little quicker.

I heard a familiar laugh suddenly. I froze, and then slowly looked over my shoulder.

Julian stood in a group of men. He wore a tux, and he was still laughing. He looked happy. Relaxed, even. And he hadn't spotted me yet.

I hurried across the room, dodging a passing waiter and another man who was very interested in my boobs. This place was full of leering assholes, apparently.

I finally made it to the bathroom. I pushed open the door and slipped into the brightly lit room.

JULIAN IS HERE, I texted Maddie as the door swung shut behind me.

"Excuse me," a voice said, and I looked up to see an annoyed-looking older woman with a helmet of blond hair trying to get past me.

"Sorry," I said, moving away from the door. A text dinged on my phone, from Maddie.

Where are you?

The bathroom.

OK, stay there for a minute. I'll tell you when the coast is clear.

I lowered my phone to see I wasn't alone. A woman stood at one of the sinks, hands braced on either side. Her dark hair was cut into a bob, and she was leaning forward so it shielded her face.

She wore a long gold dress with spaghetti straps, a sparkling diamond bracelet on one wrist.

She straightened suddenly, taking a deep breath. I saw her blink back tears, her eyes red. She noticed me in the mirror and quickly lowered her gaze.

"Are you OK?" I asked hesitantly.

"Yeah. Fine." She grabbed a black clutch from the counter and pulled out a tube of lipstick.

I stood there awkwardly as she applied it. She was beautiful, with dark eyes framed by long lashes and lightly tanned skin, like she'd just come from vacation somewhere sunny.

She glanced at me again, arching one eyebrow.

"Sorry," I said. "I would leave, but I'm hiding from my ex." I held up my phone. "My friend is running interference."

Her now-pink lips turned up slightly, and she made a sound almost like a laugh. "I just ran in here because I saw my ex-boyfriend. That's what I hate about these events. Everyone you ever knew is always here."

"Yeah," I said, like running into my ex-boyfriend at a fancy charity gala was a normal event in my life.

"He wasn't even supposed to be here—I checked—but there he was, smiling at me like I'd actually be happy to see him." She threw her lipstick back into her clutch. "And his parents just died, so I think I have to actually be polite if I talk to him. Which I do not want to do, so here I am, hiding in the bathroom like I'm at an eighth-grade dance." Our eyes met in the mirror, and she seemed to notice my startled expression.

She turned to face me. I could see the moment she recognized me. She took in a small breath.

"You're Clara," she said. I nodded. "What are you doing here?" She looked down at my phone. "Who is your friend out there?"

"Maddie. Madison St. John."

She grimaced like she didn't approve.

My phone buzzed, and I looked down at the message from Maddie.

Mom's leaving, she can't be in the same room with Julian. I'm walking her out and then I'll come to the bathroom.

I returned my attention to the girl, who hadn't given me her name yet. Her wide brown eyes flicked from my phone to my face.

"Do you know the St. Johns?" I asked. She nodded. "And you dated Julian?"

"A few years ago," she said. She paused, and then said, "I saw your video." She glanced over at the stalls, as if checking to make sure we were alone. The doors to all of them were half open. "When I saw it, and you said that Julian had gone into a rage and killed Grayson, my first thought was, *Yep, that tracks.*"

I raised my eyebrows. "Yeah?"

"Yeah," she said softly. "But no one else seemed to . . ." She cleared her throat and straightened her shoulders. "Anyway. I'm sorry about what happened. About no one believing you."

"A few people did." I gestured at her.

She blinked, and then tried for a smile. She edged around me, headed for the door. "I should get back out there."

"It was nice to meet you . . ."

"Scarlett," she said. She paused and looked back at me for a moment, like she might say more. She seemed to change her mind, pushing open the door and disappearing through it.

Maddie walked in not long after and found me leaning against the wall, scrolling through my texts. Maddie had sent a group text to me, Edan, Hannah, and Victor about Julian being at the gala, and they were all reacting.

"Do you want to go?" Maddie asked. "I sent Mom in the car, but we can get a cab."

"I'm fine if you are. We just got here."

She looked relieved. "OK. Good."

We walked out of the bathroom. I took a quick glance around, but didn't see Julian. The ballroom had filled up even more, fancy dresses and glittering necklaces everywhere I turned.

"Hey, do you know a girl named Scarlett? She dated Julian?" I asked Maddie.

"Yeah." She gave me a confused look. "How do *you* know her?"

"She was just in the bathroom. Crying."

Maddie stopped and turned to me. "*Crying?*"

"Why do you say it like that?"

"I can't imagine Scarlett crying. She's so . . ." She made a face. "Uptight."

"She was upset about seeing Julian. Which she mentioned before recognizing me."

"Oh." Maddie's expression softened. "Yeah, I guess that . . . makes sense." She scanned the room, her gaze settling on something behind me. I turned to see Scarlett standing with a handsome man who looked older than her. He was in his late twenties or early thirties, probably, and I'd have put Scarlett at closer to my age. She caught us staring and pointedly looked away.

"How long did she and Julian date?" I asked.

"Six months? Maybe longer. I don't know her super well. I wasn't exactly . . . friendly to her."

"Why not?"

"Because she was dating Julian. She's a couple years older than me, and this was back before Julian and I dated, when I was, like, fifteen. I made a habit of being a bitch to all of Julian's girlfriends." One side of her mouth quirked up. "You remember."

I gave her an amused look. "Vaguely."

The man with Scarlett said something, and she frowned deeply and shook her head.

"Who is that with her?" I asked.

"Her brother, Brian."

Brian motioned for Scarlett to follow him. She gave him an exasperated look, but trudged along behind him. They weaved around a few tables and came to a stop in front of Julian. I winced, watching as Scarlett crossed her arms over her chest. Brian greeted Julian with a hug.

"Brian and Julian are friends?" I asked.

Maddie looked surprised. "Not that I know of. Brian's a lot older."

They both smiled as they spoke. Brian laughed. Scarlett smiled stiffly and said a few words to Julian.

"Looks like they're friends now," I said.

Roman Mitchell and a familiar gray-haired man joined them.

The older man put one hand on Julian's shoulder and the other on Brian's.

"Isn't that one of the MDG dudes who's always on television?" I asked. "The older guy with Roman Mitchell."

"It sure is. That's the vice president of MDG."

"Are Brian and Scarlett invested with MDG?" I asked.

"Not that I know of, but they sure look chummy." Maddie tilted her head. "Well, Brian looks chummy. Scarlett looks ready to hurl."

The men were all talking to one another, completely ignoring Scarlett. She leaned back, as if looking for an escape route.

Maddie and I glanced at each other, and I could tell we were thinking the same thing. If this group of men hung out together often, maybe they'd spilled some MDG secrets while she was standing right there, invisible to them.

Scarlett said something to the group and practically bolted away from them. She made a beeline for the door, holding her dress up as she walked. She was impressively fast in heels.

Maddie grabbed my hand. "Come on."

We hurried across the ballroom, nearly breaking into a run as we followed her.

"Scarlett!" Maddie called.

She stopped halfway down the stairs and turned to look at us. Her expression tightened when she caught sight of Maddie.

"Hi," Maddie said breathlessly as we came to a stop.

Scarlett crossed her arms over her chest again. "Hello." Her eyes were watery, and she looked down at the lobby below instead of at us.

"Uh, I . . ." Maddie glanced at me. She clearly hadn't thought this part through.

"Listen, I don't mean to be rude, but I'm having a really bad night, and I just want to go home." Scarlett's eyes caught on something behind me, and she swallowed.

I turned to see Julian.

He stood at the top of the stairs, hands casually slid into his pockets, staring at me. He raised his eyebrows, taking one hand out of his pocket to gesture up and down my body. He approved, apparently.

I rolled my eyes and turned away. Scarlett was already at the bottom of the stairs, moving swiftly. Maddie made a move like she was going to follow, but I caught her arm.

"I think her brother might be involved with MDG," she protested. "Maybe she'll help us."

"I know. But she's clearly upset. We should let her go." I glanced back at Julian, but he was gone.

"No, let me just—"

"Maddie, please," I snapped. "Just slow down, OK?"

She blinked, clearly surprised by my tone.

"Sorry," I said, my voice softening. "I just . . . know how she feels. Let's give her some space, OK?"

She nodded, reaching down to squeeze my hand. "Yeah. OK."

"Do you have her number? Maybe you could text her tomorrow, ask if we can meet up."

"Yeah, I have it." She looked back at where Julian had been.

"Ready to go back in? We could talk shit about Julian to my mom's friends. They would *love* that."

I hooked my arm through hers. "Ready."

~

Hannah and Victor were in the media room watching a movie with Edan when we got back.

"Wow, you guys look hot," Hannah said. She was sitting on the couch next to Edan. Closer than was strictly necessary, in my opinion. They weren't touching, but she could have given him a little space.

His gaze moved from the television to me. He looked quickly away, grabbing the remote next to him. He dropped it and had to lean down to grab it before he could pause the movie.

"Yes, you both look lovely," Victor said with a smile.

"Thank you," Maddie said, flopping down in a chair. I lowered into the other one.

"How'd it go?" Hannah asked. "Find out anything useful?"

"Yes. We ran into Scarlett Wilton," Maddie said. "She's Julian's ex-girlfriend. Edan, did you ever meet her?"

Edan shook his head. He was barefoot, wearing jeans and a teal sweater that made his eyes look even greener. The sweater was old—I could see a tiny hole at the collar and the ends of the sleeves were worn—but somehow that made it look even better on him. It was very distracting.

"Well, Julian was there. And Scarlett was pretty upset about it."

Edan looked at me quickly. "Julian was there?"

"We avoided him," I said.

"He stared at her all night, though," Maddie grumbled. "It was creepy."

He *had* stared at me all night. I tried to ignore it, but every time I let my gaze wander, there he was, watching me. Once he'd even tilted his head toward the door, subtly asking me to go outside with him. He wanted me alone, apparently. I hadn't left Maddie's side all night.

"Why was Scarlett upset about him being there?" Hannah asked. "Was Julian a jerk to her too?"

"I don't know her well, but I'm sure he was," Maddie said. "But the interesting part is, she was there with her brother. Brian Wilton. Brian and Julian looked very chummy, and they were talking to Roman Mitchell and the MDG vice president."

Hannah pulled her phone out of her pocket and frowned as she scrolled. "I don't think I have Brian on my list of possible investors."

"He may not be invested yet. But he is in real estate investment, so there's a definite possibility that he's been approached. Grayson tried to get him to invest in the teams, actually, and Brian told him it was a stupid idea. So, I think it's worth talking to Scarlett, see what she knows. Maybe see if she's willing to poke around, find out where Dust Storm is."

"Do you think she'd really be willing to help us? Wouldn't that sort of be betraying her brother?" Victor asked.

"We can frame it as *saving* her brother," I said. "Tell her to get Brian as far away from MDG as possible and screw Julian over in the process."

"I like it," Hannah said. "Though we have no guarantee that she won't turn around and just tell Brian you're trying to find out where Dust Storm is, and you were trying to use her to do it."

"I'm pretty sure that Julian and everyone at MDG is fully aware that we're trying to find Dust Storm. Subtly is not our strong suit." I gave Maddie an amused look.

"You have a point." Hannah laughed. "And, hey, you can start a club! A Julian's ex-girlfriends club."

"The most depressing club of all time," I said dryly.

"I'll text her tomorrow," Maddie said. "Or maybe Clara should text her. She seemed to like you much better."

"Yeah, I'll do it. Send me her number."

"Well, you guys did excellent work *and* got to wear fancy dresses," Hannah said as she got to her feet. "I'm very jealous. I want the gala assignment next time."

"You got it," Maddie said with a smile.

Hannah walked with Victor to the elevator. "We'll see you guys later. Text us tomorrow to let us know how it goes, OK?"

"Will do," Maddie said, hopping up from her chair. She walked out of the room as the elevator door closed.

I looked at Edan. Our uncomfortable silence was back. He leaned forward, running both hands down his thighs. He seemed to be avoiding my gaze.

"It was really OK?" he asked the floor. "Seeing Julian?"

"Yeah. There were a lot of people around, and Maddie and I stuck together all night. And . . ."

"What?"

"It sounds sort of horrible."

His lips twitched into a smile as he finally looked up to meet my gaze. "Tell me anyway."

"It was actually sort of a relief to see Scarlett so upset about being in the same room with Julian. Made me feel less . . . crazy, I guess."

He cocked his head. "Do you feel crazy?"

"Maybe that's not the right word. It's just upsetting to see him. And it was nice to have it confirmed that I wasn't overreacting."

"I never think you're overreacting, for the record."

"Thank you, Edan."

He stood. "I'm going to bed. Good job tonight." He headed to the stairs, pausing to look back at me at the bottom of them. "You really do look beautiful."

14

I texted Scarlett the next morning.

Hey, it's Clara, from last night. Maddie gave me your number.

It was almost an hour before she replied with one word: Hi.

I was wondering if you had some time to talk today? Maddie and I will come to you. We can meet wherever you want.

It only took a few minutes for the second response to come through.

Fine. Come to my place around two.

She texted the address, which I sent to Maddie.

We headed downstairs and outside about an hour later. Maddie said Scarlett's apartment was only a few blocks away, so we could walk. It was a cold, sunny day, and I buttoned my jacket as we started down the sidewalk.

"So I've been working on new training plans, and I've been thinking about the possibility of adding a noncombat option for the teams. Do you think you'd be open to that?"

She looked confused. "What would recruits do if they're not fighting?"

"There are some different options. Scrabs leave a huge mess behind after they attack. People lose their homes or their businesses, they need medical care, they—"

"We're not equipped to do any of that," she interrupted.

"We could be, if we explored some different options."

"Wait, did I know you were making new training plans? I thought you were mostly working on how to boost recruitment."

"I'm working on both," I said, trying to hide my annoyance. "Recruitment is important, but I think we need to address training too, especially if we can't expand beyond combat. We might need to be a little more selective. And maybe have some sort of test they have to pass before being allowed to fight? Because I nearly got an ax to the head in that last scrab battle, and—"

"Jesus, really?" She grimaced.

"Yeah."

"Well, weapons do go flying sometimes, if they hit the scrab in the wrong place."

"Right, and we can prevent that by—"

"Fine, fine, tweak the training if you think we need it. But focus more on recruitment. We're going to need more people once we're out there."

I opened my mouth, and then shut it. This was probably the wrong time to really get into all of this. I could tell Maddie was nervous about seeing Scarlett. And it was hard to get her to listen to me about this on the best of days.

"We'll talk about it when I've worked on it a bit more," I said.

Scarlett lived in a fancy building with a doorman, and we walked into the lobby and waited while he checked his list and then pointed us to the elevator.

She opened the door as soon as we knocked. She wore a soft pink sweater and skinny black pants, her makeup perfect. Her casual elegance reminded me of Maddie.

Her expression was not friendly, but a hint of curiosity softened it when her eyes landed on me.

"Hi, Scarlett," Maddie said. "Nice to see you again."

"Uh-huh," she said, with a hint of skepticism. She stepped back, holding the door open for us.

We stepped inside the apartment, which was smaller than I'd expected. It looked like it was just one bedroom, with a tiny kitchen, a small dining area, and slightly larger living room.

She gestured for us to sit on the couch, and I lowered down next to Maddie. She sat in the chair across from us, crossing her legs and her arms, like she felt the need to defend herself.

"I think that I should say, right off the bat, that I'm sorry about that time I called you a frigid bitch," Maddie said. I looked at her quickly, surprised. "I was just drunk. And also jealous. And I'm sorry for deserting you at that party in Brooklyn because I hooked up with Logan."

"Derek," Scarlett said.

"What?"

"You deserted me at that party in Brooklyn to hook up with Derek, not Logan."

Maddie squinted. "Oh yeah. Either way, I apologize. And I'm sorry I slept with your brother and then made a really tasteless joke to you about it."

I turned to Maddie, horrified. "You slept with her brother? He's, like, thirty."

"My other brother," Scarlett said flatly. "The younger one."

"Obviously," Maddie said.

"Oh my god, Maddie," I said, pressing a hand to my forehead. "No wonder she hates you."

I heard a laugh, and I looked up to see Scarlett covering her lips with her fingers, like she was trying not to smile. She failed.

"I feel like there's more," Maddie said. "I'm just sorry for being awful in general. I was jealous you were with Julian, which is incredibly fucking stupid, in hindsight." She shifted in her chair. "Also, I feel like you should know that he was going around telling everyone that you were a crazy bitch, and I realize now that he was probably the only crazy bitch in that situation."

Scarlett laughed again softly. "A friend told me a while back that he was telling everyone that. Julian really did make me feel like I was losing my mind, though. I was convinced that he was somehow reading my texts and emails, but he always denied it. I'd end up crying and yelling at him about it, and he'd act like I was being totally unreasonable."

"He gave me a phone specifically so he could spy on everything I did with it," I said. "So, I'm sure you were right. He'd probably found a way to read them."

She stared at me for a moment, and then blinked. "He . . . really?"

"Yes. It was obvious, and he admitted it when I confronted him."

She took in a long, shaky breath. "Jesus. That makes me feel so much better." She leaned forward, pressing her palms to her forehead. "My therapist kept telling me to trust my instincts, but there was always this nagging doubt that maybe I was just crazy and paranoid, like he always said." She looked up at Maddie. "He really did kill Grayson, didn't he?"

"Yes," she said.

She leaned back on the couch again. "What do you guys want? I'm not investing. I'm sorry about Grayson, but my answer is the same as it was when he asked me. Those teams are stupid, dangerous, and shortsighted."

"We don't need money," Maddie said. "We need to know where MDG's facility is in the US, and whether they've been shipping scrabs there."

Scarlett's eyebrows shot up. "What?"

"It's a facility called Dust Storm, and we can't figure out where it is. Julian said *the middle of nowhere* once, which really isn't a lot to go on. There's a lot of nowhere."

"MDG said that facility didn't exist. They're working with the cops to figure out who was even trying to train scrabs." She stared at us. "Right?"

"They're lying," I said. "Julian told me there were facilities here. MDG is just trying to cover their asses."

"Even if they cleared it out and all the scrabs are gone, we want to find where it was," Maddie said.

"Why?" Scarlett asked.

"Because Julian is getting away with everything," Maddie said. "He killed Grayson, three of our team members, and *two* cops and still walked away scot-free. Now he's partnered with the people who are trying to normalize trained scrabs. If we don't stop him now, there's no telling what he'll do next."

The room went quiet for several seconds.

"You're telling me that you think Julian—and MDG—is building an army of trained scrabs," she finally said.

"Yes," Maddie replied.

"And you think he's going to start using them against people. Or he's already started."

"Why do you look so dubious about that?" Maddie asked. "You've seen his temper."

"Yeah, but . . ." Scarlett trailed off, her eyebrows furrowed in thought.

"Look, we could be wrong about Julian," I said. "Maybe he'll never use trained scrabs against people again. But MDG is absolutely training scrabs. Even if Julian has taken time off from MDG to stalk me full-time, they are still out there doing it."

"He's *stalking* you?"

"He called my brother. I had to quit using Instagram because he kept messaging me. And he's emailing me nonstop." Two more emails this morning. I hadn't even bothered to open them, and then I'd turned off notifications for my email. I was tired of the way my chest seized every time I heard that *ding*.

"I guess I'm not totally surprised, but . . ." Scarlett shook her head, widening her eyes.

"Is this really the kind of guy you want to have access to an army of trained scrabs?" Maddie asked.

"Of course not, but I don't know what you expect me to do about it," she said.

"I noticed that Julian and Brian seemed pretty chummy at the gala," Maddie said.

Scarlett sighed, pressing her fingers to her temple. "My parents insisted we go to the Montgomerys' funeral, and Brian reconnected with Julian. No one really wants to be around Julian anymore, and Brian felt bad for him."

"No one wants to be around Julian?" I repeated.

She shook her head. "Julian will tell anyone who will listen that Grayson's death was an accident, but everyone's still suspicious, you know? They had a weird relationship. And everyone thought it was strange that he disappeared to London right after his parents died. He didn't even need to go pick up their bodies himself, but he insisted, and then he pretty much left the funeral planning to his aunt. He acted like an asshole, from what I've heard."

"I believe that," I said.

"If you're asking me to reach out to Julian, I won't do it," Scarlett said. "I'm not putting myself in that position. Seeing him at the gala was bad enough."

"No," Maddie said quickly. "We would never ask that. I recommend you stay as far away from Julian as possible, actually."

"Then, what?" Scarlett asked.

"You and Brian are pretty close, aren't you?"

"Somewhat," Scarlett said slowly.

"Did you ever tell him about Julian?" I asked.

"He knew we dated, but I never talked to him about it in detail, no," she said. "I figured he'd either get too mad or tell me I was overreacting, and neither of those options sounded appealing to me."

"So maybe he wouldn't be suspicious if you started poking around and asking questions?" Maddie asked hesitantly.

Scarlett leaned forward, resting her arms on her thighs as she held Maddie's gaze. "You seriously came over here to ask me to spy on Brian?"

"Yes," Maddie said. "And to possibly save him."

"Save him?" she asked skeptically.

"He's invested in MDG, isn't he? I saw him talking to some of the MDG guys at the gala."

"I don't know."

"It seems pretty likely. A lot of the Montgomerys' friends seem to be involved. It's probably why they turned Grayson down when he tried to get them to invest in the teams."

"There were plenty of reasons not to invest in those teams," she said.

"Whatever. What MDG is doing is illegal, and I'm going to take them down, even if I have to spend the rest of my life doing it." Maddie's voice had gone hard. "But maybe we could help each other out. Get Brian to find out where that facility is, tell me, and then have him pull his investment before he ends up with prison time."

Scarlett blanched at the words *prison time*.

"Or skip me and go straight to the police with the information. I'll give you the number of my FBI contact, if you want. But I don't have to wait for warrants. The FBI is dealing with a lot of lawyers and powerful people who are determined to shut down any investigation into MDG. *I* give zero shits about lawyers."

"I don't know if he'll even tell me anything," Scarlett said, after a long pause. "Brian still treats me like his kid sister. We rarely even talk about his work or his investments."

"Can you tell him the truth?" I asked quietly. "About all of it? Your relationship with Julian, our suspicions, his jealousy? Just lay it all out for him and see if he'll do the right thing? He may not even know where Dust Storm is, but maybe he can find out if you tell him all of it. Get him to help us."

She considered for a moment. "Maybe. Let me think about it, OK?"

"Of course," Maddie said, getting to her feet. I did the same.

Scarlett stood and opened the front door for us. Maddie paused halfway out the door.

"Just, for the record, I wish I'd been more honest with Grayson about Julian," she said, turning back to Scarlett. "I think that if I'd told him how Julian treated me, he would have ended their friendship. He certainly wouldn't have let him be a team leader. I kept making excuses for Julian, and I kept thinking that it wasn't fair for me to break up their friendship just because things had ended badly between us. I mean, I pursued *him*."

Scarlett crossed her arms over her chest and looked away.

"But I should have told Grayson. He would have been kind about it. And maybe all of this would have turned out differently." Maddie blinked back tears. I put my hand on her arm. Scarlett's eyes followed the movement.

"I said I'll think about it."

15

I ACTUALLY SUCCEEDED IN GETTING MADDIE TO TAKE SOME time off. Maybe only because there wasn't much for us to do over the holidays. Hannah and Victor were with their families, we hadn't heard back from Scarlett, and Julian never showed up in person.

He sent emails every day, though. Eventually I changed my email settings so that everything he sent me went straight into a folder. I didn't have to see them if I didn't want to. I was tired of the constant dread.

I did, however, have to see the gifts he sent. He started with flowers, a huge bouquet that Nicole took directly to the dumpster. Then he sent me macarons (also in the trash), chocolates (trash), and several cards (Maddie shredded them).

On Christmas Eve, he sent a necklace. I took it out of the box and held it up by one finger, showing it to Maddie and Nicole, who stood in the kitchen, drinking coffee. It was a diamond pendant in a shape of a heart on a gold chain.

"I'm going to send it back to him," I said.

"Oh, no you're not," Nicole said, leaning forward to examine it. "He spent a lot of money on that."

I cocked my head, peering at it. "You think so? It's kind of ugly."

Maddie snorted.

"Trust me, I know my jewelry. He spent a lot of money that he doesn't have."

Maddie looked at her in confusion. "What do you mean, that he doesn't have?"

"The Montgomerys were broke when they died," Nicole said. "Bad investments. There were rumors they were going to declare bankruptcy soon."

Maddie appeared delighted by this. I stifled a laugh.

"Julian will probably be selling off all their assets soon. Their apartment is already on the market." She took the necklace from me. "This might have been his mother's, actually."

"What do you want to do with it?" I asked.

She took the box from me and put the necklace inside. "I say we sell it. I know a guy who will give me a great price. I'll send you whatever cash I get for it."

"I don't want his money."

"Then give it to charity," Maddie said. "Give it to one that'll really piss Julian off. Maybe that homeless shelter Edan used to stay at occasionally. Julian hates Edan *and* homeless shelters."

"What in the world does he have against homeless shelters?" I asked incredulously.

"He said they discouraged homeless people from getting a job."

"Wow."

"Yeah. We used to fight over that guy."

"Thanks for the reminder. I feel great now," I said dryly. She laughed.

Nicole smiled at her daughter, then patted me on the arm. "I'd spend it on myself, personally, but you can do whatever you want with it."

"I . . ." I trailed off as Nicole walked out of the kitchen, apparently uninterested in my protests.

"You're getting the money from that necklace," Maddie said, an amused look on her face. "There's no use fighting with her about it. She probably sees it as a way to screw over Julian, and I couldn't agree more."

"I think your mom hates Julian more than all of us," I said.

"She really does."

~

Part of me thought that Mom might finally email on Christmas, but she didn't, and I tried to tell myself that it didn't bother me. I spoke to Laurence that morning, and he said he was spending the next day with them. I changed the subject.

It was my first Christmas away from my family, and Maddie and Nicole's first Christmas without Grayson, so no one was really in the holiday spirit. We agreed not to exchange gifts, and instead cooked a meal and watched *Die Hard*, which was apparently a family tradition in Maddie's house. We'd watched *A Christmas Story* in my house, a movie I hated, so I was more than happy with this new tradition.

The day after Christmas, I sat in the media room, my laptop on the table in front of me. I pressed Accept on the incoming call from Patrick. His smiling face filled the screen.

"Clara! I feel like it's been a hundred years. How is New York?"

"I love it. How is Austin?"

"I hate it."

I laughed, and he sighed dramatically.

"OK, I don't *hate* it. But things are weird now. Half of my friends are telling me why trained scrabs are actually a great idea for our military, and shockingly, they don't appreciate me telling them what dumbasses they are."

"Wow."

"Yeah. Former friends, I guess I should say." He shook his head. "Anyway. You wanted to talk before everyone else joins?"

"Yeah. I've been working on some new training and recruitment ideas, and I wanted to get your input. Can I send you some stuff I've been working on?"

"Of course."

"I'm thinking of extending our training period by several weeks, which Maddie will hate, but I feel like might be necessary."

"It is," he said. "I'm happy to back you up there."

"Thank you," I said gratefully. "And I'm also sending you my ideas for noncombat teams."

"Noncombat teams?"

"Yeah, I got the idea from Grayson's notes. I did research into what some charity organizations are doing to help with scrab destruction, and I think we should look into creating rebuilding teams. People who go in and help with construction of new houses or businesses after they're destroyed by scrabs."

"I love that idea, but we don't even have enough people for our combat teams right now."

"I know. It would require a lot of work and . . ." I trailed off.

He looked skeptical, and I still wasn't sure that this was a good idea. He was right, we didn't even have enough people for what we'd already built.

I heard footsteps on the stairs, and I returned my attention to the screen. "I'll send you what I have and we'll talk about it later."

"Sounds good."

Edan appeared at the bottom of the stairs, smiling as he walked over to me. He sat down beside me, so close that our arms brushed. I didn't move away.

"Hey, Edan," Patrick said.

Dorsey joined the call, followed by Priya, Laila, and Noah.

"Have you talked to Saira, Laila?" I asked. "Is she still at the hostel?"

"Yeah, she's there," Laila said. "She said the UK teams are talking about pulling something together themselves if we don't ever come back. I keep telling her that Maddie isn't giving up."

"She definitely isn't. I can barely get her to take a break." I leaned away from the computer to yell up the stairs. "Maddie! Everyone's on!"

"Coming!" she called from upstairs.

"Did you get to Chicago OK?" Edan asked Dorsey.

"Yes. Thank god. Two nights in Indiana was more than enough. Both my parents are convinced that North Korea is about to invade us with trained scrabs. I feel like I just wandered into some alternate dimension."

"Oh my god! Me too!" Patrick said. "I mean, not my parents, but my friends."

"My neighbor suggested I join MDG now that the teams are dead," Priya said.

"I hope you told him to fuck off," Maddie said as she walked into the room. She slid on the couch on the other side of me.

"Maddie, I'm in Alabama. I said, '*Bless your heart*.'"

"It means the same thing," Patrick said.

"It does," Priya confirmed.

"Do you guys have any updates?" Laila asked. "My friends were asking about New Year's Eve, but I wasn't sure if I'd be here for that."

"I think you will be," Maddie said. Patrick groaned. "You're welcome to come to New York, if you want, though."

"No, that's OK," Patrick said with a sigh. "My parents throw a big New Year's Eve party every year; they'd probably really like it if I was here for it."

"We may have a lead on Dust Storm," I said. "We're just waiting to hear back."

"Hear back from who?" Noah asked. "What kind of lead?"

"An old . . . friend of Maddie's," I said, glancing at her. "She's doing a little digging. No guarantees, but it's the best we've got right now. If we don't get a solid lead, we're going to have to try something else."

"But we're going to the conference for sure in January," Maddie said. "So, we may just plan to meet up there, unless any of you want to join us here before then."

"There's plenty of room," Edan said. His arm brushed mine again when he leaned forward.

"I may take you up on that after New Year's," Dorsey said. "The buddy I'm staying with has to go back to school."

"Just let me know," Maddie said. "We'll keep you updated on Dust Storm. In the meantime, please yell at all your friends who think trained scrabs are a good idea."

"On it," Patrick said.

I waved as we ended the call, feeling a pang of disappointment as their faces disappeared from the screen. It had only been a few weeks, but I missed them. I was ready for the team to be together again.

16

SCARLETT ANSWERED THE DOOR AS SOON AS I KNOCKED, A more relaxed smile on her face than last time I'd seen her. Maybe because I didn't have Maddie with me this time.

She'd texted half an hour ago, saying she had information for us. Maddie was on Long Island with her mom, so I'd raced over alone, eager to hear what she'd found out.

"Come in," she said. "Do you want anything to drink?"

"I'm fine, thanks," I said, shrugging out of my coat.

The bedroom door opened, and a blond man, handsome and in his early twenties, emerged from within. His hair was slightly damp, like he'd just showered.

"Dan, this is Clara," Scarlett said.

He extended his hand to me. "Nice to meet you."

"You too."

He headed to the door, kissing Scarlett quickly on the way. "I'll see you later. Text me"—he glanced at me—"after."

She smiled and nodded. He glanced at me again with an expression I couldn't quite identify—suspicion? curiosity?—and then walked out of the apartment.

"Your boyfriend?" I asked stupidly. Obviously.

"Yes."

She sat down on the couch, and I lowered into one of the

chairs. I glanced back at where Dan had been. I didn't know why I was surprised that she had a boyfriend, but I was.

"You and Maddie have gotten yourselves into some deep shit here," she said.

I looked at her quickly. "Yeah? What did you find out?"

"I know where that facility is."

"Seriously?"

"The city, not the precise location. Lubbock, Texas."

I screwed up my face. *"Lubbock?"*

"What's that look for? What's wrong with Lubbock?"

"I mean, I don't know, I've never been. It's just random. There's nothing there, except a university."

"Well, you did mention that Julian said it was in the middle of nowhere," she said.

"Good point. Brian got you this information?"

"Yes. Also, this is interesting—Julian told Brian that he's no longer employed by MDG," Scarlett said.

"Really?" I asked.

"That's what he said. Apparently, he screamed something at Brian about MDG being a bunch of ungrateful bastards. And Brian heard from a friend about Julian stomping around the MDG offices right before Christmas, yelling at people."

"That does sound like Julian."

Scarlett leaned back with a snort. "It does."

"Did you call the FBI about any of this? Maddie gave you Agent Simmons's card, right?"

"She did, but I didn't call them. I don't really want to get involved with any of this. Neither of us do. Brian never invested, and he doesn't have any information that would be useful to authorities, as far as we know. Julian told Brian that the Dust Storm facility doesn't house scrabs. He claims it's just a research facility, and perfectly legal."

"We'd be happy to go confirm that."

"My point is, we have no knowledge of any crimes being committed by Julian or MDG. Just, for the record."

"Got it. If anyone ever asks, I will tell them that."

"I'd appreciate it if you didn't mention our names in the future, unless you absolutely have to. I really don't want to have anything to do with Julian, ever again."

"Of course," I said. "I don't blame you."

She hesitated for a moment, her face softening a little. "Are you sure *you* want to do this? Chasing after MDG like this keeps you in his orbit. Don't you want to just . . . stop?"

"Sometimes," I admitted. "I thought about it, for a minute, when Julian tracked us down in London. It would have been so easy to just hop on a train and disappear. That's what I did before, when I joined the teams. I just ran away. But it didn't seem like the right choice this time. Back then I only needed to save myself. There's more at stake now."

"I guess that makes sense. I wondered if maybe you were only doing this because of Maddie and your boyfriend."

I cocked my head, confused. "My boyfriend?"

"Edan? Aren't you two together?"

"No, we're just friends."

"Oh." She seemed skeptical. "Really?"

"Yeah."

"He sure has a lot of pictures of you on his Instagram for someone who's only a friend."

"He has pictures of the whole team on there."

"You're in, like, every other one."

"I don't think that's true."

She gave me an amused look. "OK."

There was a brief silence as I formed the question that had been building since I saw Dan. "I, uh, this is off topic, but I just . . ."

"What?" she asked gently, like she already knew what I was going to ask.

I took in a breath. "Did you find it hard to date again, after Julian?"

"Hmmm . . . somewhat. I definitely had my guard up more. I probably overanalyzed everything. I went on a date with this one guy who said something flippant about his mom—like he was annoyed by something she had done—and I immediately got nervous. Julian was always so rude about his mom, and about other girls in general, that even the slightest hint of that in a guy made me drop him immediately."

"That makes sense," I said softly.

"Why? Have you found it hard to date to again?"

"I just don't do it at all."

"So, yes, then."

I laughed, twisting my fingers together. "Yes. I don't know if I can trust myself not to make stupid decisions again."

"How is Julian being an asshole *your* stupid decision?"

"Because I'm the one who ignored all the warning signs. A cute guy was nice to me a couple times, and I fell head over heels."

"So did I. But I don't want to let him . . ." She trailed off, apparently reconsidering her words. "I understand where you're coming from, but for me, it was a huge relief to date other people after Julian. It helped me start to figure out how truly awful he was. I didn't have enough context before that."

I looked down at my hands. Maybe she had a point. Or maybe she just didn't know me well enough to understand. She didn't know about my dad, or my troubles making friends.

"Sorry, I didn't mean to pry," she said. "I just assumed you and Edan were together."

"It's fine," I said with a smile, and got to my feet. "Thank you so much for finding out about Dust Storm. We really appreciate it."

"Sure." She stood and walked me to the door. "Text me and let me know how it turns out." She paused. "Vague texts. Or maybe just call."

I laughed. "OK."

"And if you ever want to talk about Julian or . . . anything, you can feel free to reach out. I don't mind talking about him."

"Thanks," I said, surprised.

She smiled at me, and I shrugged on my coat and said goodbye, wondering if I'd just made another friend without even trying. I was getting good at the friend thing.

Outside, I took out my phone and pulled up Edan's Instagram. It was an exaggeration to say that every other picture was of me, but there really were a lot, now that I looked at them all together. I was often with other members of the team, or in a selfie with Edan, but I was the constant in his feed.

I was in the last photo he'd posted, on Christmas Eve. We'd

gone to Bryant Park with Maddie and her mom, and Edan and I had taken a selfie with the Christmas tree in the background, hot chocolates in hand. He'd simply written *My favorite* as the caption. I'd assumed he meant the hot chocolate, because when we bought it, he'd said he loved it when they put a giant marshmallow on top. Though it seemed like he would have just taken a picture of his cup if he'd meant that. It was very Instagrammable hot chocolate, and our cups were barely visible in the photo.

Or he could have meant Christmas in general. Or Bryant Park, though that seemed strange since he'd mentioned once that he didn't really like Manhattan.

Or he could have meant me. My cheeks went hot, despite the bitter wind whipping across my face. The thought of being Edan's favorite anything was . . . Well, it was sort of unbelievable. It was such a nice thought that I immediately dismissed it. He had to have meant the hot chocolate.

~

"Texas Tech is in Lubbock," Hannah said to her laptop screen. She and Victor had rushed over as soon as Maddie and Edan got home, and we were all in the media room, trying to narrow down possible spots in Lubbock where the facility might be.

"Do you think that's why they chose it?" Edan asked. He was lying on his back on the carpet, his gaze on his phone. Hannah was on the couch, alone, which I couldn't help but notice. There was plenty of room for him to go sit next to her.

"Texas A&M is the big scrab research facility in Texas," Victor said. "But it's possible, I guess."

"I've got another spot that might be worth checking out,"

Hannah said. "An old research lab. It's been around since, like, 2005, but could still be something."

"Yeah, put it on the list," Maddie said. "Put it all on the list. I'll check out everything."

"Apparently Julian wasn't lying when he said he was no longer employed by MDG," Edan said, still looking at his phone.

"What do you mean?" I asked, reaching for my own phone.

"He told a reporter that MDG was reckless and dangerous. Look at the news."

I clicked on a news site and found the breaking story about Julian at the top. The headline read JULIAN MONTGOMERY CUTS TIES WITH MDG, CRITICIZES THEIR METHODS.

"Sounds like he's scared that we're onto something," Maddie said with a grin. "I'm buying these plane tickets now. Edan, Clara, you're in?"

"In," Edan said.

"Of course," I said.

"What are you going to do there? Just look for the facility?" Victor asked.

"Yep, exactly," Maddie said.

"All of these spots are just guesses," he said skeptically. "We've only narrowed it down to the entire city, which could pose a problem."

"It's not that big of a city," Maddie said. "And I think we have some pretty good leads. Plus, Julian just ran scared after we found out that Dust Storm is in Lubbock. I am *definitely* going." She hammered at her keyboard. "I'll let the rest of the team know what we're doing. They can join us if they want."

"They'll want to," I said.

Maddie nodded approvingly. "Good. Then we can all drive to Dallas together for the conference. Actually, we should just fly to Germany from Dallas when we're done. That's a big airport. We can probably get good flights."

"Wait, what?" I traded a confused glance with Edan. "We're going to Germany?"

"Yes! Sorry." She typed as she talked. "I meant to tell you that I've been in contact with some people there. I think it's the best place to get the teams going again. The police in London aren't being particularly cooperative, so I think we should probably cool it in the UK for a while."

"But . . . that would mean we'd be in Germany in, like . . . a week? Two, maybe, if we have to go back to Lubbock after the conference?"

"Yeah, exactly. We can get going again right away."

"We can't do that."

"Sure we can. I'll just fly all the recruits who are still in London over once we're there. I'm excited. I've never been to Germany."

"But, Maddie, I haven't finished our new training program, or recruitment strategies, or talked about some changes in the teams. We could—"

"We don't need to change anything," she said, glancing up at me from her laptop.

"We haven't even discussed—"

"I have it handled, promise. If you want to help, maybe look at where we could stay in Berlin. I haven't decided if we should go the hostel route again. I'll send you some rough recruit numbers."

I let out an annoyed breath. Edan looked from me to her, clearly picking up on the tension, but Maddie was staring at her screen, oblivious.

"Yep, lots of good flights out of Dallas to Germany," she murmured. "It'll work out perfectly."

Part Three

DUST
STORM

17

Maddie, Edan, and I flew to Lubbock the next day. Maddie solved the problem of being too young to rent a car by just buying a giant van, which was ridiculous, but also pretty good problem solving. Being rich seemed like it made everything so much easier.

"What are you going to do with it when we're done?" Edan asked as we walked out of the salesman's office.

"Donate it to charity, probably. I'm sure someone could use it." She caught the amused looks on our faces. "Oh, come on. It's used! It was a steal." She squinted through the sun at the beige van. "Also, it's really ugly."

"Grayson said once that the two of you would be personally responsible for draining the St. John fortune, and I'm beginning to think he's right," Edan said.

"Oh, he's totally right." Maddie opened the driver's door. "Future generations of St. Johns are shit out of luck."

~

Our boxes full of weapons packs were waiting for us at the hotel. Maddie had shipped them, since we figured the TSA would not appreciate us bringing machetes and axes on the plane.

Edan took the boxes up to our rooms, and I went with Maddie back to the airport to pick up the rest of the team.

"Have you told Laurence you'll be in Dallas later this week?" she asked as she pulled onto the highway.

I looked out the window at the flat earth. You could see for a long way here. "Not yet."

"Are you going to?"

"Y . . . yes? I mean, yes. I am. Going to do that." I tried to smile at her.

She glanced at me and cocked a judgmental eyebrow.

"It's just awkward, when we talk," I said. "I've been putting it off."

"You know who you could talk to about that?"

"Maddie, please give it a rest with the therapist thing."

"Never gonna happen."

She was quiet for a moment, tapping her fingers on the steering wheel. "Are you OK with going to Dallas next? I wasn't thinking when I booked our tickets that this might not be a good idea for you."

"Why?" I asked. "Just because my parents are there?"

"Yeah. It just occurred to me that maybe it could be kind of upsetting for you? Or even dangerous? What if your parents realize you're there and report it to police? Your permission slip was forged, and you're not eighteen for another four months. What if the police pick you up?"

"They're not going to do that," I said, even though my chest had tightened, just a little. "Laurence said they weren't going to make a big deal out of the permission slip, remember?" He'd told me he talked to them about it not long after I posted that video.

Mom had made noises about trying to get me home, and he'd really let them have it. Told Mom and Dad he'd tell the police everything if they tried to do something.

"Right," she said. "That's true. But if you feel weird about it all, you're welcome to go back to New York. Or go ahead to Germany, if you wanted."

"Actually, we should talk about Germany."

She let out an exasperated sigh. "Why are you being weird about Germany?"

"Because we're not ready."

"We will get ready."

"How long do you plan to take before you put teams on the street in Berlin?"

"I think we can get the more experienced teams out within a few days of arriving."

I stared at her.

"What?" Her voice rose a little. "*You* are part of a more experienced team. You don't think you're ready to be out fighting scrabs again?"

"Not without excellent teams backing me, up, no. You're rushing into this without thinking. I have some ideas about changes we could make, but we would need time—"

"We need to get the teams off the ground again before we start talking about changes."

"That doesn't make any sense. We have a better chance of success if we make some changes, *then* recruit and start again."

"And just leave everyone to die in the meantime?" she snapped.

I reeled back, surprised by her sharp tone. "There are other people fighting scrabs. Rushing in and getting *all* of us killed isn't going to help anything."

"Don't be dramatic. Our team is a well-oiled machine, and so are several of the others. Even if we have to start small, it'll be fine."

I made an exasperated noise. "Why won't you ever listen to me about this? You won't even hear one of my ideas—"

"I listen to you!"

"No, you don't. You don't want to talk about changing things even a little bit. It's like you've decided my ideas are stupid before you've even heard them."

"Fine, tell me your ideas." The words came out clipped and angry.

I crossed my arms over my chest. My heart was pounding, and I wasn't sure if it was because I was angry or upset or scared. I wasn't scared of Maddie, but I wasn't sure if my body knew that.

She turned into the airport and moved into the arrivals lane.

"Never mind," I said. "You're right, it was probably stupid anyway."

"I never said it was—"

"Just forget it." I pointed to the team, standing together with their luggage in the pickup area. "There they are."

Her eyebrows drew together, but she didn't argue as she pulled up to the curb. I hopped out as soon as she stopped, grateful that we couldn't continue the conversation.

Priya rushed up to hug me first, and then the rest of the team followed. We helped them pile their luggage in back, and then I quickly climbed into one of the rear seats, far away from Maddie.

"So, what are we doing first?" Patrick asked as Maddie pulled onto the road. He was sitting up front in the passenger's seat.

"We have a pretty long list of possibilities," Maddie said. "I'll send it to you guys when we get back to the hotel. I think the best option is for us to just start at the top, because we honestly don't have any leads except that the facility is somewhere in the city."

"And who is it that got you this information?" Noah asked.

"She's someone from Maddie and Julian's circle in New York, and she asked that we don't spread her name around," I said. "She asked her brother to get it out of Julian."

"And Julian is probably aware that we know, so we should move quickly," Maddie said. "I thought we'd split up into teams of two, and I'll drop you guys off at a possible location. You'll check it out—discreetly—and then, if you think we can rule it out, you'll move on to another one. Sound good?"

We all nodded.

"Good," Maddie said. "We start first thing tomorrow."

I caught Maddie's eye in the rearview mirror. I quickly turned to look out the window.

I swallowed around the lump in my throat. Part of me wished I hadn't said anything. But a bigger part of me knew I was right, and I wouldn't be able to live with myself if I didn't say something and people got hurt. I just hoped that I hadn't ended my friendship with Maddie in the process.

18

I WAS PAIRED WITH EDAN THE NEXT DAY. MADDIE DROPPED US off at a Starbucks, where we ordered coffees and food and took a seat at the window so we could watch the building across the street. It was a tall structure that housed some kind of research lab. It was probably too centrally located to have scrabs anywhere nearby, but we were checking everything.

I glanced at Edan, who had his eyes on his phone. Maybe Hannah was texting him again. She seemed to be doing that a lot. Would Edan even tell me if they were dating? I felt like he would.

My phone rang, and I looked down to see Laurence's name.

"I'll be back in a minute," I said to Edan, scooping up my phone and walking quickly outside. I swiped to answer the call.

"Hey, Laurence."

"Hey. I saw I missed a call from you earlier."

"Yeah." I blew out a nervous breath. I'd tried calling him before we left the hotel this morning, and now I'd lost my nerve.

"How's New York?" he asked, after a brief silence.

"Uh, it was good. But I'm actually not in New York anymore."

"Where are you?"

"Lubbock."

There was a brief pause. "Why in the world are you in *Lubbock?*"

"It's a scrab thing. Kind of hard to explain. But we're going to be here for about a week."

"Oh. OK."

It was quiet for another moment.

"Everything OK?" he asked.

"Yes. I mean . . . yes. We're tracking MDG and trying to figure out some stuff . . . Are you working a lot right now?"

"Am I . . ." He sounded puzzled. "I just finished a job. Still looking for the next one. Why?"

"I just, uh . . . You can say no."

"What?"

"You can say no. I mean, I won't be insulted if you say no."

"You haven't told me what you want."

"Right." I paused.

"Clara, do you need something? Do you need money? I'm happy to send you some, just give me your bank—"

"No," I interrupted. "I don't need money. I mean, thank you, but I'm fine on money."

"Then . . . ?"

"After Lubbock, the whole team is going to Dallas. To this conference thing. We'll be there a few days, at least. And I was wondering . . . if you had time and you wanted to, you know, meet up, I wouldn't mind. I mean, I would like to see you. If you wanted."

"I would like that." He actually sounded like he would.

"Oh. OK. Good. Um, I can text you?"

"Sure," Laurence said.

"OK. I'll do that, then. Bye, Laurence."

"Bye, Clara." I ended the call and walked back inside. Edan looked at me curiously.

"Laurence," I said, sliding back into my seat.

"Are you guys going to meet up in Dallas?"

"Yeah." I paused, staring out the window at a guy standing at the corner, waiting for the bus. "I really don't appreciate those assholes choosing Dallas for their conference."

He let out a short, startled laugh. "What? You said it was no big deal."

"I know, but I lied. It sucks, and I don't want to go back, but I have to, so I'm just lying to everyone to try and make myself feel better." I sighed, leaning forward to rest my head on one hand. "And Maddie and I had a fight."

"I thought things seemed weird between you guys. What happened?"

"I got mad because she won't ever listen to me about the teams or Germany or anything I have to say about the future of the whole St. John operation."

He cocked an eyebrow.

"What does that look mean?"

"It's just, if you're looking for someone to tell you that you're totally right, you've come to the right person. I was wondering when you were going to get mad about that."

"Really?"

"Yeah. She dismisses it every time you bring it up. I don't think she means to, it's just kind of her personality. Full steam ahead."

"Full steam ahead is going to get us all killed."

"I agree."

"You do?"

His lips quirked up. "Of course. We've both been doing this for months; we know our stuff. But I'm really not the right person to ask if you're looking for, like, an objective opinion." His cheeks reddened, and he looked out the window.

"What do you mean?"

"I'm always inclined to be on your side." He glanced at me briefly with a smile, and then returned his attention to the lab across the street.

I felt my cheeks heat as well. "Thank you." There was a short, awkward pause.

"What did you want to tell her?" he asked. "About the teams. I know you think we're not ready for Germany, and you're definitely right about that. What else?"

"We need to overhaul our training program, for sure. Recruits need more time and training before being sent out to battle scrabs. I've been working on some ideas with Patrick and Noah."

"Our training strategy could definitely use some work."

"And I think there should be other options for people besides fighting. There are a lot of people who want to help but aren't equipped to fight scrabs. I saw a note from Grayson about non-combat teams on an exit interview, and it got me thinking. Did he ever talk to you about that?"

Edan shook his head.

"We've lost a lot of recruits who never should have been out there to begin with, honestly. And I feel like, with Maddie's resources, we could focus on other things as well. Like rebuilding homes and businesses. Pair people like us — recruits who can fight—with rebuilding teams. Our recruit numbers would sky-rocket if we had a nonfighting option. Investors might be more interested too."

"I think that's a great idea."

"Yeah?"

"Yeah. Grayson was very focused on the fighting aspect, prob-ably because that's what *he* was good at. But that doesn't have to be the only thing we do."

"I know Maddie will say that there are already charity organi-zations that do exactly what I'm talking about. But even if there are other charities, most of them don't have the money and resources that she does. And the name recognition. *And* teams of people who already have some scrab-fighting training."

"You should definitely tell her this. It's a good idea. And you're right about needing to overhaul our training program, even if she doesn't want to hear it. I'm sure Patrick and Noah will back you up on that."

"Thank you," I said, and I could feel myself blushing again. I hadn't realized I needed someone to tell me I was right until Edan said it. I didn't even care if he wasn't objective. I liked having him on my side.

"Are you going to go to Germany?" I asked. "Even if she doesn't listen?"

He turned his attention from the window to me, a small smile on his face. "I told you before that I go where you go."

My breath caught in my throat. It was the first time either of us had talked about that night we spent in his bed, and I suddenly felt off balance. I fumbled for my phone to avoid looking at him, and another heavy silence settled between us.

~

We spent the next two days staring at random buildings around Lubbock, getting nowhere. Dorsey and Patrick got a visit from the police once, who shooed them away from a lab that conducted animal research testing. They got a lot of angry visitors, apparently.

"How far down the list are we?" Noah asked, leaning forward to look at the list over Edan's shoulder. All of us were in the van after taking a break for lunch.

"Halfway or so," Edan said.

"That's just the first list," Maddie said, looking in the rearview mirror as she pulled out of the parking spot. Our eyes met briefly, and she quickly looked away. We'd been avoiding talking about anything but possible facility locations since our fight. "We put all the most likely stuff on the first list. The labs and research facilities and all that."

"We're going to end up lurking outside every building in this town, aren't we?" Dorsey asked from behind me. "I'm going to get a weird reputation."

"You already have a weird reputation," Patrick said. Dorsey whacked his head.

Maddie dropped off Priya and Laila, and then Patrick and Dorsey. She drove for about fifteen minutes toward the edge of town before turning down a street.

"Maddie, there's nothing out here," Edan said.

"The building's right there," she said, pointing to the

nondescript one-story white building at the end of the road. The sign said SUNBURST LABS. It was a biomedical research facility.

"It looks abandoned," he said.

He was right. The parking lot was completely empty except for some trash and a big lump of something that looked suspiciously like a dead animal. I craned my neck, trying to see.

Beside me, Noah suddenly leaned forward. I drew in a sharp breath.

"That's a scrab," Edan said. Noah grabbed his weapons pack.

"What the hell?" Maddie pressed on the gas, and then came to a quick stop next to the scrab. "Clara, hand me—"

I was already holding a sheathed machete out to her. She took it, pulled the cover off, and opened her door. She poked the scrab with it.

"Definitely dead."

"There's another one," Edan said, pointing.

I followed his finger. There was a dead scrab at the entrance of the building, face-down, propping the door open.

"Well, that looks like an invitation to go inside," Maddie said, hopping out of the van.

"What? Maddie, no," Noah said. "Shouldn't we call the cops?"

"Of course. Let's just go take a peek around inside real quick. The door's open! It's not even breaking and entering."

"Plus, there could be people inside who need our help," I said, grabbing my own weapons pack from the floor.

Noah still looked skeptical as we all piled out of the van.

"You can stand out here and keep watch if you want," Maddie said to him. "But I don't trust the cops. MDG could have been paying off police in this area for years." She gestured to the scrab on the ground, as if to prove her point.

"No, you're right," Noah said with a sigh. "Let's go."

We followed Maddie to the entrance, carefully stepping around the dead scrab. We were in a bright, sun-drenched lobby, the tile floor streaked with dirt and grime and some kind of disgusting brown mucus-looking substance. There was an empty security desk at the far end of the room. Just beyond it was a stairwell door.

Maddie tried the handle to the stairwell, and it easily opened. We went down two flights of stairs until we came to another door that had been propped open by a dead scrab. Or a piece of scrab. It was just its severed leg.

"Is it suddenly occurring to anyone else that someone might have left these scrabs here to bait us into coming inside?" Edan said.

"It sure is," I murmured.

Maddie didn't acknowledge that she'd heard us. I edged around the scrab leg and through the door.

I stopped. Beside me, Noah sucked in a breath.

It was a huge facility. We were on a walkway, looking down at a lab below. To my left and right were cages. Hundreds of them. They wrapped around to the other side, and when I looked up, I saw another row of them. Another row below us.

They were all empty. There was a dead scrab on the ground outside one of the cages to my left, but other than that, they were all gone. Blood was splattered across them.

I gasped as I spotted the bodies. Five people lay dead on the floor, blood pooling around their bodies. I could see evidence of scrab claw and teeth wounds.

"What the hell?" Maddie breathed.

I leaned over the railing, looking at the scrab cages. These were not the quick, makeshift cages I'd seen in France and the UK. These had sturdy metal bars, and I didn't see a single one that was broken. Still, something had clearly gone wrong.

"They left all the computers on," Noah said quietly.

He was right. Laptops were still open, monitors bright with whatever they'd been working on last.

Maddie walked slowly toward the stairs and started down.

"Maddie, are you sure we should go down there?" I called. "There are dead bodies."

She paused, turning back to look at us. "Does anyone have gloves?"

Noah nodded, reaching into his jacket pockets and producing black gloves. He walked down the steps and handed them to Maddie.

"No one else touch anything," she said, pulling them on. Noah followed her down to the lower level; Edan and I were close behind.

"The cages were opened," I said, pointing. There was a bright green light at the front of every one. "The scrabs didn't escape."

Edan looked down the rows of cages. "Do you think this place was full?"

"Yes," Maddie said. She was leaned over a laptop, scrolling through it. "There's a daily log here. There were five hundred."

"Shit," Noah muttered.

"These logs . . ." Maddie frowned. "They go back fifteen years."

"What were they doing down here fifteen years ago?"

"It seems like . . ." She looked over her shoulder at us with a baffled expression. "They were housing and training scrabs back then too."

"They couldn't have been," Noah said. "The first scrab sighting was, what? Eight years ago?"

"They were down here way before that. There are pictures. And video." She clicked on something and moved away from the screen. I edged closer.

Two men in lab coats stood on either side of a metal table. A small, hairless animal sat in the middle of it, motionless.

"The last product of R-256 died today, aged three months. Lungs were underdeveloped. Subjects from R-257 and R-259 continue to thrive."

The video ended. We all stared at the screen.

"MDG *created* the scrabs," Noah said, eyes wide.

"Those assholes." Maddie reached for the laptop. "We're taking this. We're showing every—"

"No, no!" Edan rushed forward, pushing her hand away from the laptop. "We can't take it. If we move it out of here, they can say we tampered with it."

"He's right," I said.

"Take some pictures and videos on your phone," Noah said. "Then we'll go outside, call the cops, and call your contact at the FBI. Let them come and collect the evidence. We'll send our stuff to reporters if we have to."

"Yeah, OK," Maddie said, pulling her phone out of her pocket.

I looked up, turning in a circle. "There should be security footage, right? Maybe we can see what they did with those scrabs."

Edan pointed to the camera in the corner, which was in pieces. "Looks like someone didn't want anyone to know who took them."

I sighed.

"Everyone, quiet for a minute. I'm going to record a few of these videos," Maddie said.

We all waited as she took a few videos and then pictures of the logs.

"There's more in here, but it's password protected," she muttered, squinting at the screen.

"That's enough," I said. "We have some proof. The cops can do the rest."

She wrinkled her nose like she didn't trust the cops to do anything. I couldn't say I blamed her, after watching Grayson's murderer walk free.

We headed back up the stairs and outside. Maddie dialed 911 as I walked around to the side of the building.

I shielded my eyes from the sun, squinting out at the flat earth beyond the building. I didn't see any scrab holes. Hundreds of scrabs could have fit in those cages, but I didn't see any evidence of a massive scrab escape.

"No scrab holes!" I called.

"I don't see any either," Noah said.

"So, they didn't just set them free," Edan said.

"They couldn't have," Noah said. "That many scrabs, in an open area like this . . . Most of them would have started tunneling immediately."

I walked over to the dead scrab in the middle of the parking lot, and kneeled down to look at it. There weren't any puncture wounds. No sign of how it had died.

"Why leave a dead one out here like this?" I asked.

"Maybe they escaped after everything?" Noah guessed.

"Doesn't explain why they're dead." I stood, glancing over at the other dead scrab in the doorway.

"Someone has those scrabs," I said. "And they left these out there so someone would find what was inside."

19

Three police cars showed up, and even though we'd told them about the dead scrabs, they were horrified when they saw the bodies. One of the officers actually screamed when he spotted the scrab in the parking lot. They made us move far away, and then spent a really long time making sure the scrab was dead. We could have told them that it definitely was, but they seemed intent on doing it themselves.

We all had to go to the station to answer questions, and Maddie gave them Agent Simmons's number at the FBI. The Lubbock police were thoroughly baffled by us. But they didn't seem to suspect that we were responsible for the deaths of the people in that lab, which had been a real concern of mine, especially since we went inside. We pointed them to the computer where we'd found the evidence that MDG created scrabs, since we'd already admitted to going inside. Seemed best to give them a solid reason to take every computer in the place.

My second concern was that they'd insist on calling my parents, since I was the only minor in the group, but no one seemed particularly worried about that. One officer asked me after the interview if I needed for her to call them, but didn't press when I said I was fine.

Maddie told the officers we'd be in town for at least a few

more days if they had more questions. They asked us not to talk to reporters for the time being. Maddie said that she couldn't make any promises. The Lubbock police didn't seem to like us much.

Agent Simmons was exasperated, as usual, and asked us to go home to New York. I didn't think she actually expected us to do that, though. She was realistic at this point.

The rest of the team was waiting for us in the parking lot of the police station when we were finally done, gathered around the van. Maddie gave them a quick rundown of what we'd seen.

"So, you told them what you saw on the laptop?" Laila asked. "The FBI?"

"I told Agent Simmons that I'd seen some logs on the computer that went back at least fifteen years," Maddie said. "I told her there might be some information there worth looking into."

"What'd she say?" Laila asked.

"She said she'd pass that on. They're sending some people out here."

Her phone buzzed, and she pulled it from her pocket and held it out. "Hey, Hannah. You're on with the whole team."

"Hey, guys. Maddie texted me earlier. Holy shit, huh?"

"To put it mildly," Dorsey said.

"OK, so this is probably nothing, but I just got a tip, and I needed to pass it on. Julian's going to that conference in Dallas in a couple days."

"Why?" I asked.

"One of my Reddit bros said that he's a surprise guest speaker. He's always been a hero to that crowd, since he's constantly defending them."

"True," Maddie said. Edan made a face.

"I don't think we're going to the conference anymore," I said. "Our first priority is finding those missing scrabs."

"No, I know," Hannah said. "But get this. Julian's already in Texas. He was photographed in the Dallas airport yesterday. Which is really early to get to the city if he's just going to the conference."

A brief silence settled over the team. Maddie and I exchanged a look.

"He . . . Did he stay in Dallas?" Maddie asked.

"I don't know," Hannah said. "There's a picture of him arriving at the Dallas airport yesterday afternoon. That's all I've got."

"That drive is . . ." Patrick looked at me. "What is the drive from Dallas to Lubbock?"

"Five hours," Hannah said before I could answer. "I checked."

"So, there's a possibility that he jumped in a car, drove to Lubbock, and stole all those scrabs last night," Maddie said slowly.

"It is very possible."

"He knew we were coming," Edan said. "It can't be a coincidence that right after we discovered where Dust Storm is, he shows up and takes all the scrabs."

"Or could have told someone at MDG," Maddie said. "Or Brian did. They had a couple days to get all those scrabs out before we found it."

"Wouldn't they have destroyed all the evidence too, though?" Edan asked. "If MDG knew in advance that we were coming, they would have just blown that place up like they did in France."

"True," I said. "And Julian doesn't even work for them any-more. So, he had no reason to give them a heads-up."

"And also, no reason to take those scrabs," Priya said.

"Except he's chummy with these league guys who are all about trained scrabs," Hannah said. "You should see some of the shit they post. I have to wonder if Julian would be willing to help some of them get their hands on a few."

"Especially if they were willing to pay," Maddie murmured. She bounced on her heels. "OK. New plan! We're going to Dallas tomorrow. Hannah, see if you can find out which hotel Julian is staying at."

"Got it," Hannah said.

"We'll tail Julian and see if he leads us to the scrabs. If he doesn't, we'll come back here or follow the next lead. Hannah, stay on the Reddit bros and see if any of them say anything suspicious."

"Got it."

"Good," Maddie said. "Everyone else, get ready to go to Dallas."

~

I went downstairs that evening and found a quiet corner of the hotel's patio. Maddie was in our room, and we were still avoiding talking about anything important. It was getting awkward, and I worried that if I stayed, we'd end up fighting again.

I sat in one of the chairs, buttoning my jacket as a cold wind whipped across my face. I dialed Scarlett's number and pressed the phone to my ear.

She picked up right away. "Hey."

"Hey."

"You guys OK?"

"We're fine. I just wanted to let you know that we found it."

"Really." She sounded impressed.

"Yeah. I'm not sure how much you want to know . . ."

"Not much, honestly."

"I'll just say that we are eternally grateful to you. And you should maybe keep an eye on the news."

She laughed softly. "I'll do that."

"Your brother hasn't heard from Julian, has he?"

"Definitely not."

"OK." I leaned back in my chair.

"Everything OK otherwise?"

"Yeah . . ."

"That was the least convincing *yeah* I've ever heard."

I sighed. "We're going to Dallas tomorrow. My family is there, and it's just . . ."

"Complicated?" she guessed.

"Yeah. And Julian is there too. It's like the universe hates me."

"Are you coming back to New York anytime soon?"

"I don't know. I hope so."

"Call me if you do, OK? We'll go get lunch or something."

"I would like that." I paused. "Hey, I've been meaning to ask you about something you said about not investing in the teams. You said they were shortsighted?"

"Yes. That's what I told Grayson last year when he approached me about it."

"What did you mean?"

"I don't really understand how sending a bunch of amateurs

out to fight scrabs hand to hand is that helpful. I think that his time and money could have been better spent elsewhere."

"Like addressing some of the problems scrabs leave behind? Like homelessness and destroyed businesses?" I asked.

"Exactly like that."

"If the St. John teams built a program that did that, do you think that more people would want to invest?"

"Oh, definitely. Are you doing that?"

"I don't know. I'm hopeful that I can change some things."

"Let me know. I'd be very interested in hearing about that."

I smiled. "I will." I spotted Edan walking through the door to the patio, and I straightened. "I should let you go, OK? I'll update you in a couple days."

"OK. Good luck."

"Thanks." I hung up the phone as Edan began to make his way across the patio.

"Hey." He pointed to the chair next to me. "Mind if I join you?"

"No, of course not." I slipped my phone into my pocket. "I was just updating Scarlett on what happened today. Sort of, anyway."

He sat down, stretching his legs out in front of him. "Sort of?"

"I think she wants plausible deniability. I left out the details."

"That's probably for the best. I have talked to far too many police and FBI officers over the past six months. I'm really over it."

"Same."

"Did you talk to Maddie yet?"

"Not yet. I will. We've been polite to each other, though, so at least we're not fighting anymore. Maybe."

"Ah yes, the avoidance route. Pretending the problem isn't

there and just hoping it goes away. Also a favorite of mine." He turned to look at me. "Never works out the way you want, though."

"I know," I said, pushing my hair back with a sigh. "I'm going to talk to her. She was just really focused on finding that facility, and now with the missing scrabs . . . I'm waiting for my moment."

"Or avoiding your moment." He grinned.

"I am strategically waiting for the best time."

He laughed. "As someone who is also very good at running away from problems, I sympathize."

"Thank you, I appreciate that."

His phone buzzed, and I looked over to see him reading a text. His lips twitched as he answered it.

"Hannah?" I guessed.

"Yeah." He was still typing.

We sat in silence for several seconds, a lump forming in my throat. I suddenly needed to know. Desperately. Knowing seemed better than always stressing about it.

"Are you and Hannah dating?" I blurted out.

He looked up with a start, nearly dropping his phone. He caught it and put it on the table between us. It buzzed with another text.

"Are Hannah and I . . ." He trailed off like he didn't understand the question.

My cheeks burned, and I regretted this already. "I was just wondering. You know. If you were."

He blinked. I'd never seen this expression on his face before, and I didn't know what to think. It was like a mixture of confusion and . . . annoyance? I could have sworn he looked annoyed, like he didn't want to be asked this particular question. Maybe he thought it was none of my business. Maybe it *was* none of my business.

"I, uh, I didn't mean to pry, I just . . ." Why had I opened my mouth? His confusion seemed to be intensifying, and I had no idea how to get out of this without looking like a total idiot. Or more of an idiot.

"It's fine!" I blurted out the lie too loudly. "If you and Hannah are dating. I was just wondering."

"It's *fine?*" Now he looked truly bewildered.

"Sorry. You don't need my approval on your dating life." I tried to laugh, but it came out kind of weird and strangled. "I didn't mean it like that."

"How did you mean it?" he asked.

My heart was beating too quickly, and it was making me feel sick. "I was just wondering. You guys seemed to have hit it off."

His eyebrows drew together. He slid forward in his chair like he was going to bolt, but he just angled his body so that it was facing me. "But . . . you'd be fine with me dating Hannah?"

Well now I'd really screwed things up. "I, uh . . ." I couldn't bring myself to lie again. A long, familiar awkward silence stretched out between us.

"I'm not dating Hannah," he finally said softly. His gaze was downcast, but he glanced up at me as he spoke the next words. "I was waiting for you."

My breath caught in my throat. Waiting. For me.

I opened my mouth. No sound came out.

"It's OK, you don't have to say anything." He laughed a little, but it sounded more embarrassed than joyful. "I probably shouldn't have just sprung that on you like that, I just . . ."

The buzzing in my brain was making it hard to think. Part of me wanted to jump up and down and celebrate because he wasn't dating Hannah. He'd been waiting for *me*.

But the other part of me felt terrified, because I hadn't planned this. I hadn't made a decision about whether or not I was going to date Edan. Part of me had liked that limbo we were in, and I'd just gone and destroyed it.

"I, uh . . ." Nope, I still didn't have any words.

"It's OK, Clara," he said gently. He stood, grabbing his phone and avoiding my gaze. His cheeks were pink. "I'm going to go back upstairs and try to get some sleep."

I considered stopping him, but he practically bolted away from me. I would have done the same, and I couldn't bring myself to haul him back and embarrass him even more. Not to mention that I still had no idea what to say to him. I could tell the truth—that I actually wasn't at all OK with him dating Hannah—but then that would lead to more, and I hadn't decided on more yet. More still felt dangerous.

So I watched him walk across the patio and disappear into the hotel, and then I sat in the dark by myself until my fingers were frozen.

20

I sat in the very last row of the van on the way to Dallas.
It was the farthest seat from Edan, who was up front. He was
pointedly avoiding me. Or I was avoiding him. Hard to say.

The rest of the team chatted happily. Noah edited on his laptop, putting together a Lubbock video that he was going to post
after all this was over. It made us all look so focused and happy,
and I sort of wished I lived in that world instead. Fake YouTube
World seemed much nicer than the drama I had going on with two
of my best friends.

I texted Laurence on the drive, and we made plans to have
dinner together. He said he was free any night, so I suggested that
evening. Fleeing for the night seemed like the best option at the
moment.

Maddie got us several rooms at a hotel downtown and put the
two of us together again. Maybe she thought it would be too awkward to suddenly change things up. But she left after dropping off
her bag and only returned right before I left.

"You're meeting up with your brother?" she asked.

"Yeah," I said, pausing at the door to look back at her. I wasn't
sure if we were still fighting. I didn't know how to fight with her.
Maybe we weren't even fighting. Maybe she'd decided to just put
some distance between us. A lump formed in my throat.

"I got a tip that some of the league guys are meeting up for happy hour at a restaurant tomorrow," she said. "Dorsey and Patrick are going to go check it out, and the rest of us are going to tail Julian, see if he goes anywhere interesting. You're welcome to invite Laurence, if he doesn't mind sitting in a van all day."

"I'm not sure he'll want to . . ." I had no idea if he wanted to. I wasn't sure if Laurence was just being polite when he asked me questions about the team or if he was truly interested.

She shrugged and turned away from me. "Whatever you want."

"Maybe I'll ask." I tried to sound casual.

She nodded. I stared at her back for a moment, and then walked out the door.

Laurence was waiting in the lobby, leaning against the back of a chair. He looked mostly the same as the last time I'd seen him—tall and broad, with dark hair and a nervous expression on his face. Maybe I was projecting the nerves. But Laurence often looked like he wished he was someplace else—*any*place else—and I thought I saw that familiar expression now.

But he smiled when he spotted me. Maybe I really was projecting. *I* was nervous, and honestly, a little shaky. I couldn't stop thinking about Edan's downcast gaze as he walked away last night. And Maddie shrugging and turning away from me, like she didn't even care if we were fighting.

I took a deep breath and tried to focus on Laurence, who had straightened as I approached. I could at least try not to fail at *this* relationship.

I stopped in front of him, unsure if I should greet him with a hug. I couldn't remember the last time I'd hugged Laurence.

Probably when we were kids and Mom would make us hug after we fought. But that must have been at least ten years ago.

He didn't make a move like he was going to try to embrace me, so I just stood there awkwardly.

"Hi," I said.

"Hi."

"Thanks for coming."

"Thanks for inviting me."

And then we just stood there staring at each other for several seconds. This had probably been a horrible idea. We'd barely gotten to a point where we could talk on the phone for fifteen minutes. Spending an entire evening together was going to be painful.

"I saw a restaurant down the road that looked pretty good," he finally said. "You up for Mexican?"

"Sure."

I followed him out of the hotel and to his truck, and we managed small talk about Lubbock on the five-minute ride to the restaurant. I didn't fill him in on what we'd found at the facility. The news hadn't broken yet, and we were giving the police a little more time to announce it.

We were seated at a booth, and I opened the menu, grateful to have something to look at besides him. It took a moment for him to speak as I stared at the taco section.

"So, the whole team is here? In Dallas?" he asked.

"Yeah. They went home for the holidays, but we all met up again in Lubbock."

"And what exactly are you doing here?"

"We're . . ." I took a quick glance around the restaurant, not sure how much I should share within earshot of other people. The news of the missing scrabs hadn't hit the media yet. I decided to go with a half-truth. "We're following a lead. Maybe going to the Scrab Defense League conference."

His eyebrows shot up. "Don't those guys hate you? I mean, all of you on the teams," he clarified quickly.

"They do. But we'll all be together, and it's in public. Not much they can do."

The waitress appeared to take our orders, and I took a long sip of my water as she walked away.

"Have you thought about what you're going to do about finishing high school?" he asked.

"What?"

"High school. Are you going to finish or get a GED or . . ." He ran his finger down the condensation on his water glass, maybe so he wouldn't have to look at me.

"I looked into the GED, but it's complicated since I'm only seventeen and not living here anymore."

"Can you take it in New York? Or even abroad?"

"I don't know."

"I'll look into it for you."

"Thanks?" I gave him a confused look.

"Why are you looking at me like that? You don't want me to look into it?"

"No, I mean, that's nice, I just didn't realize you cared that much about whether I finished school."

"I do."

"OK."

"I want you to finish or get a GED or whatever the equivalent is if you decide to live in another country."

"I'll give it a go, but you know I'm kind of a dumbass, so it may take a few tries."

"Clara." He leaned forward, looking at me seriously.

"Yes, I know, I'm not dumb just because I didn't do well in school, Maddie tells me all the time."

"She's right; you should listen to her. But I was going to say that you should stop thinking that you're dumb, if only to spite Dad."

I raised my eyebrows, silently asking him to go on.

"Making you and Mom feel dumb was his favorite pastime. Don't let him win by actually believing it."

I folded the paper from my straw over and over until it was tiny. Maybe he had a point.

"Imagine if you went to college," Laurence said. "He'd be mad about it forever."

I laughed. "That's honestly one of the best reasons I've heard to go to college."

"Some of your friends are going, right? They talk about it sometimes on Noah's YouTube videos, or on Instagram. Several of them deferred college?"

"Yeah. Noah, Laila, Priya . . . I don't think Maddie applied to any colleges since she knew she was joining the teams with Grayson, but yeah, she'll definitely go one day."

"You and Maddie are close, aren't you?"

"Uh . . ." My throat closed, and my expression must have given away something, because he suddenly looked alarmed.

"What?"

I stared at the table. "We're sort of fighting."

"About what?"

"It's . . . complicated. Just some teams stuff. But things are also really weird between me and Edan, and I just . . ." I glanced up at him. "I'm failing at the friends thing right now."

"I'm sure you're not *failing* at it. Friends fight sometimes."

"I guess, but I don't know what to do to make it right," I said. "Maybe go to therapy. Maddie's always annoyed with me that I don't go to therapy."

"Do you even have the time or the money to go to therapy? Do the teams offer health insurance?"

"Maddie got some therapists for the teams, free of charge. She's mad I didn't take advantage."

He raised his eyebrows.

"I know, she has a point." I let out a long sigh and pressed my palms to my forehead. "I guess she wants me to go tell some doctor all about Mom and Dad and talk about my feelings, and I don't know how to do any of that. I mean, what am I supposed to say?"

He let out a short laugh. "I really can't help you there. My last girlfriend dumped me because she said I never talked to her." He cocked his head, thinking for a moment. "Actually, all my girlfriends have said that."

I moaned. "We're doomed, Laurence."

"No, we're not," he said with a chuckle. "Maddie's right; you should have taken advantage of the therapist. I'm sure you can work through whatever it is that makes us like this."

"I wish Maddie was here so she could hear you keep saying she's right. She would really enjoy that."

"I would like to meet her sometime, if she's around. I wouldn't mind meeting the whole team, if you're up for it."

I looked at him in surprise. "Uh, yeah, we can do that. Maddie did actually tell me to invite you to come with us tomorrow, if you want. Some of the team will be scoping out those league guys. The rest of us will probably be tailing Julian, maybe some of his buddies too. Fair warning, a few of them might try to punch us."

"I can take a hit," he said, his lips turning up.

"I know you can."

"I'd like that. Not the getting punched, but meeting everyone. Seeing what you do."

"Yeah?"

"Yeah."

I smiled at him. Now I really wished Maddie were here, because she'd also been right about me calling Laurence. It was definitely a good choice.

21

Maddie wasn't in our room when I got back, and I didn't see her until the next morning. I suspected she and Noah had snuck off together for a while.

I hadn't gone looking for Edan, and apparently, he wasn't looking for me either. Of course, we'd already established that we were both master avoiders, so I shouldn't have been surprised.

Maddie was on her bed when I emerged from the shower, and she looked up from her phone and then quickly back down.

I really couldn't handle things being weird with Maddie *and* Edan. I took a deep breath, pulling the towel from my hair.

"Are we ever going to talk about this?" I asked.

She looked up with a smile. "Are you ever going to tell me your ideas, or do I have to beg?"

I returned the smile. "Are you going to listen?"

"Yes. I'm sorry that I didn't. And I never meant to imply that you were stupid."

"I was maybe projecting some things there."

"You're not stupid, you know. I've never thought you were."

"I know. Laurence reminded me yesterday that I have some hang-ups about that. I invited him to come with us today, by the way."

Her eyes lit up. "Seriously?"

"You said I should invite him."

"I know, but I didn't actually think you'd do it!" She bounced onto her knees excitedly. "Can I make him tell us lots of embarrassing stories about you?"

"You can try, but I don't think he has many."

She clapped her hands and grabbed her phone. "I'll text the team. They'll be excited."

I sat down on my bed, twisting my towel in my hands. "Things got really weird between me and Edan. I've been dying to tell you."

"Weird how?" She tossed her phone aside and got up to sit next to me.

"It was our last day in Lubbock, and I guess I lost my mind briefly, because I asked him if he was dating Hannah. And then I told him that I was fine with it, which isn't even true. I'd be devastated if he started dating her. And then he seemed sort of upset or confused or something, and he said he'd been waiting for me."

Maddie put her arm around me. "Clara, hon, I'm sorry to have to say this to you, but—no shit. Anyone with eyes could see he was waiting for you."

I moaned, leaning against her. "I screwed it up. I froze up and didn't say anything, and he just left, and now he's obviously upset."

"Listen, you're going to have to be honest with him. You can't just keep avoiding it and hope that it goes away."

"I know."

"Tell him that you *do* feel weird about him dating Hannah, but since you're not ready to date, you're going to suck it up and be happy for him. Or tell him you love him and you lied and you want to jump his bones immediately. But maybe say it more romantic than that." She waved her hand. "I don't know. I've never been good at that part."

"Is there a third option, where I just keep doing nothing and hope it all goes away?"

"Sure. That option ends in the two of you no longer being friends."

I moaned again.

"I'm going to be totally honest with you, I've really tried not to be pushy, but I don't get why you're still waffling about Edan. You're obviously into him. He's into you. It's been months since Julian. Do you seriously still think you can't be trusted to make good dating decisions?"

I straightened. "It's not just that. It also really annoys me that Julian is the thing that defines me to a lot of people. To all the recruits, to people I've never even met. I'm just Julian's ex-girlfriend. I wanted to be seen as someone who has her shit together and is totally independent and isn't just someone's girlfriend."

"Who cares what other people think?" she said. "No one gets to define you but you. If you don't want to date, fine. Don't date. But just because you don't *need* a guy doesn't mean you can't want one. It doesn't make you less of a badass."

"Yeah," I said softly.

"But you know who you should really be talking about all of this with?"

"A therapist?" I guessed with a smile.

"Yep."

"That one I saw back in May does Skype sessions, doesn't she?"

"She sure does. You want me to schedule an appointment for you?"

"Yeah."

She wrapped an arm around my shoulders and squeezed. "I'm a really good influence on you, you know that?"

I burst out laughing. She grinned.

"What? I am."

~

Laurence was waiting in the lobby, talking to Edan, when Maddie and I stepped off the elevator. Edan caught my eye briefly as we approached and quickly looked away.

"I see you roped your brother into following league guys around all day," he said, looking at Laurence instead of at me.

"I figured he'd want to see firsthand the exciting life I lead," I said. A hint of a smile crossed Edan's face, but vanished quickly.

"This is Madison," I said, gesturing to her. She extended her hand.

"Laurence. Nice to meet you."

"You too." She released his hand and looked him up and down. "You guys don't look alike."

We really didn't. Laurence looked a little more like Dad, and I resembled Mom.

The rest of the team arrived with a ding of the elevator, and I introduced them to Laurence. Priya held his hand for a moment after shaking it.

"We've heard a lot about you," she said.

Laurence looked skeptical, and then worried. "You have?"

"Well, Clara has mentioned you more than once, which for her is basically gushing."

"Priya," I said with an embarrassed laugh. Laurence looked at the ground.

She finally let go of his hand. "What? It's true."

"Come on," Maddie said, heading to the door and leading us all outside. She stopped in front of the van and looked at Laurence. "Do you have a gun?"

He didn't answer for a moment, like he didn't realize she was talking to him. "Me? No." He glanced at me in confusion. "Why would I have a gun?"

"You're a Texan," Maddie said. "Don't lots of people here carry guns?"

"I guess some do. Were you hoping I had a gun?"

"No!" she said quickly. "I was going to tell you not to use it if you did. They're pretty ineffective against scrabs; you'd just end up shooting us by accident. And Clara's already been shot once."

He looked at me in horror. "You were *shot?*"

"Not really. The bullet barely grazed me."

"Who shot you?"

"It was an accident. The bullet ricocheted off a scrab."

"Whatever happened to that guy, anyway?" Patrick asked. "What was his name?"

"Hunter. Grayson sent to him to join the teams in China. None of them have guns there." Maddie returned her attention to Laurence. "Do you have any other weapons on you?"

Laurence looked confused. "Uh . . . no? I have a pocket knife on my keychain, but it's not very big."

"Maddie," Edan said with a laugh. "Why are you concerned that he's armed? Are you expecting trouble?"

"I'm always expecting trouble," she replied. "But seriously, if we run into scrabs today, you might want a weapon. We have extra machetes in back."

Laurence glanced behind him. "You do?"

"Of course."

"We're probably not going to run into scrabs," I said.

"We are literally headed out to *look* for scrabs," Maddie said.

"That's a good point." I glanced nervously at Laurence. I'd assumed we'd just be in the van all day. Now I wondered if it had been stupid to bring him.

"It'll be fine," Maddie said, clearly noticing my expression. "We can protect you if we need to. And you had combat class in high school, right?"

"Y—yes." He looked worried suddenly. "Wait, you're looking for scrabs? In Dallas?"

"Get in," I said, pulling the van door open. "We'll explain on the way."

~

"You regret agreeing to come today, don't you?" I asked Laurence after I finished telling him about our discovery in Lubbock.

"Five *hundred*?" he repeated incredulously. He was sitting next to me in the first row of the van behind Maddie. "You think Julian stole five hundred scrabs and brought them to Dallas?"

"Or one of his league buddies," Edan said, glancing back at us briefly from the passenger's seat.

"So now you're tailing Julian and these league guys to try and find the scrabs?" Laurence asked.

"Yep," Maddie replied. "If the Lubbock police find something, then we'll head back there, but for now, Julian and the league is the best lead we have."

"What would Julian even do with them?" Laurence asked.

"Our best guess is try and sell them," I said.

"Or he could have just moved them," Patrick said. "Dropped them at a different MDG facility, since he knew we were closing in on Dust Storm."

"Hopefully not," Maddie said. "And I'd be surprised if they had two huge facilities in Texas. Or even two huge facilities in the whole country. It's incredibly risky."

"It was there for fifteen years?" Laurence asked. "And the police never noticed?"

"I mean, I'm sure they noticed," Maddie said. "But they either didn't know they had scrabs in there, or they paid off a few officers to keep it quiet."

"They still haven't released the news about the facility yet, which is highly suspect," Patrick said.

"I'm giving them a few more hours, and then I'm sending my pictures and videos to my contact at the *Post*," Maddie said.

"Do you think they're trying to cover it up?" Laurence asked.

"I really don't know," Maddie replied. "I'd like to get proof that Julian did it before I leak it, but if we can't get anything today, I think I'm going to do it anyway. At least it will put some pressure on him."

She pulled into the parking lot of a restaurant and came to a stop. Dorsey and Patrick climbed out.

"You forgot your hat," Noah said, throwing it to Dorsey.

"I didn't forget it so much as deliberately leave it behind," Dorsey said, wrinkling his nose as he turned it around in his hand.

"What do you have against baseball caps?" Patrick asked. He was wearing one too, an attempt to fly under the radar at the happy hour.

"They're not my best look. We should have gone with a cowboy hat. We're in Texas, and I think I'd be cute in a cowboy hat."

"No one actually wears cowboy hats here. Unless you're going to the rodeo." Patrick looked at me for confirmation.

"It's true," I said. "You'll draw attention to yourself by wearing a cowboy hat, which is the exact opposite of what we're going for."

Dorsey sighed and put the hat on. "Fine. I still think we should have gone with a fake mustache, though."

"You're not actually in disguise here—we're just trying to stay under the radar so we don't get our asses kicked," Patrick said. "Also, I'm sorry, but you would look terrible with a mustache."

Laila raised her eyebrows like she agreed. Noah laughed.

"Hey!" Dorsey looked insulted. "Now I'm going to grow one just to prove you wrong."

Patrick snorted. "I hope you do so I can make fun of you for it every day."

"Text us updates, OK?" Maddie said. "Split up when you get in there—they're more likely to place you if you're together."

"And don't be too obvious," Priya said. "Try to be casual while you gently inquire whether they stole five hundred scrubs."

"Casual prodding, got it." Dorsey pulled the door shut, and they both waved before turning to walk toward the restaurant.

Maddie drove about ten minutes down the road, to the conference hotel. Laila unhooked her seat belt and reached for the door. She was going to the lobby to wait for Julian to come out.

"Are we sure she should go by herself?" Noah asked.

"I'll be fine," Laila said. "Trust me, Julian doesn't even remember me. He barely said two words to me when I was on his team. And he looked right through me when he saw me in London. No recognition at all."

"He really was the worst team leader, wasn't he?" Priya said.

I looked down at my hands. Sometimes I was still hit with a wave of shame about Julian—I'd been so wrapped up in how he treated me that I hardly noticed that he could barely pretend to care about the rest of the team.

"Their meeting is supposed to end at five," Maddie said as Laila hopped out. "Maybe poke around the conference rooms if it's possible to do so discreetly. And text us updates."

"Got it," Laila said. She hopped out and closed the door behind her. I watched as she walked across the parking lot and disappeared through the front doors.

Noah looked at his phone. "It's only four thirty."

"I know, but I didn't want to miss him, in case they finished early," Maddie said. She twisted around in her seat to look at Laurence. "I hope you weren't expecting excitement."

"I was hoping for the opposite, honestly."

I smiled at him. It felt a bit awkward having him here, but not entirely terrible.

Priya leaned forward, resting her chin on the back of our seat. "Why did I think you lived in Oklahoma?"

"I did, but only for a few months," Laurence said.

"Why'd you come back?"

Laurence and I glanced at each other briefly, my uncertainty reflected in his eyes.

"Our mom asked him to," I said, after a silence that had stretched out a bit too long.

"Oh," Priya said. She knew enough about my family not to pry further.

Our phones all buzzed, and I looked down to see a message from Laila to the team.

Julian was running late, they just started the meeting. Going to be a while.

Maddie sighed. "Of course Julian was running late." She looked out the front window, at the huge, mostly empty, parking lot. Her face brightened suddenly. "Oh! Let's teach Edan to drive."

"What?" Edan straightened, alarmed. "No."

"Yes!" Priya clapped.

Maddie pointed out the front windshield. "Look. It's perfect. There's tons of space."

Edan shook his head. "I don't want to learn to drive. I'm an avid pedestrian."

"Too bad," Maddie said, starting the van. "You're in Texas now. Land of gas-guzzling trucks and terrible public transportation. You're learning to drive."

Laurence chuckled and glanced at me. "Did you ever learn to drive? I only took you out once."

"Yeah. I sort of learned just by doing it."

"When they stole an MDG van after getting kidnapped," Maddie said, driving to the emptiest part of the parking lot.

"And then Patrick taught me to drive stick a few months ago," I said.

"See?" Maddie said. "You have it easy, Edan. It's automatic."

"Fine, but if I wreck the van, I don't want to hear shit from any of you."

"How are you going to wreck the van in an empty parking lot?" She pulled in, put the van in park, and hopped out. Edan reluctantly got out and trudged over to the driver's seat.

Maddie slid into the passenger's seat and hooked her seat belt. "OK, Edan, let's go." She waved her hands forward.

"Let's go?" he repeated. "That's it?"

"I mean, do you really need me to tell you to put your foot on the brake and put the car in drive?"

"Maddie, you're terrible at this," I said with a laugh.

Noah looked up from his phone. "Maybe the rest of us should get out."

"Shush," Maddie said, waving a hand at him without turning around. "Fine, Edan, ease your foot off the brake slowly or whatever."

"Or whatever," Edan grumbled, but he put the van in drive and we began to inch forward, very slowly.

"Well, we clearly don't have to worry about you wrecking anything, because it's going to take us all day just to get to the other end of the parking lot," Maddie said. Priya giggled.

"I could do without the commentary, thank you very much."

His phone buzzed in the cupholder.

"Do you want me to see who that is?" Maddie asked.

"It's fine, it's probably just Hannah."

My chest tightened, and Maddie stole a quick look back at me.

"You know you have to press on the gas to actually make it move faster, right?" she said, returning her attention to Edan.

"I'm getting there."

Maddie looked back at Laurence. "So, Laurence, how was Oklahoma?"

"It was fine. Boring."

"Do you like Dallas? Are you going to stay?"

He shrugged. "It's fine, I guess."

Maddie looked from me to him. "I see the family resemblance now," she said dryly.

~

Laila finally spotted Julian leaving the hotel an hour later, and she jogged out of the hotel and hopped into the van.

"You see the black car?" she asked Maddie.

"I see it," Maddie said, easing the van across the parking lot. A black town car was turning out of the hotel parking lot.

"I heard some of the guys talking about dinner tonight," Laila said. "But not until eight."

"And Dorsey and Patrick said that the happy hour is wrapping up," Noah said, glancing down at his phone. It was nearly six. "So, he's probably not going there."

"Hopefully he doesn't notice us," Maddie murmured as she pulled onto the street. "I probably should have bought another, more discreet car."

Laurence and I exchanged an amused look.

"She *bought* this?" he asked me quietly.

"It's used!" Maddie exclaimed. "Actually, do you want a fifteen-passenger van? You can have it after we leave, if you want."

"Uh, I think I'm OK, thanks," Laurence said, trying not to laugh. Edan looked back at us and rolled his eyes in Maddie's direction.

We followed Julian down the street, through heavy traffic for about fifteen minutes. The car turned into a parking lot next to a white brick building with a sign that said THOMLINSON MARKET on the front.

Maddie slowed the van. "What is that?"

"Hold on, I'm . . ." Noah typed quickly on his phone. "A butcher! And convenience store. But from the reviews, people mostly come here for the meat."

Maddie turned in to the parking lot next door. It was a deserted donut shop that looked like it had been closed for years, and we were the only car in the lot.

"Scrabs eat meat, don't they?" Laurence asked. He looked nervous.

Across the road, Julian climbed out of the back seat of the car. Two young men, maybe in their early twenties, climbed out of their pickup truck. The door to the market opened, and a man pushed out a cart full of something packed in brown paper bags. Another man followed behind him with another overflowing cart.

"They sure do," Maddie said. "And if you have five hundred scrabs in one place, you're going to need a lot of meat." She grabbed her phone, aiming it out the windshield. She snapped a few pictures. She lowered it suddenly. "Shit."

Julian was staring straight at us. He started walking in our direction, so fast he was practically running. I could see the fury on his face as he got closer. He looked both ways, and then began across the street.

"Uh, Maddie, this guy already tried to kill me once," Edan said nervously.

"You're right, I'm going." Maddie tossed Edan her phone and threw the van into drive. She hit the gas, and we peeled out onto the street, leaving Julian in our dust.

~

We picked up Dorsey and Patrick, who'd come up empty-handed at the happy hour, and headed back to our hotel.

"These photos don't prove anything," Patrick said, scrolling through Maddie's phone as we walked across the parking lot. He handed it back to her. "We should find out who those two guys are, though."

"That's what I was thinking," Maddie said. "I would have stayed longer, but Julian had his murder face on."

"He sure did," Edan muttered, and then shivered. Laurence glanced at me with an expression I couldn't quite read.

"I'll hold off on sending this to my guy at the *Post*. I'm going to go call him with everything else, though. I'm done waiting for the police to get their act together." Maddie turned to face us. "Laurence, are you coming up?"

He stopped as we reached the hotel entrance. "No, I should head back. Thanks, though. For . . ."

"Terrifying you with Edan's driving skills?" Maddie guessed.

"Hey!" Edan looked insulted.

"Or terrifying you by following around a guy with five hundred scrabs?" Maddie guessed again.

Laurence laughed. "Uh, both. It was nice to meet you guys."

The team said goodbye to Laurence, and I hung back as they walked inside.

"Thanks for coming today," I said. "I know it was kind of boring."

"I'm not sure that *boring* is the word. Is this what you guys usually do?"

"No, there's usually a lot more scrab fighting. And blood."

He cocked his head, squinting through the sun, setting behind me. "I don't think I realized exactly what you guys were doing out there. This is some intense shit. And Julian . . ."

I looked at him expectantly as he considered his next words.

"He's scarier in person," he finally said. "I got a bad feeling from him on the phone, but I thought maybe that was just because you'd told me what he did. But that's the sort of dude I would turn and walk the other way if I saw him coming."

"That is a good instinct."

He hesitated for a moment, glancing up at the hotel. "You know someone took a picture of you guys here and put it on social media, right?"

"Yeah, Maddie mentioned it. A group shot of us checking in, right? People often notice us when we're together like that."

"Yeah." He slid his hands into his pockets. "It's just that if I know, then Julian may know."

"He may, but we stick together. I won't go taking any walks by myself or anything."

He nodded. "I try to steer clear of talking about you with Mom and Dad, so I don't know how much they keep tabs on you. What do you want me to say if they ask if I've seen you?"

"You can tell them you have. I wouldn't be surprised if they didn't keep track of me at all, though." I looked past him. "Mom's never even emailed or tried to make contact once since I called her from Atlanta."

"Do you want her to?"

I sighed. "I don't know. I liked the space at first, but then it just started to feel like she didn't even care."

"She does," he said quietly. "She's always going to choose Dad, but she does care about you. In fact, she said something once that kind of made me think she was proud of you."

"What?"

"She said that you were a lot like her, but braver. She said, 'I don't know why I was surprised when Clara joined those teams. I always knew she was the brave one.'"

"I kind of wish she'd called and said that to me."

"I think she's not sure if you want her to."

"I'm not sure if I want her to either." I blew out an annoyed breath. "I told Maddie I'd go to therapy. Maybe they can help me sort it out."

"Tell me what they say—maybe we can both sort it out." He

laughed, though it wasn't exactly cheerful. "I'm not doing any better than you. I'm just getting sucked back into everything."

"We're a mess."

"We are." He laughed again, and then looked back at his truck. "I should get going."

"Thanks for coming today."

"Sure. It was fun, actually. In a way."

I smiled, and we both just stood there for a moment. I didn't know if we were supposed to hug, but I was surprised to discover that I actually *wanted* to hug him.

I wasn't exactly sure how to go about that, though. I could have just stepped forward and hugged him, but the potential awkwardness of that kept my feet rooted to the ground.

He took a step back. "I will . . . talk to you soon, then?"

"Yeah," I said. I lifted a hand. "Bye, Laurence."

22

THE NEWS BROKE THE NEXT MORNING.

MDG FACILITY IN TEXAS HOUSED LIVE SCRABS, the headline screamed. All the cable news stations picked it up immediately, and the team gathered in our room to watch.

"They're not reporting about MDG *creating* the scrabs," Priya complained.

"My guy at the *Post* said they needed another source before they could report that," Maddie said. "But he's on it, trust me."

I glanced at my phone. "Maddie, it's ten. We need to leave for the conference soon."

She slid off the bed. "I take it that means you want me to get dressed?" She was in sweats, her hair still damp from her shower earlier.

"It couldn't hurt."

"Wait, wait, it's the Lubbock police," Noah said. He grabbed the remote and turned the volume up. The news switched to a live feed of a news conference. A police officer was walking toward a podium.

"He doesn't look pleased," Maddie said with a laugh.

He began by giving them a quick summary of what had happened a few days ago—receiving a call and discovering the dead scrabs and people inside an MDG facility. Cameras flashed wildly as he talked.

"This investigation is still ongoing, so I only have limited information for you at this time," he said. "But we have determined that the facility was used for the housing and training of scrabs. And approximately five hundred scrabs that were being kept in that facility are currently unaccounted for."

A ripple went through the crowd in the room. The officer held up his hand to quiet them.

"We are working with individuals at the Monster Defense Group to determine where these scrabs are, and we have set up a tip line for anyone who has any information. We ask that you call if you see anything suspicious. We have had some scrab experts out here to survey the city, and they've determined that it's unlikely the scrabs are currently burrowing underground anywhere nearby."

"Are you saying that someone stole the scrabs?" a reporter shouted.

"Yes, right now we are working off the assumption that the scrabs were stolen," the police officer said. "Again, we urge anyone with any information to come forward. That's all for now. Thank you." He walked away amid shouted questions.

"They don't believe that Julian took them?" Priya asked.

"Agent Simmons seemed skeptical," Maddie said. "But she promised she'd look into it." She walked to her suitcase and began digging through it.

"What do they think Julian was doing with all that meat?" Dorsey exclaimed. "Having a barbecue?"

"I mean, we are in Texas," Priya said.

"Whatever, they can be as skeptical as they want," Maddie said. "We have it covered. Laila's going to wait for Julian in the hotel lobby again, and we'll look for those other two guys at the conference. Or anything else suspicious."

"They're all suspicious," Dorsey muttered.

"Have you thought about what we're going to do after we find the scrabs?" Patrick asked.

Maddie glanced at me. We'd talked some about my ideas to expand training and possibly start up other programs, but we definitely hadn't made any decisions yet. I wasn't sure if she was just humoring me.

"Uh, the plans are still in flux," she said.

"You're planning on Germany next, aren't you?" Noah looked confused.

"Yeah, but maybe we should go back to New York instead of going straight to Germany."

"Why Germany?" Laila asked. "What's up with the UK?"

"I'm not totally sure the UK wants us back. I've been talking to some people, and they're not crazy about the idea," Maddie said.

"The UK recruits are pissed, but a lot of them are willing to work in another country for a while," Patrick said.

"Did they find out if MDG sent those scrabs on our last assignment in London?" Dorsey asked.

"I asked Agent Simmons about it, and she said they're claiming they have no knowledge of it. They admitted to losing a good number of their trained scrabs that night we tried to stop the shipment, so it's possible it was just some of those."

"But you want to wait on Germany?" Noah asked.

"I don't know." Maddie glanced at me again. "I know we have some work to do, but I really don't want to let the teams languish for too long. People will lose interest, and they won't come back. I mean, we're already losing some of our own team."

I blinked, surprised. "We are?"

Priya blew out a long breath. "I don't know. I told Maddie before I left that I was wavering about going back, but I missed you guys. And you had fun without me. I have fomo."

"What is fomo?" I asked.

"Fear of missing out," she said. "I think it's too strong for me to stay in Alabama."

"I'll go back, but only until the summer," Laila said. "I deferred college for a year, and I want to start next fall so I don't lose my place."

"Oh," I said, my heart sinking a little.

"And Noah is about to become a star, so he'll be leaving us," Maddie said, lips twitching. I looked at him quickly.

He flushed. "I'm not about to become a star."

"Because you already are one?" Maddie guessed.

He shot her an amused look. "A producer reached out to me about doing a docuseries about fighting scrabs. They want me to travel around to different parts of the world and talk to people about interesting things they've done to fight off scrabs in their communities."

"That's awesome," Patrick said. "Why didn't you tell us?"

"I'm still deciding. I'd have to leave the team. They said they'd like to shoot some stuff with you guys, if you're up for it, but then I'd have to leave for six months to shoot the show."

"Scrabs aren't going to disappear in six months," Maddie said. "You are always welcome back."

He smiled at her, and they exchanged a look that made me think there had been more to this discussion when it had been just the two of them.

"Well, I'm going to Germany," Patrick said. "Whenever that is. Clara's been working on some new training plans with me and Noah, and I think we could be in good shape if we really make some changes." He looked pointedly at Maddie.

"We'll make the changes!" she said, putting her hands up. "Some of the other stuff Clara is working on is still up in the air, but we'll implement a new training program. I promise."

I smiled at her.

"I'm in for Germany too," Dorsey said.

I glanced at Edan. His eyes were already on me, and he quickly looked away.

"Uh, yeah," he said slowly. "I intended to stay with the teams. I think that's still the plan."

My stomach dropped. He sounded hesitant. Maybe he was rethinking his decision to stay with the team too. He'd said that he went where I went, but that was before I cheerfully told him to date another girl. I wouldn't blame him for changing his mind.

Maddie grabbed some clothes from her bag. "Just give me, like, fifteen minutes," she said, walking into the restroom and closing the door behind her.

Edan stood and headed to the door. "I'll meet you guys in the lobby."

I tried to catch his eye before he left, but he was already turned away. He disappeared into the hallway.

~

Patrick pulled the van into the empty corner of the hotel parking lot and turned the ignition off. I climbed out, followed by Laila, Maddie, and Noah.

I'd expected the parking lot to be full today, considering it was the first day of the conference, but there were only a few more cars than there had been yesterday. It was still half empty.

Edan opened the passenger's side door of the van, shielding his eyes to look past me. "Why is it so hot? It's January."

Priya hopped out, arms spread wide. "I like it. I'm going to sit out here and pretend it's summer."

Edan frowned at the clear sky like he disapproved of the seventy-degree weather.

"Is that why you've been so cranky since we got here?" Dorsey asked. "You don't enjoy summer weather in January?"

"I haven't been cranky." Edan paused, his lips twitching. "I prefer *moody*."

"Oh, yes, that's much more manly." Dorsey reached up to whack the side of his head.

Laila gave them an amused look and then stepped back. "Let's go. I want to stake out a good spot in the lobby so I don't miss Julian."

I turned to look back at Edan as we started across the parking lot. He was watching us go, and he lifted one hand with a smile when our eyes met. I returned the smile.

Inside, the hotel wasn't as crowded as I was expecting. We left Laila in the lobby and headed up to the second floor to check in. A few men wandered around, wearing matching red badges.

"I'm here at the first annual conference of the Scrab Defense League," Noah said, holding his phone out and doing a circle to get the full picture, "and it is a sad sight so far. Not sure how many attendees they were expecting." He lowered his phone and glanced at us. "Instagram story. I figured it's best to post throughout the day in case anyone tries to murder us."

"Good thinking," I said.

Noah smiled at me. "It's so nice how you never tell me I'm overreacting when I say stuff like that, Clara."

~

We spent the next several hours attending panels that alternated between excruciatingly boring and terrifyingly stupid. We went to one about Second Amendment rights, and another about scrab defense theory. I had to stop Maddie from standing up and telling the speaker off when he started in about how scrabs would be really helpful to local police.

We split up for the last session, and Maddie and I went to a useless session on scrab training, while Dorsey and Noah went to a panel about scrab combat. We met up in the hallway after it was over.

"Anything interesting?" Maddie asked them.

"It was mostly just talk about how to use guns against scrabs,"

Dorsey said, running a hand through his hair. "I'm kind of rooting for everyone in that room to actually go up against a scrab one day, because they for sure are going to accidentally shoot themselves. I hope there's video."

"What about you guys?" Noah asked.

"There was nothing . . . new." Maddie cocked her head, her attention on something behind Noah and Dorsey. She hit my arm. "Aren't those the guys who were with Julian at the butcher yesterday?"

I followed her gaze to the end of the hallway, where two familiar men stood in front of the elevator. One was talking on his phone as they stepped on.

Maddie grabbed her phone, dialed, and pressed it to her ear. "Laila? Those two guys who were with Julian yesterday just got on the elevator." She paused, waiting for several seconds. Her face lit up. "Yeah? You see them? Are they leaving?" She listened for a moment. "Yes! We're headed down now." She took a step forward, and then stopped. "No, go. Don't wait for us." She moved the phone away from her mouth. "They're already in their car, we won't make it down in time." She listened for a moment. "OK, great. Call me back when you figure out where they're going. And tell Patrick to try and keep a good distance from them. Julian may have told them to watch out for us." She hung up and slipped her phone into her pocket.

"Are we going to Julian's session, or should we try to follow them?"

Maddie chewed her lip, considering. "We probably can't follow them until I have an address to give the Uber driver. Let's just go to the session. Plus, if Julian sees us, maybe he won't think we're following those other guys."

"Speak of the devil," Dorsey said, nodding down the hallway.

Julian was stepping off the elevator, which caused everyone in the area to turn and look. A large, red-haired man in a black suit followed him, scanning the area as he walked.

"Does he have a bodyguard?" Maddie asked with an eyeroll.

"He sure does," I said.

"I mean, there are probably quite a few people in world who want to punch Julian in the face," Dorsey said. "Present company included. I'd get a bodyguard too, if I were him."

"That's a good point," Maddie murmured.

"I think we could take that guy, though, if anyone wants to give it a go." Noah looked at me expectantly.

"Come on," I said with a laugh. Julian had just disappeared into the ballroom.

We followed the crowd inside. Though perhaps *crowd* was the wrong word. There were maybe two hundred people at this entire conference. The panels were half empty. This ballroom was far too big for the event, and I noticed that Julian glanced back at all the empty space as he made his way to the raised platform at the front. His bodyguard stood off to the side.

"Can I boo?" Dorsey asked.

Maddie patted his arm. "No, but I appreciate that attitude."

"Hey, guys," Julian said. "You don't mind if I don't use the mic, do you? Why don't you all come in close? We'll keep this informal."

The crowd shuffled forward a bit. Julian sat down at the edge of the platform, legs dangling off. He had an easy smile on his face. If I hadn't known him, I'd have thought he seemed friendly.

"As you all know, I'm Julian Montgomery. I just wanted to drop by to say thank you all for coming to the first annual Scrab Defense League conference."

The crowd clapped, and a few people cheered.

"People don't really understand this movement yet. And that's OK. People are always slow to accept change. But not you guys. You guys see the future."

More cheers.

"Scrabs have been a part of our lives for nearly ten years now, and it's time to accept that they're not going away. It doesn't matter how they got here, it matters that they're here now and we have to deal with them. It's time to innovate. It's time to figure out how to put these things to use before someone else does it first. That's what Americans are known for, right? Innovation?"

Julian's gaze caught on me suddenly, and he stopped talking, clearly surprised. His eyes bounced to Maddie, followed by Dorsey. He looked back at me, head tilted to one side, a smile playing on his lips. I cocked an eyebrow.

He gestured to his bodyguard, and then at us. The man frowned at us, and a few people turned.

"We should probably get out of here now," Maddie said.

"Yep, good plan." I said.

~

We walked outside and down the street to avoid a run-in with Julian or any of his admirers. My phone buzzed, and I looked down at it to see a message to the group from Edan.

They've stopped. We're out at a salvage yard. I don't think they noticed us following them.

Maddie typed out a reply. Any sign of scrabs?

I haven't seen or heard them, but these guys just started hauling buckets of raw meat out of their car. This has to be it.

"Oh my god," Maddie said, typing frantically.

Text me the address. Take pics and video. Calls the cops once you spot the scrabs. We're coming to you.

23

"Do you want me to get an Uber?" Noah asked. He pulled his phone out.

Maddie shook her head. "I've got it."

Edan sent the address, and an Uber pulled up a few minutes later. Maddie jumped into the front seat, and I got in back with Dorsey and Noah.

Maddie dug through her wallet, eventually producing several twenties. She put them in the cupholder. The driver, a young white guy who was wearing at least half a bottle of cologne, looked from the money to her.

"That's a thank-you in advance for getting us there as fast as possible," she said.

"Ooo-kayyy," he said, pulling out onto the road. "I can do that."

He hit the gas, and I quickly reached down to buckle my seat belt. My phone buzzed with another message. It was from Priya this time.

I think they're in the big truck at the south side of the yard.

Edan replied a moment later. We're headed your way. Are the guys over there?

Yeah, but they're just on their phones. They haven't opened the truck yet.

"We are going to nail those bastards!" Maddie said excitedly.

The driver glanced at her uneasily, and then at us in the rear-view mirror. "So are you guys, like . . . visiting, or—"

"Yep," Dorsey said. "We're tourists. Seeing . . . you know, the . . . nice weather."

The driver squinted and hit the gas as a light changed. "Right."

Patrick texted. I saw several trucks that looked just like that going the opposite direction when we came out here. You could probably fit about 100 scrabs in each truck, if you really packed the cages tight.

They must be feeding them before moving, Priya wrote. That's what I would do, if I were transporting scrabs. Feeding them makes them less antsy.

We sat in silence for the next ten minutes, our driver really picking up speed as we moved away from downtown. I glanced at the map on the phone mounted on the dashboard. We were only about five minutes away.

Ok, they're opening it, Priya texted. I can't see from this angle. Anyone else?

A message from Edan popped up. I see them. Scrabs in cages. Patrick just called 911.

"We're going to need you to drop us off a bit before you actually get there," Maddie said to the driver. "I'll let you know when." He nodded.

Another message from Edan popped up. They're feeding the scrabs. These guys have no idea what they're doing. They look terrified. They're just throwing the meat in the cages and it's making the scrabs go wild.

"Maybe they'll get eaten," Dorsey said cheerfully.

"Maybe *we'll* get eaten," Noah mumbled. Dorsey gave him a confused look. "Our packs are in the van," Noah explained.

"The rest of the team has theirs," Maddie said. "And we'll grab them if we get the opportunity."

The driver turned, the salvage yard coming into view at the end of the road.

"You can stop here," Maddie said, and he hit the brakes. We climbed out with a "thanks," and he did a quick U-turn and sped away.

Maddie ran onto the grass, gesturing for us to follow her. We ran toward the salvage yard, which was a massive stretch of junk cars behind a wooden building.

There wasn't much around to cover us, but maybe the building out front shielded us from view. I could see several trucks on the other side of the yard.

I heard Priya yell suddenly. I weaved in between the cars, Noah's footsteps pounding right behind me.

I heard an engine rumble, and I looked right to see an eighteen-wheeler peeling out from the back of the yard, its rear doors swinging open. Laila ran right beside it, hot on the heels of a man who was desperately reaching for the passenger's door. The truck slowed, and he managed to hop in, narrowly escaping Laila's grasp.

Our van shot across the yard. I could see Patrick in the driver's seat, Priya beside him. Edan was running from the other side of the yard, headed for us.

The truck blew past us and took the turn onto the road so quickly that the end swung out, the back door flying open again.

The cab swerved dangerously, and for a moment, the whole truck looked in danger of toppling over. The driver managed to stay upright, but not before three scrab pens tumbled out. They bounced onto the road. One flew open. The scrabs ripped open the other two damaged pens.

I heard heavy breathing as Laila and Edan skidded to a stop next to us. They both had their weapons packs, machetes poised. Laila tossed me her machete, and then grabbed an ax from her pack and took off running.

Patrick slowed as he neared us, but Maddie waved him on.

"Go, go!" she yelled, pointing at the truck. "Follow them! We've got the scrabs!"

Edan tossed Maddie a weapon and took off after a scrab that was lumbering toward the salvage yard. I glanced at Dorsey and Laila, who had already killed their scrab, and at Maddie and Noah, who had theirs cornered. Laila moved to help them.

I sprinted after Edan, weaving in between the cars. The scrab smashed into a car, slowing from the force of the impact. Edan was gaining on it, and it turned and snarled at him.

The scrab lunged at Edan, swiping its claws alarmingly close to his face. Edan took a step back as he swung his machete, his foot catching on a discarded car part behind him. He stumbled. The scrab swung again, and I couldn't tell if he'd made contact that time. My heart stopped.

I darted in between them, grabbing Edan's arm with one hand and driving my machete into the scrab's neck with the other. It collapsed into the car and then slumped to the ground.

And then I was falling too. Edan and I hit the ground with

a thump, and I landed on top of him, catching myself before our heads crashed together. I straightened, my hands going to his chest to look for blood.

"Did the scrab get you?" I asked, frantically grabbing for his arms. I held both wrists, examining them for scratches.

"No, Clara, I'm fine," he said, a hint of amusement in his voice.

I let out a relieved breath, and then glanced back at the scrab behind me. It was motionless, blood pooling on the ground under its neck. Definitely dead.

I returned my attention to Edan and released his arms. "Jesus. I thought it got you."

"I'm slightly offended that you thought *one* scrab could take me out."

"I didn't—"

"It wasn't even a very big scrab, it was kind of slow, actually, so I don't—"

"I just saw you lose your balance, and I got—"

"I'm just saying, I think you might have forgotten how great I am. At scrab fighting, I mean." A smile spread across his face.

I laughed quietly. "I could never forget how great you are, Edan."

His smile changed, softening a little, and I felt his fingers brush my hand. I was still on top of him, a fact that hadn't escaped my notice for even a second. I didn't want to move. I wanted him to keep looking at me the way he was now, like every problem we had no longer mattered. I wanted to kiss him.

I leaned down and pressed my lips to his. He took in a breath, his arms circling around me.

Kissing him wasn't how I expected. For me, kissing a boy for the first time was sort of like those seconds before a scrab burst up from the ground. When you could feel the rumbling, and you were full of nerves and excitement and a little bit of fear.

This wasn't like that. This was all the heart-pounding excitement without the sinking feeling that it could go wrong at any second. I didn't need to spend so much time debating whether Edan was the right choice. I could have just kissed him.

When I pulled away, he sat up, his arms holding firm around my waist. We were so close I could feel his breath against my mouth.

"I'm sorry that I . . ." I tried to find the words. My brain was buzzing, and he'd just put his thumb at the edge of my lip. It was distracting.

"Can you hold that thought for a second?" he asked quietly, and I was smiling as I nodded and he kissed me again.

When we pulled away for the second time, I had my fingers tangled in his hair and his heart was thumping wildly next to mine.

"I was going to say I'm sorry that it took me so long," I whispered.

He shook his head. "You don't have to apologize for that."

"I was lying when I said I was fine with you dating Hannah. I just said that because I felt awkward, and I thought . . ." He brushed my hair away from my face, making me lose my train of thought for a moment. "I thought I wasn't ready to date again, or I thought maybe I would ruin everything, because apparently I'm a disaster at relationships and kind of a mess in general."

"What, in our time together, gave you the impression that *I'm* not a total mess?"

I laughed softly, and he leaned forward like he was going to kiss me again. He stopped suddenly, pulling back a little to meet my gaze.

"Are you ready to . . . ?" He trailed off. "I didn't mean to be an ass after that night in Lubbock. I was just kind of embarrassed, and I started to think that maybe I'd read the signals wrong and I . . ." His cheeks went a little pink. "I didn't mean to rush you. I'll wait, if you're—"

"No," I said quickly. "I don't want to wait. I just want to—" I cut myself off by kissing him again, and he smiled against my lips and pulled me closer.

"Oh, they're over here!" I heard Dorsey yell suddenly. "Making out next to a dead scrab, which is a weird choice, honestly."

We both laughed and pulled away, turning to find Dorsey. He stood behind a nearby pickup truck, peering over the top so he could see us.

"Andrew, get lost!" Edan called.

He grinned, and then turned and bounded away.

"He does actually have a point, though," I said, glancing over at the bloody scrab.

"Yeah, he does, we should get out of here."

We both got to our feet, and I pulled my machete from the scrab's neck, slipped it into its sheath, and put it back into my weapons pack.

Edan took my hand as we walked out of the yard and back to the team. They were near the road, and Maddie was on her phone.

Probably with 911. She turned and smiled at me when she saw our interlocked fingers.

"Shit," Noah said into his phone.

"What?" Laila asked.

"Patrick says they lost the truck. But they've given the police a description and the last location."

Maddie let out a long sigh, and then lowered her phone. "Clara, you and Edan need to start walking. Now."

"What?" I asked, confused.

"We are not taking the risk that the Dallas police see you're a minor and decide to drive you home."

"It wasn't a problem with the Lubbock police," I said, though I gripped Edan's hand a little tighter.

"Your parents weren't twenty minutes away in Lubbock," Maddie said. "Do you really want to risk them running your name through the system?"

"Good point."

She pointed down the road. "There was a gas station that way." She looked at Noah. "Can Patrick come pick them up?"

"Eventually, but they're headed to the police station now."

"We'll get an Uber," Edan said. He pulled gently on my hand.

"Text us updates," I said, looking at Maddie over my shoulder. She nodded, waving me away. Edan and I took off at a brisk pace, only slowing once we'd put a bit of distance between us and the team.

Once we'd slowed, I looked down at our fingers, laced together, and let out a quiet laugh.

"What?" he asked.

"We just lost track of five hundred scrabs, but I still feel really happy."

A smile spread across his face, and he leaned over and brushed a quick kiss to my lips. "Me too."

24

Edan and I took an Uber back to the hotel. A text popped up on my phone from Maddie as we waited for the elevator.

Going to the police station to give them a statement. The FBI is already here and wants to talk too. We'll probably be a few hours.

Edan reached for my hand, sliding his phone back into his pocket. "You want to go outside?" He gestured toward the back of the hotel. "They have a nice patio out there."

I laced my fingers through his. "I'd like that."

We walked through the lobby and to the patio. It was nearly dark, and a chill had returned to the air. Edan steered us toward the fire pit, where some empty chairs sat near the flames.

"It's barely cold enough for a fire," he said with a laugh.

"Does this weather really make you cranky?" I asked.

He turned, still smiling. His cheeks were slightly pink. I'd never seen Edan blush so often, and I realized with a happy jolt that it was because of me.

"Sort of. I don't appreciate nearly eighty-degree weather in January. But mostly I was just mad at myself for making things awkward between us."

"*I* made things awkward between us by lying about not caring if you dated other girls."

He wrapped an arm around my waist, pulling me close and

pressing his lips to mine. I took in a breath, my heart pounding so hard I was sure he could feel it. It hadn't stopped doing that for the past hour.

He pulled away a tiny bit, so that our foreheads were almost touching. "I was trying to play it cool, but I was clearly being an idiot if you thought I was at all interested in dating anyone else."

I smiled and he kissed me again, pulling away when my phone buzzed. I pulled it out to find a text from Maddie.

Julian is texting me and Noah, asking to talk to you. I just wanted to give you a heads-up.

I sighed, and Edan gave me a curious look. I considered saying nothing, to avoid ruining the mood or seeing that look he always got when Julian was mentioned. But I'd never gotten anything but confusion and sadness from lying to Edan.

"Julian is texting Maddie and Noah. He wants to talk to me."

He raised his eyebrows. "Do you want to talk to him?"

"God no."

He laughed, leaning forward to kiss me again before tugging me closer to the fire pit. He sat in one of the chairs and pulled me in with him. It was a tight squeeze, but we made it work.

"Can I be honest?" I asked quietly, playing with the collar of his shirt.

"Of course."

"I don't like bringing up Julian with you, but I'm going to have to occasionally."

His eyebrows drew together. "You can talk to me about Julian anytime. Did you think you couldn't?"

"I could tell it upset you to talk about him. And honestly, I don't *want* to talk about him. I want to go back in time and tell myself to run the other way. To go give that thief who threatened to puke on me a second chance." I smiled at him.

"What? I never threatened to puke on you."

"Yes, you did. On the bus ride back from tryouts."

He squinted, thinking. His lips curved up into a smile. "I remember politely warning you that I might need to puke out the window."

"Well, it made an impression."

He laughed and pressed his lips briefly to mine. "I really made a great first impression, huh? You thought of me as the thief who threatened to puke on you."

"I imagine you thought of me as the scary girl who tackled you."

"Well . . . yes, actually. But I deserved it, so mostly I was just impressed."

We both laughed, and then we were kissing again, his arm slipping around my waist. I hooked my fingers into his collar, pulling him even closer.

We were breathless when we pulled away, and I took a moment before I spoke.

"Yesterday, when we were all talking about going to Germany, you seemed hesitant," I said. "Was it because of the weirdness between us or . . . ?"

"No, it wasn't that," he said. "I was still planning to hang around you until you told me to go away, honestly."

A smile spread across my face. "Really?"

"Of course. I thought I was being obvious." He took my hand, lacing our fingers together.

"Are you OK with going to Germany?"

"If you're there."

I smiled, leaning forward to kiss him. "What do you want?" I asked softly, pulling away just enough to speak.

"You mean besides never leaving this chair?" We were so close that his lips almost brushed mine when he spoke.

"Besides that, yes," I said with a smile. "What do you want to do next? Or in the future?"

He brushed my hair back, thinking for a moment. "I'd like to travel."

"That's right. Mexico and South America."

"Yeah. I'd never been out of New York City before I went to Atlanta for tryouts. There are a lot of places I'd like to see. Like that city in Mexico you were telling me about. Where you have to walk because the streets are too narrow to drive."

"Guanajuato."

"Right. Actually, now that I think about it, I'd like to go lots of places that don't require me to use my new driving talent."

"I wouldn't call it a *talent*," I said with a grin.

"I tried to tell you people that I was an avid pedestrian."

I kissed him and then we were both quiet for a moment, my gaze on my hand on his chest.

"I've been thinking about calling my mom," I said.

"Yeah?"

"Do you think that's a bad idea?"

"It doesn't matter what *I* think. If you want to call her, then you should."

"But you didn't call your mom. Even though she kept reaching out to you."

"It's not the same," he said. "I know that letting my mom back in my life is going to be a shit show. She just wants money or someone to scream at and blame for all her problems. Even her messages to me aren't about me. She hasn't even asked what I did in the three years since I left home. If she actually cared, she would want to know."

"I'm sorry," I said softly, reaching for his hand and lacing our fingers together.

"I feel OK about it. I gave up on her a long time ago. But it sounds like you haven't given up on your mom?"

"When I talked to Laurence about it, he said that Mom would always choose Dad, and I totally agree. I don't expect to talk her into leaving him. And I don't forgive her for letting him terrorize us. But I do wonder if I could have some kind of relationship with her now. Something that doesn't involve Dad. Even if that's just talking to her on the phone every once in a while. I . . . miss her, as dumb as that sounds."

"That doesn't sound dumb." He rubbed his thumb gently across my hand.

"You wouldn't think I was weak, if I reached out to her at some point?"

"Of course not."

I smiled at him, and he leaned forward to kiss me. I dropped his hand, letting my fingers trail up his neck and into his hair.

When we pulled away, Edan's eyes caught on something. He went very still. I followed his gaze, past the fire pit and to the man standing near the door.

Julian.

We both scrambled to our feet, and I grabbed Edan's hand, holding it tighter than necessary. My heart pounded as Julian drew closer.

There were two doors back inside—the one he'd just come through and another down near the restaurant. We could turn and bolt for the second one. Of course, that wouldn't help us much if he had a gun.

He was close enough now that I could see his face, the firelight flickering across his horrified features.

I couldn't see a gun, but he was wearing a bulky jacket. There was no way to tell what he had underneath it.

"Seriously?" he whispered.

"Julian, we're going to go back inside, OK?" Edan said. His voice was calm, but I heard the slight tremble of his words. "Let's all go inside."

Julian stared at me like Edan hadn't spoken at all. "You said there was nothing going on. You *swore* there was nothing going on."

I considered trying for logic. I could explain to him that there truly hadn't been anything going on with Edan, not when Julian and I were together, and not even when we'd last spoken in London. I could point out that it had been seven months since we broke up, and that my relationship with Edan didn't have anything to do with him.

But it wouldn't matter. I could get on my knees and cry and insist I was telling the truth, and he would never believe it. And I didn't care if he believed it. Part of me wished I *had* cheated on him with Edan. That would have shown excellent taste on my part.

Through the windows, I saw a hotel employee round the corner and walk down the hallway. I tugged on Edan's hand and moved forward. We had to get close to Julian to use this entrance, but it seemed like the safest option. At least someone in the lobby would see if he lunged at us.

He stayed rooted in place as we edged closer to the door. Only his head moved, his eyes following us.

I grabbed the door handle and pulled it open.

"Did you never even care about me?" Julian asked quietly.

I didn't stop. I walked through the door, Edan's hand still clasped in mine. The lobby was just ahead, and we walked quickly toward it.

I heard the door open behind us.

"Were you just laughing at me?" Julian called, anger beginning to edge into his voice. Edan's hand tightened around mine. "I don't know why I even wasted my time."

I could hear his footsteps gaining on us, but I didn't turn. Two men sat in the chairs in the corner of the lobby, and a teenage girl in a bright pink sweater stood near them, scrolling through her phone.

"You showed me that you were a lying bitch months ago, but I thought you deserved a second chance." His words were bitter now, and loud. The men and the girl looked up, alarmed.

We stepped into the lobby. There were two people behind the front desk, a man and a woman, and an older woman checking in.

"At least look at me!" Julian screamed.

The lobby went silent. I turned around to face him.

"Please don't do anything," I whispered to Edan. He nodded. His expression was tight, his shoulders stiff.

"You never gave me an answer," Julian said, his voice slightly calmer. "I asked you why he deserved a second chance and I didn't."

Edan's eyes flicked down to me, his fear giving way to a hint of curiosity.

"I'd like you to leave," I said to Julian, and moved toward the elevators. At the other end of the room, the girl in the pink sweater held her phone up, like she was filming. One of the men made a gesture like she should stop, but she waved him off and kept the phone pointed at us.

"I want an answer!" Julian yelled.

"I gave you an answer!" I said. "You just didn't like it."

"You just enjoy toying with me, don't you?" Julian sneered. "You're a selfish, lying bitch, you know that?"

The older woman gasped, putting a hand to her chest.

I turned to face the front desk. The man was already coming out from behind it, headed for Julian.

"Can you call the police?" I asked the woman. "He's not a guest here."

She nodded, picking up the phone.

"Sir, please calm down. Let's go outside," the man said. He

gestured with one arm toward the door, like he thought Julian might just need to know where it was.

"Why am I always the bad guy?" Julian yelled. "I'm just trying to talk to her!"

"You're insulting her," Edan said quietly.

"Yes, we have an unruly man in our lobby," the woman at the front desk said into the phone. "He's screaming at a guest and—"

"I have done nothing but be kind to you!" Julian screamed, drowning out the rest of the woman's words. "I helped you and I loved you and you spit it back in my face! You didn't even care that my parents died! I needed you, and you didn't even care, you fucking bitch!"

The older woman looked absolutely horrified. Like she'd never heard someone speak like this before. I felt sort of happy for her. I almost wanted to say, *Congratulations, you must have had a nice family and chosen lovely partners throughout your life.*

Julian's expression twisted as he watched me. I knew exactly which expression I had on my face—nothing. I was good at nothing. I had a lot of practice.

My nothing used to make Dad so mad. Half the fun of this was watching me crumble, and if he couldn't get that, then what was the point? He was just a hysterical man screaming in a hotel lobby, frightening an old woman and delighting a girl who was definitely still filming him.

I even sort of felt nothing, right now, in the moment. I'd feel it later. As soon as he left, I'd start to shake. Maybe I'd even cry.

The man edged a little closer to Julian. "Sir, I need you to—"

Julian lunged suddenly. He'd always been a nimble fighter, able to move faster than most people.

Most people. But that didn't include Edan, and it didn't include me, not after the months we'd spent as sparring partners.

Edan shot in front of me, reaching back to grab both my wrists. Julian threw a punch and missed spectacularly, his fist finding only air as we both darted away just in time.

It would have made me laugh if I hadn't been terrified. Julian's punch was wild, and when he missed, he nearly fell, tripping over his own feet.

"Oh my god," the girl with the phone whispered with a giggle.

Edan and I moved away from Julian as he righted himself. He made a move like he was going to lunge at us again, but the two men at the other end of the lobby had shot across the room as soon as Julian tried to punch us. They grabbed him by either arm and shoved him to the ground. The man working the front desk had to help hold him down.

"I'm going to kill you, bitch!" Julian screamed. "I'm going to fucking kill you!"

~

The men held Julian down until the police arrived. He screamed for a while, and then gave up and lay limply on the floor.

The police arrested him. Watching Julian being escorted to a police car in handcuffs might have been one of the nicest moments of my life.

The officers took our statements, and the girl who'd been filming—Tori—showed them the video. Edan and I sat on the couch, holding hands. Tori's dads asked if there was someone they could call for us, and then stared at us worriedly when we said no. I'd texted Maddie about what happened, but they hadn't made it back to the hotel yet.

I stood as the police walked out the door. Edan slipped an arm around my waist, kissing the top of my head.

Tori left her dads standing at the elevator and jogged over to me. "Hey, is your AirDrop on?"

"What?"

"Your AirDrop. Turn it on. I'll send you the video."

"Oh." I grabbed my phone from my pocket. "Thank you."

"I see you. There, I sent it." She smiled at me. "I already put it on Twitter, by the way."

"Tori!" one of her dads exclaimed.

"What?" She turned around and walked back to them. "Do you know who that guy was? There was no way I was *not* going to put that on Twitter."

Edan laughed softly, and I waved at Tori and her dads as they disappeared into the elevator.

"You think Julian will even spend the night in jail?" I asked.

Edan glanced down at the time on his phone. "Maybe. It's late. But he'll post bail first thing tomorrow, for sure. Unless the police can prove he took the scrabs, of course. Then maybe he won't get out for a very long time." His expression brightened.

I rose up on my toes to plant a kiss on his cheek. "Let's hope."

25

I woke up early the next morning, my body buzzing with excitement and anticipation.

Edan texted me as I was getting ready, and I smiled as I opened it. It was a link to a Twitter account from a guy I didn't know. *"She tried to tell y'all what Julian was like. NOW do you believe her?"* it read, with the video of Julian in the lobby last night below it. It had thousands of likes and retweets.

I didn't know if I cared if people believed me or not. I wanted Julian to pay for what he'd done, but mostly I just wanted people to stop mentioning my name with his.

Want to grab coffee? I typed to Edan.

Yes, he replied immediately.

Maddie's phone buzzed, and she emerged from under the blankets to grab it.

"Any news about the scrabs?" I asked, pulling my hair into a ponytail.

She rolled over, rubbing her eyes. "Not yet. It's just Mom."

"I'm going to go grab coffee with Edan. Do you want anything?"

"No." She glanced away from her phone for a moment to grin at me. "Have fun."

~

Edan was waiting by the lobby doors, a frown on his face as he looked down at his phone. It disappeared when he looked up and spotted me.

He put both hands on my cheeks and kissed me, making every thought fly out of my head. I smiled at him as we pulled away. My eyes caught on the front desk behind him, where both of the people working there were staring at us. They weren't the same ones from last night, but they were looking at us like they'd heard (or seen) everything.

I took Edan's hand, and we walked outside into the cool morning air. It was sunny, but a bit chillier than yesterday.

"Is something wrong?" I asked. He looked confused. "You looked worried when I came down."

"Oh! Right." A small smile crossed his lips. "I got distracted."

I grinned, and he leaned over and kissed me quickly.

"TMZ posted a picture of Julian being released from jail this morning," he said, almost apologetically.

"Great." I glanced back at our hotel. "Do you think maybe we should ask Maddie to change hotels? It doesn't seem safe to stay here since he knows where we are."

"Yeah, we probably should. And we maybe shouldn't walk through the lobby together at the next place."

"Yeah, we're pretty obvious in a big group."

We walked to a nearby coffee shop, and found a table in the corner.

"I've been wondering about something Julian said last night," Edan said.

"What's that?"

"Julian said that he asked you why I deserved a second chance and he didn't. You said you gave him an answer and he just didn't like it."

"I told him that you'd never hurt me. Or spied on me. Or tried to manipulate me. It's not even fair to compare the two of you. It only makes sense in his twisted brain."

The edges of his lips turned up. "Thank you." He laughed softly. "Is that a weird response? I just appreciate that you know that about me."

"Of course I know that about you."

He took a sip of his coffee and seemed to consider his words carefully. "Do you feel OK about everything? The things he said to you were really mean, and I couldn't tell if you were just pretending not to be upset or if you really weren't."

I looked at him in surprise. "Upset? About what Julian yelled at me?"

"Yes," he said, with a slightly confused laugh. "He was awful to you."

I cocked my head, considering. "I guess he was. But no, that didn't upset me. It scared me—I keep looking out that window, checking to see if he's coming for us." I pointed to the front of the coffee shop. "But otherwise I'm fine. If *you* yelled at me like that, I'd be devastated. I don't care what Julian thinks of me."

"I would never yell at you like that. I would never yell at *anyone* like that."

I smiled at him. "I know."

~

Maddie texted me as we were walking back to the hotel.

Are you watching this??? Where are you?

I typed out a response. **Walking back to the hotel with Edan. What's going on?**

Come up to our room now! Julian took the scrabs and MDG just ratted him out! This is the best day of my life!!

"Oh my god," I said with an incredulous laugh. I passed my phone to Edan so he could read the messages.

We raced upstairs and found the team crammed into the room, glued to the television. Maddie waved us over with a grin and we moved closer.

The chyron on the bottom of the screen said *Julian Montgomery implicated in scrab theft.* An anchor was behind the desk, talking to the camera.

"An arrest warrant has been issued for Julian Montgomery this morning in connection with the missing scrabs in Lubbock, Texas. Multiple witnesses have put Mr. Montgomery in Lubbock when the theft occurred, and sources tell us that he had recently been fired from his role at MDG.

Mr. Montgomery was in police custody in Dallas until early this morning, when he posted bail after being arrested on disorderly conduct and misdemeanor assault charges last night. Those charges are unrelated to the scrab theft."

Tori's video flashed on the screen, showing Julian lunging at me and Edan.

"Police ask anyone with knowledge of his whereabouts to come forward immediately."

"Holy shit," I breathed. I sat down on the edge of my bed. Edan lowered down beside me, slipping an arm around my waist.

"My thoughts exactly," Laila said.

"Have they mentioned the Scrab Defense League guys yet?" Edan asked.

"The *Post* is reporting it," Maddie said, looking at her phone. "I talked to one of their reporters last night, and he definitely didn't seem surprised when I said I'd seen guys from the conference go fetch the scrabs. And they have a source that confirms Julian's exit from MDG was nasty. Multiple people saw him screaming and throwing a fit when they fired him."

"That's why he didn't warn MDG to empty out Dust Storm," I said. "He just grabbed the scrabs and let us find everything to screw them over."

Maddie's eyes lit up as she looked at her phone. "Oh my god, one of the Scrab Defense League guys just confirmed to the *Times* that Julian stole the scrabs because he had an interested buyer. He'd promised the league guys that they could have a few if they helped him."

I leaned into Edan's arm, overwhelmed by the flood of information. He pulled me a little closer.

"That asshole is going to prison for sure this time," Maddie said. "And you should look at Twitter. Everyone has changed their tune after seeing that video. Lots of people are saying you're owed an apology."

"Edan sent it to me. And Julian going to prison will be enough of an apology for me." I turned to smile at Edan, who gently pressed his lips to mine.

"Hey," I heard Priya say in a loud whisper. "Edan and Clara are kissing!"

We both laughed as we pulled away. Everyone was looking at us. Priya silently clapped her hands, a delighted expression on her face.

"Thank you, Captain Obvious," Maddie said dryly.

"They've been doing that since yesterday," Dorsey said.

Priya looked insulted. "What? How come no one told me?"

"Sorry, forgot," Laila said, her eyes still on the television.

"Finally," Priya said. "I was about to say something to one of you, because the tension was starting to get to me."

"Same," Dorsey said.

"Plus, we all already have enough stress trying to pretend we don't know Maddie and Noah are hooking up," Laila said.

Noah's head snapped up from his phone. Priya clapped her hand over her mouth to suppress a giggle.

Maddie shot Laila an amused look. "I guess you're tired of pretending, then?"

Laila waved her hand. "Please, we all know."

"It's true, we do," Patrick said.

"Well, it doesn't matter because Noah's about to tell us he's leaving in a week anyway," Maddie said.

We all looked at Noah, who nodded sheepishly.

"I decided to take that job," he said. "The scrab documentary? They want me to go to China with them in a week to start scouting locations."

"That's awesome," Priya said.

"It's going to take several months," he said. "But I plan on coming back when I'm done. Wherever you guys are. I think I'm going to hold off on college for a couple years."

"You're always welcome back," Maddie said. Noah shot her a smile.

"So, you're leaving from here?" Dorsey asked.

"Yeah, they bought me a ticket out of Dallas. But I have a few days to keep looking for those missing scrabs, and Maddie said you guys aren't going anywhere."

I looked at her in surprise. "We're staying in Dallas?"

"*You* are not staying in Dallas," Maddie said, pointing to me. "Not with Julian still on the loose. Not to mention that your parents might have seen that video and decided to change their minds about making you come home. I'll buy a ticket for you and Edan to go back to New York tonight."

"But the scrabs are still unaccounted for," I protested. "We can't just leave you guys."

"Julian screamed repeatedly that he was going to kill you, and I really believe him," Priya said. "You can't stay here. We can handle the scrabs if we have to."

"The governor already deployed the National Guard here, and they're trained in scrab combat," Maddie said. "And the FBI sent a bunch of people down too. We probably won't even have anything to do."

I frowned, still hesitant to leave them.

"Go somewhere closer, if you don't want to go back to New York," Patrick said. "Go to Austin. It's only, like, three hours by bus. You can come back and help if we need it."

I brightened. That was a better plan. Plus, I didn't hate the idea of spending time alone with Edan. Alone in a city without scrubs, without the rest of the team. I loved them, but I certainly wouldn't mind a hotel room with just the two of us.

"What do you think?" I asked Edan.

"I'm game if you are," he said. He smiled, and I got the impression he was just as excited at the prospect of being alone as I was.

"We'll do it," I said, squeezing his hand.

"Perfect," Maddie said. "I'll book you guys a hotel where you can't get upstairs without a room key. And lie low while you're there. Just in case." She scooted off her bed. "Everyone go get dressed. We're going for a celebratory breakfast."

Edan leaned over to kiss me and then followed the rest of the team out of the room. Maddie swiped at her phone.

"Go ahead and pack your bag. There's a bus that leaves at noon. We'll drop you guys off after breakfast. And do you want one room or two at the hotel?"

"One."

She grinned at me. "Good choice."

"What are you going to do?"

"Hang around, wait to see if the police find the scrubs. Noah flies out on Wednesday, so I'll at least stay until then."

"And then?"

She sighed. "I haven't decided about Germany. You're right about a lot of stuff, but Patrick's been coordinating with Connor about the teams still left in the UK. There's a decent amount left who are willing to jump right back in."

"A decent amount isn't a *safe* amount," I said.

"I know. Just give me a few days. I feel sort of overwhelmed by everything right now." She rubbed at her forehead. "If Grayson were still around, he'd already have figured out a way to turn the MDG revelation about them creating scrabs into a big recruitment effort."

"We can definitely do that. I imagine the news will be reporting it any day now."

She smiled. "Send me any ideas you have. And hurry up and pack, because I am eating an entire mountain of pancakes to celebrate Julian's upcoming jail time."

~

We went to a diner down the street for breakfast. The news about Julian was playing on the televisions, the reporters all speculating about what Julian had planned to do with the scrabs and where they were now.

I hadn't seen Maddie so happy in months. Her phone kept dinging with interview requests and apologies from people back in New York, but she ignored them. She must have really been thrilled if she didn't even want to gloat.

All the reporters on television were saying that it probably wouldn't be long before Julian surrendered. They suspected he was just strategizing with his lawyers before turning himself in. They also said that bail was unlikely, given his wealth and resources. Which meant that I could relax soon. I was going to shut down the email account with all of Julian's emails and maybe (hopefully) never hear from him again.

Edan slipped his arm around my shoulders, and I leaned into him. I still needed to finish my plans for noncombat teams and present them to Maddie, but I'd decided to enjoy a few days with Edan first. A few days without scrabs or Julian or MDG.

Maddie drove us across town to the bus station after we finished eating. It was the same bus station where I'd joined the St. John teams back in May. The whole team piled out of the van to say goodbye, even though we would see them in a few days.

"Eat tacos for me," Priya said as she hugged me.

"I will," I said with a laugh.

"What?" I heard Noah say softly, and I turned to see him looking at Maddie worriedly. She was staring down at her phone.

"It's Julian," she said, her eyes flicking up to mine. "He's calling me."

"Answer it," Noah said.

She swiped to answer the call and put it on speaker. "Julian?"

"Hi, Madison." He sounded calm. Almost cheerful, actually.

"What do you want?" she asked.

"Is Clara with you?"

Maddie looked up at me, clearly unsure if she should answer that honestly.

I stepped closer to the phone with a sigh. "Yeah, I'm here."

"Oh, perfect. Hi, Clara."

An uneasy feeling began to creep into my chest. He sounded almost . . . happy? It was unsettling. I felt Edan's hand brush mine, and I gripped it, weaving my fingers through his.

"Your neighborhood is a real shithole, you know that?" Julian said. "When you told me you grew up in Dallas. I was picturing a big suburb with those houses that all look alike. You know the ones. Kind of tacky, but still nice enough. But this is definitely not that."

The blood drained from my face. "Julian, wh—what are you—"

"You kept treating me like I was some kind of monster. No matter what I did or how many times I tried to apologize, you refused to see me as anything but this horrible guy. Even after my parents died, you didn't have one ounce of sympathy for me. So, I just figured, what the hell?" He laughed hollowly. "If you're going to insist that I'm the bad guy here, I might as well be one, right?"

I heard screams in the background, followed by a crashing sound.

"Everyone here is running from the scrabs, which is an . . . interesting choice," Julian said. "But I guess there have never been any scrabs in Dallas, huh? People don't know what to do." Distantly, I heard gunshots. "Yep, that dude just tried to shoot a scrab. That did not work out for him, let me tell you."

Patrick grabbed the van keys from Maddie and ran around to the driver's seat. The engine roared to life. Edan guided me into the van as I talked into the phone Maddie was still holding.

"Julian, what are you doing?" My words came out frantic. "You're hurting innocent people, you can't—"

"You have no one to blame here but yourself, Clara. If you'd just listened to me, none of this would have happened. If you hadn't been such a selfish, judgmental bitch, we could have avoided all of this! Instead, the whole world has turned against me and everyone thinks you're some kind of hero."

"Clara, which way is your neighborhood?" Patrick asked, hitting the gas.

"Her brother's apartment is at 385 Iris Spring Road," Julian said. "Don't be fooled by the pretty street name—the place is a real dump."

My blood went cold. I fumbled for my phone in my pocket.

"You assholes are so convinced you're heroes, so come on out here. Save everyone." The call abruptly ended.

Part Four

HOME

26

I FRANTICALLY SWIPED OPEN MY PHONE AND SCROLLED DOWN to Laurence's number as Patrick peeled out of the parking lot. "Someone needs to call the police," I said.

"Already on it," Noah said, his phone against his cheek.

I pressed my phone to my ear and listened as it rang. I closed my eyes briefly, willing Laurence to pick up. Edan reached around and buckled my seat belt for me.

"The weapons packs are in back, right?" Dorsey asked, twisting around in his seat to try and see in the back of the van.

"Yes," Maddie said.

The phone was still ringing. Edan was watching me worriedly. Patrick was driving incredibly fast.

"Hello?"

I let out a huge whoosh of air at the sound of Laurence's voice. "Oh my god, Laurence, are you OK? Where are you right now?"

"I'm outside my apartment. Clara, there are scrabs everywhere." He was breathing heavily, like he was running. I could hear screams and a siren in the background.

"I know," I said. "Julian did it, he—" I shook my head. "Not important. Are you in a safe place?"

"A safe place? I don't even . . . I don't have anywhere to go. I just got back home, and there were scrabs crawling through the window of my apartment. They weren't going in any other windows! Just mine!"

"That . . . Thank god you weren't home. Listen, you need to try and get somewhere safe. And you need to be on the lookout for Julian, because it is not a coincidence that all those scrabs targeted your apartment."

"Jesus. Seriously?"

"Yes. We are on our way, but we're still, like . . ." I looked out the window. "Maybe five minutes away. Get in your truck and start driving north on Iris Spring. You'll—"

"I can't, the scrabs completely destroyed the street. I couldn't get my truck out of the parking lot. I'm just running—wait, do you think he sent scrabs over to Mom and Dad's too?"

"Maybe," I said, trying to keep my voice calm. It seemed like he would start panicking if I did. "We'll go straight there once we pick you up, OK? Are you running north or south?"

"South." I heard screams in the distance. "Holy shit, there—" His voice suddenly cut out. I lowered my phone to see that the call had ended. I cursed and redialed.

"He's running south on Iris Spring," I said to Patrick. I listened to the ringing until it went to voicemail. "He's not picking up."

"He can't talk and fight scrabs at the same time," Maddie said, turning around in the passenger's seat to look at me. "He told us he had combat class in high school, right? He's probably just finding a weapon, like they taught him."

I knew she was just trying to make me feel better, because we both knew that most people, when faced with their first scrab attack, completely panicked. But maybe Laurence would be different. He never was one to lose his cool.

Dorsey grabbed the weapons packs and started distributing them. I took mine, pulling out a sheathed machete and putting the pack on my back.

Patrick turned the corner and gasped. A pickup truck was on its side in the middle of the road.

He hit the brakes hard, turning the wheel as fast as he could to avoid it. The van scraped against the tires before coming to a stop.

"Oh shit," Patrick breathed.

The truck was mangled, only a few feet away from several big holes in the ground where scrabs must have tunneled out from the earth.

"Can you get around it?" Maddie asked.

"I think so. Going to be a tight squeeze, though." He backed up and then edged around the truck, bumping it lightly.

There were several more scrab holes in the road, and Patrick weaved around them as he headed down Iris Spring. The holes weren't a great sign—Julian would have released the scrabs aboveground, so it meant that a bunch of them had tunneled under and would pop up anywhere around the city.

I spotted several dead bodies as we neared Laurence's apartment. I knew that they couldn't be him—he was farther down the street when I talked to him—but my chest still clenched painfully.

Patrick slowed the van, and I leaned over to look out the front window. The road in front of us was completely destroyed. A huge number of scrabs had all popped up in the same place. In the distance, I could see people running. A fire hydrant spewed water into the air.

"We're going to have to get out and run," Maddie said, unhooking her seat belt. "Everyone has their phone on them, right?" We all nodded. "Try to stay together, but if we get separated, head back to the van if you can. The cell phone towers are probably going to be overloaded on and off, so no one panic if we can't get in touch. OK?" She climbed out of the van. "Let's go kill some scrabs."

We piled out of the van, and I broke into a run, Edan beside me. We skirted the edge of the giant holes in the ground and ran faster. There were more dead bodies on the road, and I tried not to panic every time we approached one that looked even vaguely like Laurence.

I spotted three scrabs suddenly. One of them tossed a woman like she was a doll. I spotted a dark-haired man dart out from behind a car and make a run for it. Laurence.

I pointed. "There!"

"I see him," Edan said, picking up speed and pulling slightly ahead of me. Patrick, Laila, and Priya cut in front of us, making a beeline for the scrabs.

"Laurence!" I yelled. He didn't turn.

He was nearly at the end of the street when he skidded to a sudden stop, arms flailing out as he almost fell. He whipped around and started running back in our direction. I could see the moment he spotted me, when he was close enough that I could make out his expression. A flash of relief crossed through his terror.

Several scrabs came screaming around the corner, making

it clear why he was running back in our direction. I gripped my machete in my right hand, using my left to point to an overturned car on the side of the road. Laurence veered to the right and made a dash for it. The scrabs followed him.

Beside me, Dorsey whistled loudly and stomped his feet, drawing the scrabs' attention away from Laurence and to us instead. They all changed course.

My heart pounded a frantic rhythm in my chest as I took my first swing, ripping open a scrab's throat. I realized too late that in my panic, I'd forgotten to put on my leather arm coverings.

I moved to help Edan take out a scrab. In the distance, I could hear faint sirens. Noah had given the police my parents' address and Laurence's address, though Julian couldn't be their top priority at the moment. Even finding him among the scrabs was going to be a challenge.

A scrab claw ripped across my forearm, and I gasped, darting backwards. Edan jumped in, swinging his ax directly into the scrab's belly.

"Are you OK?" he asked. Blood had started pouring from the gash.

"I'm fine." I heard a thud and glanced over my shoulder to see two scrabs fall. Another broke away from the team, galloping straight for the car that Laurence was hiding behind.

"Laurence!" I yelled. I broke into a run.

The scrab slammed into the car, sending it skittering into the bushes. Laurence was sprawled out on the concrete, and he scrambled backwards on his hands and feet as the scrab lumbered toward him.

I darted in front of the scrab just as it was about to strike. I drove my machete into its side, and it lurched away from Laurence, swiping at me. I ducked the claws, slashing my blade across its throat. It fell.

I whirled around to find Laurence getting to his feet. "Clara." He was breathing heavily. "Thank you."

I practically launched myself at him, grabbing him around the waist and pulling him into a hug. I tried to keep my bloody machete from touching his clothes.

"Don't die, OK? Please don't die."

He made a sound almost like a laugh—a laugh tinged with panic—and hugged me back.

"Thank you for coming," he said breathlessly.

"Anytime."

I smiled as I released him, then took a quick glance behind me to make sure there weren't any more scrabs. They were all dead, the team standing over their bodies.

"Are you OK?" Laurence asked, his gaze on my bloody arm.

"Yeah. It's just a scratch."

His eyes flicked over the rest of the team, and he lifted a hand. "Hi."

"Hi, Laurence!" Priya said, waving enthusiastically.

"Did you call Mom and Dad?" I asked Laurence.

"I tried, but they didn't answer, and then I got a busy signal." He squinted down the street, where the fire hydrant was still spewing water into the air. "It's not that far . . ." He trailed off, turning back to me. "I understand if you don't want to go."

"I think we're going that way anyway," I said, looking at the rest of the team. "Right?"

Noah had already taken a few steps down the road, in the direction of the scrabs. He turned to look at us. "Yeah. I have to try and help. It's going to take the cops at least another twenty or thirty minutes to get enough officers down here, and that's assuming they don't run into roadblocks like that." He pointed at the giant holes behind us.

"Yeah, we're going," Laila said, striding up beside Noah.

I looked at Laurence. "We were in a van, but we couldn't get it down the road. I can give you the keys, if you want, and you can make a run for it."

He shook his head. "I'll stay with you."

I smiled at him, and then pulled the foldable ax out of my weapons pack. I unfolded it and handed it to him.

"The neck," I said, touching my own neck. "Or the stomach, if you can see a soft spot. But the neck is the most reliable place to hit a scrab. Don't just swing wildly—the ax will get stuck in the scrab's hide or bounce off and you'll lose your balance. OK?"

He gulped. "OK." We took off running behind the rest of the team.

I spotted evidence of more scrab attacks as we headed down the street. An old convenience store had completely cratered, and a trail of blood formed a path where the scrabs had apparently run away after demolishing it. I spotted a few people standing on the roof of a three-story building in the distance, which was a smart idea. Scrabs could usually make it up a one-story building, but not much higher.

A scrab staggered into the road not far ahead of us, and Noah, in the lead, came to a stop. The scrab must have been injured, because its body lurched as it walked, its head ducked into its neck. Drool poured out of its mouth.

I frowned, moving closer. "Noah, wait," I said, as he aimed his blade at the scrab's throat. The scrab toppled to the ground and made a gurgling noise. Noah hadn't touched it.

I walked to it, motioning for Dorsey to come look. Brown mucus poured down the scrab's eyes.

"It's like the one in London," I said, pointing. The rest of the team had gathered around. "The MDG scrabs we saw in London were sick like this."

"It is," Dorsey said, wrinkling his nose.

"Is that stuff coming from its eyes?" Patrick asked, leaning down to get a better look. The scrab squeaked like it wanted to protest.

"No, it's from the stuff they put in its head," I said. The scrab had the usual MDG sensors across its forehead, though one had fallen out, pus oozing out of the hole.

Screams sounded from in front of us, and I quickly sliced my blade across the scrab's throat. We broke into a run again.

I could hear the occasional scrab roar, but the majority of them must have had their vocal cords cut, because mostly the only sound was humans screaming. I could tell where the screams were coming from—the busy four-lane road a block over.

"That way!" I yelled, pointing to an alleyway between two buildings. "We can cut through!"

We raced through the alley, and I skidded to a stop as we

crossed into the street. It was chaos. There was a huge pileup of cars in the middle of the street, blocking traffic both ways. Looking south, the line of cars was already wrapped around the block, and scrabs galloped in between them, headed for us.

"Clara?" Laurence called, a note of panic in his voice. I turned to see several scrabs coming for us from the opposite direction, leaping over dead bodies and cars.

"Edan, Clara, Maddie, and Priya, go that way," Noah said, pointing north. "Everyone else with me."

We split, breaking into a run as we headed north.

"Stay behind me, but just in case," I said to Laurence.

The gash on my arm burned, but I barely felt it as I swung my machete at the approaching scrab. It was slower than scrabs I'd encountered in London, and it went down easily with a grunt. It also had brown liquid seeping from its sensors.

There was another scrab right behind it, this one at full strength, and then another. Laurence swung his machete at a third one and missed. Edan jumped in to help us.

I stepped back as we finished off all the scrabs in the immediate area, surveying the scene. It was noisy, the air full of screams and car horns and the sounds of people's feet hitting the pavement as they ran. All the scrabs in the general area would be attracted to this exact spot.

A scrab leapt over a car and made a beeline for me. I swung, but the scrab dodged it, and I barely escaped a swipe of claws across my good arm. Laila jumped in front of me, swatting the scrab away and digging her machete into its stomach.

"Thank you," I said breathlessly as the scrab toppled over.

"No problem."

I heard a scream, and I turned to see a scrab with a woman in its teeth. It tossed her and lumbered toward a family climbing out of their smashed car. There were two more scrabs just behind it.

Noah shot forward, whistling to distract the scrabs. He swung his machete into the first one. We'd finished off all the scrabs in our area, and I broke into a run, heading for him.

He took out two scrabs and then dove in front of the third, which was lumbering toward the family. A fourth approached from his left. Beside me, Laila gasped.

"Noah, watch out!" I yelled.

The scrab lunged at him. Noah turned, but not in time. He was on the ground. I couldn't see him anymore. The scrabs swarmed around him.

Maddie got to him first, taking down one scrab. Then Patrick was there, and so were Laila and I, but I had a sinking feeling that it was too late. I blinked back tears as I drove my blade into a scrab's neck.

"Noah?" Maddie whirled around as the last scrab fell. She scrambled to him. "Noah?"

He was motionless on the ground, blood dripping from a gash on his neck. And another in his chest.

Maddie put her fingers to his neck, her face crumpling.

Tears spilled onto my cheeks, and I had to turn away. I could hear the rest of the team realizing Noah was gone, and I couldn't look at them. I couldn't look at Noah. I surveyed the general area instead, looking for more scrabs. I could hear the pounding of their feet somewhere to the north, but I didn't see them. Edan's fingers intertwined with mine, and I took in a shaky breath.

In the distance, I heard sirens. The police would be here soon. I hoped, anyway. I couldn't handle losing anyone else.

The thumping of feet grew louder, accompanied by screams. Beside me, Laurence's eyes widened.

A swarm of people were headed our way. They were panicking, weaving in between cars and clearly trying to outrun something.

"Quick, move him!" Patrick yelled, reaching for Noah. Edan dropped my hand to help. They grabbed him by the shoulders and legs and began hauling him to the side of the road.

The crowd reached us, bumping against me and nearly knocking me over. A woman tripped when she passed me, and I had to shove several people out of the way as I helped her to her feet.

I felt an arm around my waist as I straightened. It was Maddie, trying to pull me away from the thick of the crowd. I grabbed her arm and let her lead me out.

"What were they running from?" I gasped, whirling around to look for Laurence and Edan. I found Laila and Priya stumbling toward us as the crowd thinned, and then Dorsey, on the other side of the street with Laurence and Edan. In the distance, I spotted several scrabs galloping over the cars, chasing the screaming crowd.

The ground between us began rumbling, and Edan's eyes met mine. He put his arm out in front of Laurence and nodded once. I gave him a grateful look. If there was anyone I trusted to keep Laurence alive, it was Edan.

A scrab split the earth, blocking them from my line of sight. Dorsey raced forward, swinging his ax.

The ground beneath my feet shifted, and I gasped, grabbing Maddie and pulling her out of the way. We both stumbled as the scrab burst up through the earth. I scrambled to my feet, but Laila and Priya were already there, slashing a blade across the scrab's throat.

"There's another one," Priya said, eyes wide. "Feel that?"

I did. The ground was moving. In the distance, I saw Edan and Laurence running.

"Move back, move back," Maddie said, pulling on my arms. We began running too.

I heard yelling behind me suddenly, and I turned to see men and women in military combat uniforms flooding the area. Behind them were dozens of police, all dressed in riot gear. Several scrabs burst up from the ground.

"Everyone clear the area," a voice on a bullhorn said from somewhere.

"I vote we let the National Guard handle those," Laila said.

"Seconded," Maddie said. She pointed past them. "Edan and Laurence went that way, but I don't think we should try and cut through those scrabs."

"They're headed to my parents' house," I said. "Come on, it's only a few streets over."

I broke into a run, and the girls followed me. I'd been trying not to think about my parents, and what I was going to find at their house, but now, with the streets quiet, it was hard to keep the thoughts at bay.

I didn't want to see Dad, and my feelings about Mom were complicated, but I didn't want them *dead*. It was an especially cruel move by Julian, to send scrabs after them. It would be hard not to feel guilty about their deaths forever. He probably knew that.

My phone rang suddenly, and I pulled it out to see Edan's name. I pressed Accept. "Edan? Are you OK?"

"I'm fine. Clara—I've got them. Your parents."

I came to a sudden stop. The girls stopped as well, all of us breathing heavily.

"What?" I said.

"Laurence spotted them on the street. They're with us now. They're fine. Dorsey's with us too. Patrick stayed with Noah's body, but the police were helping him get to an ambulance. We're all fine."

I nearly crumpled with relief. "Where are you?"

"We're . . . I don't even know. But the soldiers aren't letting us go back the way we came. They're putting us all on a bus and taking us to some church. They don't want anyone on the streets until they can get the scrabs under control."

"OK," I said. "Text me the address of the church, and we'll meet you there. Have you heard anything about Julian?"

"No, nothing. With any luck he was killed by his own scrabs."

"Now, there's a nice thought."

"Listen, one question before you go." His voice was quiet, and I had to strain to hear him. "Am I supposed to be nice to your dad? He's being overly friendly to me and it's weird and I want to tell him to go throw himself into traffic but that seems like the wrong thing to say to my girlfriend's father. I feel very confused about how to act in this situation."

I let out a surprised laugh that turned into a moan. "I'm so sorry. You shouldn't have to deal with this."

"No, it's fine, I just don't want to make things weird if you'd prefer that I keep the peace."

"I want you to act however you want. You don't have to play nice if you don't want to."

"I really don't want to. I have this very strong urge to practice my confrontation skills."

"Then go nuts. Make things super awkward. Laurence will love that."

"He does look kind of terrified right now."

"Thank you, Edan."

"For making things awkward with your family? Anytime. Happy to do it."

"You know what I mean," I said affectionately.

"I do. I'll text you that address. Come quick, OK?" His voice turned serious, and I knew he was thinking the same thing as me. We'd already lost one team member.

"We will." I slipped my phone back in my pocket and looked at the girls. "They're all OK." My voice wobbled a bit when I said it, because when I said *everyone*, I no longer meant Noah. Maddie, Priya, and Laila all had looks on their faces like they knew exactly what I was thinking. I took a deep breath. "The cops are shuttling everyone to a church. I say we hightail it out of here—" I heard a woman scream, and I stopped, turning to look for the source of the noise.

"That way, I think," Maddie said, pointing to the next street over. We broke into a run again, rounding the corner onto the street. It was a mess, the road completely destroyed by multiple scrab holes. One of the homes was leaning dangerously to one side, something clearly damaged structurally.

Another scream, and I turned to find the source. A few homes down, a girl was high up in an old tree, squatting on a branch. A scrab was clawing its way up the trunk. It roared, and I couldn't see any MDG hardware on it.

We ran for the tree, Maddie whistling as we approached. The scrab, distracted, lost its hold and tumbled to the ground. It sprang to its feet, healthy and fast like a normal scrab. I drove my machete into its exposed belly while Laila slit its throat.

"Clara?"

I stepped back, squinting through the sun and leaves at the girl. "Adriana?"

Her mouth dropped open. "Oh my god! What are you doing here?"

"You know her?" Maddie asked, tilting her chin up to look at her.

"Remember how I told you I had friends in middle school who I sort of abandoned?"

"Oh, right. This is one of them?"

"Yep."

Maddie waved to Adriana, then pointed to the dead scrab. "They can climb trees!"

"I see that now!" Adriana called.

"Do you need help coming down?" I asked.

"No, I think I . . ." She trailed off, clinging to the trunk as she took a cautious step onto a lower branch. "I think I've got it."

She climbed down the rest of the way, jumping off the lowest branch and edging away from the dead scrab. Her dark hair was loose around her shoulders, and she pushed it out of her face as she walked to me.

"What were you even doing up there?" I asked, glancing at the unfamiliar home. "Did you move?"

"No, it's my boyfriend's house," she said. "I was waiting outside for him, and then there were scrabs, and I couldn't get inside. Going up the tree seemed like the safest option. I thought if I was quiet it wouldn't notice me, but I guess not."

"The National Guard is evacuating people to a safer spot until they can get all the scrabs out," I said. "We're headed over there, if you want to come with us."

She nodded, her eyes skipping from me to Maddie.

"Oh, sorry," I said. "This is Madison, and Priya, and Laila. This is Adriana. We went to school together."

"I know who you guys are. It's nice to meet you," Adriana said with a smile, then turned her attention back to me. "And it's nice to see you again. I saw on the news that you were in Dallas and I was kind of shocked. It sounded like you were never coming back again in the emails."

"Well, the scrabs," I said, gesturing to the dead one.

"Sure."

Somewhere nearby, a scrab roared. Laila and Priya exchanged a look.

"We're actually going to let the army and the police take it from here." I glanced down at Adriana's shoes. Black boots. "You OK to run?"

"Away from the scrabs? Yes."

We jogged in the opposite direction of the scrab roars, all of us silent as our feet pounded the pavement.

Maddie slowed as she pulled her phone out of her pocket, and then came to a stop. I called for Priya and Laila, who were slightly ahead of us, to wait.

"It's Julian," she said breathlessly. She swiped her phone to answer, putting it on speaker. "What, asshole?" Adriana blinked, clearly startled.

"Is Clara with you?" He sounded significantly less cheery than he had earlier.

"Yes," I said.

"I want to talk to you. Take me off speaker."

I sighed, reaching out to press Mute on Maddie's phone. "Let me talk to him. Maybe I can find out where he is."

"It's up to you," she said, offering me her phone.

I took him off speaker and mute and pressed the phone to my ear. "You're off speaker. What do you want?"

"I'd like you to come talk to me."

"No."

"I'm in your old bedroom. There's a very cute stuffed pink elephant here."

"Yeah? Did they replace the door? I've been wondering."

"There's no door at all. Guess they didn't think you were coming back."

"Good guess," I said.

"Come see me."

"No."

"Your parents aren't here, if that's what you're worried about."

"I know where my parents are. And Laurence. Nice try, jackass."

"OK, I admit that sending those scrabs into Laurence's apartment was a bit much. But come on, you wouldn't be that upset if your parents died. You never would have admitted it, but I would have done you a favor." I heard a rustling sound. "Listen, I don't know if you already have Maddie calling the cops to come after me, but I'd put a pause on that."

I *should* have told Maddie to call the cops. I hesitated, waiting for him to continue.

"I released half the scrabs. I've got the rest on standby in a *very* populated area. And I can release them from here. Come see me or I push the button."

My breath caught in my throat, and I looked up at Maddie with wide eyes.

"If I see police outside, I'm pressing it. And please don't bring Maddie with you. I do not need that right now."

I paused, thinking about the destruction I'd just seen a block over. The holes where the scrabs had tunneled underneath the ground.

"Half is two hundred and fifty, right?" I asked.

"That's right. That's a lot of scrabs. Have you ever seen the destruction that hundreds of scrabs can do in a highly populated area?" His voice lowered. "Come talk to me. Just one more time. I have things to say to you, and I just want some time to say them."

I blew out a long, slow breath, and looked up to meet Maddie's eyes. "OK. I'm coming."

27

I WAS OUT OF BREATH FROM RUNNING, AND THE GASH ON MY arm was starting to ache. My heart pounded frantically in my chest.

I couldn't stop thinking about my doorless room. It made sense that Mom and Dad took the door completely off. I'd destroyed it beyond repair.

But I kept hearing what Julian had said—*Guess they didn't think you were coming back.*

It took me a moment to identify the emotion I felt when he said that. I wasn't sad. Or guilty.

I was proud.

Dad didn't go out and buy a tough, sturdy door that locked from the outside. Mom didn't put another cheap one in because she'd feel too guilty asking me to sleep in a room without a door. They didn't bother, because they knew I wasn't coming back.

And maybe they just thought I was going to die. Dad had made it clear that he thought that was my fate when I left. But maybe there was a little more to it also. Maybe they knew that I was done, that I was never going to live the life that they'd chosen.

"Are you close?" Julian's voice was in my ear, the phone still pressed to my cheek. He'd insisted on staying on the phone with me until I arrived.

"Yes," I lied.

Ahead of me, Adriana pulled open the door of an apartment building. We'd run several blocks to it. Priya and Laila followed her inside. Maddie held the door open for me.

We followed her to the corner of the building and up the stairs, through the door that said it was alarmed. No alarm sounded. We stepped onto the roof.

Adriana pointed. She'd said that she came up to the roof of this apartment building all the time, and you could clearly see my house from here. She was right. I could see the brown roof, the huge tree in the neighbor's yard, our dead grass. The bars on the windows.

The street was torn up—a scrab hole, cars overturned, even a dead body on the pavement. I spotted several people standing on the roofs of their houses.

"I'm looking out the window and I don't see you," Julian said.

"I'm almost there," I said, still out of breath. "We'd gotten a good distance away, and I don't have a car."

Priya pointed at something, and I turned to look. It was a huge black SWAT truck turning onto the street. The vehicle stopped in front of the scrab hole, unable to go around it. Armed police officers piled out.

"Is that . . . ?" Julian's voice went cold. "I told you what would happen if you called the cops."

"You did," I said. "But I don't think you actually have two-hundred-and-fifty scrabs waiting somewhere."

"That's one hell of a bet, Clara. All those people will be dead because of you."

"No, because of *you*. But you don't have them. I saw how sick some of the scrabs are out here. There's something wrong with MDG's scrabs, isn't there? All that stuff they put in their brains is killing them."

He didn't reply.

"You said it yourself when you asked if I'd seen the destruction that hundreds of scrabs could do on a neighborhood. That would be catastrophic in a populated area. What I just saw here, in my neighborhood, was maybe fifty scrabs, at most. But you said that you released half of them."

I watched as the officers surrounded the house.

"I've been fighting these things for six months, Julian," I said. "Do you think I can't tell when a scrab is sick or wounded or somehow not at full strength? Do you really think I don't know what it looks like when a nest of over a hundred attacks? More than half would have immediately tunneled underground when you released them at Laurence's apartment, and there aren't enough holes for that. Not to mention that I'm extremely dubious about this claim that you can just push a button to release scrabs in some unknown location. Where did you put them? How did you hide them if they're in a highly populated area? Are they just hanging out somewhere and miraculously no one noticed? I'm not an idiot, Julian."

The sound of his breathing was the only noise I could hear from his end.

"Tell me the truth, Julian. You don't have any more scrabs, do you?" I held my breath as I waited. I was so confident that he was bluffing, but my heart still pounded.

He was silent for a long time. "No," he finally said quietly. I let out a rush of air. "But you didn't know that for sure. You really just risked the lives of hundreds—maybe thousands—of people on a hunch? You really could have lived with yourself after that?"

"I took a risk, yes. And it could have been a disaster. But it wouldn't have been my fault. You're the one making the decisions here. And I'm certainly not going to let you manipulate me into being alone with you."

"You can make all the excuses you want, but you know that you could have prevented this," Julian said, his voice shaking. "I came to you for help after my parents died and I apologized to you and I tried to make things right. But you wouldn't even *listen*—"

"So you only meant the apology if I accepted it and forgave you for everything? That's not how apologies are supposed to work."

I heard a sniffle. "I was drowning and I just needed someone to pull me out and tell me everything was going to be OK."

"I'm not responsible for you or your choices," I said. "I am not here to save you."

"You can't—"

"Bye, Julian." I ended the call.

28

WE STOOD ON THE ROOF AND WATCHED AS THE POLICE LED
Julian out of my parents' house in handcuffs. Maddie sat down
and cried, either out of relief, or because of Noah, or both. I sat
down next to her and put an arm around her shoulders.

Once the police had left, we took the stairs back down and
walked to where we'd left the van. I drove us to the church where
they'd shuttled everyone. We had to take a long route to circum-
vent all the damaged or closed roads.

I spotted Edan as soon as I pulled up, sitting on the steps at
the front of the church. He stood as we approached, and I took a
few quick steps as I drew closer, throwing my arms around him.
He held me tightly, and I buried my face in his neck, taking a
shaky breath.

"Your family's inside," he said when I pulled away. "Dorsey
grabbed a ride with some people who were going to the hospital.
He's meeting Patrick there. They both need stitches." He gingerly
touched my hand, examining the gash on my arm. "You should
probably get checked out too."

I nodded, my eyes catching movement at the church door. It
was Laurence. He lifted one hand.

"Give me a minute?" I asked, squeezing Edan's hand. He nodded and squeezed it back.

I walked to Laurence and pulled him into a hug. He circled his arms around me, a bit loosely. I didn't think he hugged people very often.

"We hug now," I said. "I hope that's OK."

He laughed softly. "That's OK."

I smiled as I pulled away from him. His eyes flicked back to where Edan had gone to join Maddie, Priya, Laila, and Adriana. They were all sitting in the grass.

"I'm sorry about Noah," he said, his gaze returning to me.

"Thanks," I said around the lump in my throat.

He slid his hands into his pockets, a hint of awkwardness crossing his features. "It was really nice of you to come. I don't think I would have made it out of there alive if it weren't for you. And the rest of your team."

"Well, you're the only brother I have," I said.

He smiled. "Unfortunately."

"You're not so bad," I said, returning the smile. My eyes slid to the door. "Mom and Dad are inside?"

"Yeah. Do you want to see them?"

"In a minute. Can I say something first?"

He turned back to me. "Sure."

"I don't think you should stay here just because Mom wants you to. If you like Dallas and you have friends here, then fine, stay. But don't let her make you feel guilty for the choices she made. For the choices she continues to make."

He swallowed, his eyes flicking to the ground. He nodded.

"I don't think I'm going to see Mom and Dad much for a while. Maybe forever," I continued. "But I just want you to know that

I'm always going to want to see you, OK? Even if you decide to stay here and you see them all the time. You can have whatever relationship you want with them, and you and I can still see each other. Often, I hope."

His expression shifted to surprise. "I would like that. I . . ." He trailed off, and it took him a few moments to find the words. "I don't particularly like it here. I had regrets when I came back, but I don't really know where else to go, you know?"

"Well, Edan and I were talking about going to Guanajuato sometime soon. Our tía is always bugging us to visit. We could start there."

"Yeah." He smiled. "That sounds nice." He paused. "And it would make Dad really mad, so that's a bonus. You know how he hates Tía Julia."

"That alone is a great reason to go," I said with a laugh. I glanced at the door again. "OK. I'm going to talk to Mom. Do me a favor?"

"Name it."

"I'm going to ask her to come outside. Make sure Dad doesn't try and ambush me?"

"You got it." He grabbed the door and held it open for me.

I stepped inside, surveying the crowd. It was packed, the chattering creating a dull roar. Laurence crossed in front of me and walked a short distance to the corner nearest me. I spotted Dad first, standing stiffly with his eyes on his phone, brow furrowed. I saw Mom second. She'd already seen me, her mouth forming an O.

"Mom?" I called, not moving from the door and raising my voice to be heard over the noise. "Can I have a minute?"

Dad's head popped up. His eyes swept over my face, to my bloody arm, to the sheathed machete sticking out of my back pocket. I thought he might look horrified, or even angry (it didn't take much), but he just stared, a shadow of embarrassment crossing his features before he lowered his eyes. Laurence was beside him, but he didn't have to stop Dad from doing anything. He didn't make a move toward me.

Mom hurried over and pulled me into a tight hug. She was crying, talking so fast it was hard to understand her. She wanted to know why I was in Dallas. Why I didn't call her. What had happened to my arm.

"Let's go outside," I said, extracting myself from her grip and turning to walk back outside. I led her down the church steps and to a quiet piece of grass. My friends were within view, and they turned to look. Mom glanced at them and then at me.

"Those are the kids from the videos, right? The ones you were in London with?"

"Yes."

"When did you get back? How long have you been in Dallas? Why didn't you call me, mija?"

"I haven't heard from you since I left," I said. "I wasn't actually sure that you would want me to call."

"Of course I want you to call," she said, exasperated.

"Why didn't you ever try to contact me? You never even emailed."

"Well . . ." She shifted, clearly uncomfortable. "You made it clear that you didn't want anything to do with us when you left. I didn't know . . ." Her gaze was on my arm. "What happened?"

"A scrab claw."

"It looks bad."

"I'm going to the hospital in a minute."

"Your brother said that you saved him."

"I had help," I said, tilting my head toward my friends.

"You've kept in touch with him." It wasn't a question. I nodded. "That's good," she said softly.

"Listen, I'm not going to give you my phone number because I don't trust you not to give it to Dad. But I'm going to send you my new email address soon, OK? Maybe we can . . ." I shook my head. "I don't know." I really didn't know what kind of relationship I wanted with Mom, and it was probably going to take me a while to figure it out. "I wouldn't mind hearing from you occasionally," I finally said.

She blinked back tears. "I think you should come for dinner. We should talk this out, as a family. Your father—"

"No," I interrupted.

"Just one dinner, all four of us. You don't just give up on family, you work things out, you try—"

"No," I repeated.

"Why not?"

"Because I don't want to."

She frowned deeply but didn't argue further. She was quiet for several moments, her gaze shifting to my friends.

"That boy . . ." she said, trailing off.

"Edan?"

"Edan. He looks very . . . rough. With the tattoos and the way he talked to your father." She returned her attention to me. "He treats you well?"

"Yeah, Mom," I said gently. "He treats me well. Thanks for asking."

Edan noticed us watching him, a small smile crossing his lips. It was strange to me that anyone thought he looked *rough*.

I returned my attention to Mom. "I should go." I gestured at my arm. "I think I need stitches." And we had to call Noah's parents. I took in a shaky breath.

Mom looked disappointed, but she hugged me tightly and then turned and quickly walked back inside. Laurence appeared at the door a moment later.

"We're going over to the hospital," I said. "I'll call you later."

"OK."

I walked back over to Edan, slipping my arm around his waist as we headed to the van. I waved to Adriana, who had joined Laurence on the church steps. She smiled as she waved back.

"Everything OK?" he asked quietly.

"Yeah," I said. "Everything's OK."

29

We all went to Charlotte for Noah's funeral. Maddie got permission from his parents for us to attend, but confessed to me that she was worried about Noah's family being hostile to us. I wouldn't have blamed them.

But they seemed genuinely pleased that we were there, and his mom even invited us to their house after the service. His brother and sister wanted to hear stories about the team, and they didn't seem surprised when I told them that Noah was the best one and we all assumed he'd been added to keep the rest of us alive. Apparently, he'd been famous at his high school for taking down football players twice his size in combat class.

I stood in the doorway of the kitchen, listening as Priya told the crowd gathered around the table about Noah saving her on one of our first assignments. I turned to the living room, where the news was playing on a television no one was really paying attention to. It was muted, but the subtitles were on.

"The president of MDG was arrested today, along with several others, in connection with their scrab creation program," the man said to his two guests. "And Julian Montgomery has denied any knowledge of MDG creating the scrabs. He was Roman Mitchell's protégé in the security division, and it's been revealed that Mitchell was fully aware of the program. Do we believe Julian?"

"I really don't know at this point," a blond woman said. "I'm honestly still trying to figure out why he released the scrabs in Dallas. He was from a good family, he had a good education, he basically had everything going for him. What causes someone like that to turn around and suddenly stage a violent attack against a bunch of innocent people? It's mind-boggling."

"I can't imagine," Maddie said, and I turned to see her standing on the other side of the door frame, eyes on the television. "Completely shocking. Who could have seen it coming?" She rolled her eyes. "By the way, I just heard from Victor that he's been bombarded with requests for you to go on these shows and talk about Julian. Do you want him to send them to you?"

"No," I said, turning away from the television. Behind Maddie, I could see Edan standing in the kitchen, and I smiled as our eyes met. "I'm done talking about Julian."

~

After the funeral, we all went back to New York with Maddie. Partly because none of us really knew where else to go, but mostly because we just didn't want to split up yet. Noah's death had left a huge hole, and it felt like sticking together was the only way to fill it. It wasn't working, but at least we had one another for a while.

I woke up the morning of our seventh day back in New York to the steady sound of Edan's breathing. He was asleep next to me, rolled over on his side, his back to me. We'd gone to our original, separate rooms for about thirty minutes our first night back. My bed hadn't been touched since.

I had to resist the urge to reach out and trace my fingers down his spine, or over the tattoo on his shoulder. I didn't like to wake him up, but it was hard not to touch his skin when it was so close.

His phone chimed and he stirred, reaching for it and missing the nightstand completely.

I laughed softly and reached past him, turning off the alarm. He rolled over and pulled me against him. I slid my arm around his waist and pressed a kiss to his neck as I settled into his arms.

"Did you sleep OK?" I asked. "Why did you set an alarm?"

"Better than yesterday," he said. "And I have that doctor's appointment this morning."

"That's right." Edan was running low on his anxiety meds, and his doctor was in the UK.

When Maddie's mom heard that, she made him a whole slew of appointments, including with a sleep therapist, a profession I'd never even heard of.

He slipped his hand into my shirt, pressing his palm to the bare skin of my back. "I may have set it a little earlier than necessary."

I smiled against his neck.

~

I sat on Edan's bed later, watching as he finished lacing up his shoes. I was dressed too, my hair still wet from the shower.

"I think I need to talk to Maddie today," I said.

He straightened, grabbing his wallet off the nightstand. "Yes, you do." He walked over to me, leaning down to press a kiss to my lips. I caught his belt loops, keeping him in place.

"I will. I'm going to."

He slid both his hands onto my neck. "She's going to understand."

"I hope so," I said, tilting my chin up to kiss him again. I smiled as he pulled away.

"I'll be back in a couple hours," he said.

I watched as he walked out of the room, and then left to find Maddie. She was in the dining room off the kitchen, her laptop in front of her. She'd started working in earnest yesterday, and had been talking about going to Germany in the next two weeks.

I slid into the seat next to her. "Can I talk to you for a minute?" I asked.

"Sure." She glanced up from her laptop, doing a double take when she saw my expression. She slowly closed the computer. "Is something wrong?"

"No, nothing's wrong." I turned so I was facing her. "But we need to talk about Germany."

"I've actually got a pretty good group together," she said quickly. "And your plans for recruitment and training are amazing, so I think we'll get a lot of new people once we put the word out. Plus, Scarlett said Brian will invest if we do the rebuilding teams."

"She told me. And that's great. But I'm not going to Germany."

She swallowed, but she didn't look surprised.

"Not if you go in the next two weeks," I said. "We don't have the numbers yet. And Noah was going to be a huge part of the new training, wasn't he? Even with the show?"

She blinked back tears. "Yes."

"We can't jump back in right now. We don't have the people, and we don't have the resources. You haven't even found housing for everyone yet. Or a gym. We haven't even started figuring out how to make rebuilding teams and where to put them."

"I can't just abandon all the work Grayson did. He believed in it, and I believe in it, and I just want to keep it going." She took in a shaky breath.

"I believe in it too, and we can keep it going. In fact, I think we have a much better chance of keeping the teams together if we take a step back and restructure everything. And I really want to help you do that. But I won't go to Germany in two weeks."

She let out a long sigh and wiped a tear away. "Dammit, Clara, you know I won't go without you."

"Yeah, I know." I put my hand over hers and smiled. "You know what I'm really good at?"

"What?"

"Staying alive. And I know that if I follow you to Germany, and we build teams with so few people, with most of the experienced recruits gone, there's a really good chance that we're all going to die. So, I'm saving myself. And you."

She blew out a long breath, and then tried for a smile. "OK. We'll wait."

"Good."

"You're very bossy today, you know that?"

"You rubbed off on me."

"I really am a great influence on you." She let go of my hand and turned in her chair, looking at me seriously. "You have to promise me something, though."

"What?"

"You're staying here. You and Edan aren't moving out."

I hesitated, because Edan and I had definitely discussed

moving out. We had money saved, and neither of us was comfortable living off Maddie and her mom indefinitely.

"We can't stay here forever," I said. "And isn't your mom selling this place?"

"Eventually, but not right now. She's waiting a bit."

"Because of us?"

"And financial reasons, or real estate reasons, or something." She waved her hand dismissively. "Doesn't matter. Even if we did move someplace else, you'd come with us. I'm not taking no for an answer. My mom is super serious about it."

I shifted in my seat. "Edan wouldn't stay here before with Grayson because he doesn't like taking advantage of people and—"

"OK, first of all, it is not taking advantage to accept an invitation to stay with a friend," she interrupted. "Second of all, Edan will stay this time because you're here and he's not going anywhere without you."

I smiled, heat blooming across my cheeks.

"And I am counting on you to help me rebuild the new teams," she said. "So, you have to stay."

"I can still help you build the teams if I'm living somewhere else."

"That's true. Let me be clear. I want you to stay because you're my best friend and I love you and I want you to stay."

A lump formed in my throat, and I had to blink back tears. "OK," I said quietly.

"Yeah?"

"Yeah. Thank you, Maddie." I scooted forward in my chair, pulling her into a hug. "And I love you too."

She wrapped her arms tightly around my waist. "I know."

~

The next evening, Edan and I made dinner for everyone. Hannah and Victor came over, and everyone gathered in the large dining room to eat enchiladas. I emailed Mom for her recipe. They actually looked pretty good, considering Edan and I tore so many tortillas we had to send Dorsey out to buy more.

After we told everyone that we were putting off Germany indefinitely, they started talking about going home for a bit. Laila and Priya would probably leave in the next couple days, and tonight's dinner felt like a goodbye. For now, anyway.

Victor was playing his favorite video on his phone when I walked in with a huge bowl of rice. It was the one of Maddie doing an interview in Dallas, after a reporter had found us outside the hospital. He'd asked if she ever could have guessed that Julian was capable of doing something like this.

"We told you assholes repeatedly that he was violent and dangerous, and none of you would listen," she'd said. "Don't act all fucking surprised now."

People really should have known better than to put Maddie on live television at this point.

Edan brought in the salad and then slid into the chair next to me, throwing his arm around the back of it. Priya shoveled enchiladas onto everyone's plates and continued her campaign to try and get us all to come to Birmingham. Apparently, all her friends wanted to meet us.

"Alabama is not as bad as you've heard," she said.

"I'm skeptical," Maddie said, then laughed and dodged Priya trying to smack her shoulder.

I leaned into Edan, and he turned to press a kiss to my temple. We were staying put in New York for a while. Here, with Maddie and her mom. And Dorsey and Patrick, for now, though they were already talking about meeting Connor and a few of the other guys from the UK teams somewhere in Europe. Maddie said it could be helpful to have them there, available to scout possible locations for training and housing.

I didn't really have a plan, beyond helping Maddie put together new teams. And enrolling in high school equivalency classes, which Nicole had already looked into for me.

It was a strange feeling, just existing for a while. I'd told my therapist that I felt out of sorts, almost restless, and she'd said I'd gotten so used to living in a constant state of fear that normal life didn't feel quite right.

I thought sometimes about that night I joined the St. John's team. Laurence staring at me through smoke, the painting of Texas burning in the barrel. My choice could have gone either way, honestly. I was on the edge of just shrugging and saying "fine," to his offer to stay and going back inside.

I tried to imagine how life would have unfolded if I hadn't gone — summer school, and then senior year, and then there was just a giant blank. I had no idea what I would have done.

I didn't think I would have stayed, though. The St. John teams were the first really good excuse that came along, but there would have been others. I was smarter than I gave myself credit for, and if it hadn't been fighting scrabs, I would have found another way to escape, eventually.

Patrick went for a separate helping of enchiladas, declaring them the best he'd ever had. I smiled at him.

I didn't know if I would have ended up with friends like them if I hadn't joined, though. There was something special about a friend who helped you pull scrab guts out of your hair.

My therapist had asked me yesterday if I had any goals, anything I was going to do to combat the restless feeling I was experiencing. I told her that the only thing I really wanted was to keep the friends I'd made. To not let Laurence drift away. To confide in Maddie, even when it made me uncomfortable. To always let Edan know how much he meant to me.

To learn how to actually live a life, not just survive it. That was my goal.

Epilogue

EIGHT MONTHS LATER

CLARA PRATT'S FACE APPEARED ON THE SCREEN. SHE SAT AT A wooden table, a bright red wall full of family photos in the background behind her. Her dark hair was pulled back in a ponytail which swung to one side as she cocked her head at the camera.

"Uh, I think I'm live? Yes? Maybe?" She turned, showing the camera the small tattoo of flying birds on her left shoulder. "Edan!"

The camera caught only Edan's midsection as he walked into the room—his jeans and gray T-shirt.

"I'm live, right?" Clara asked.

Edan slid into the chair next to her. He cast an amused look at the screen. "Yes, you're live. You're still the worst at social media, you know that?"

"I'm getting better!"

"Yesterday your cousins told me you reminded them of their abuela."

"I like to think they meant that as a compliment." She pointed at the screen. "Everyone is sending laughing emojis now. I'm glad I amuse you guys." She glanced at Edan. "Do I just start whenever?"

"Yes," he said with a laugh.

Clara faced the screen again. "OK. Hi, guys! Thanks for

coming or tuning in or whatever you call it. As you have probably seen here and on Edan's Instagram, we are back in Guanajuato after spending the last month traveling around South America."

A voice off camera murmured something in Spanish, mostly indistinguishable. Edan and Clara turned to look for the source of the voice.

"Hey!" Edan said with a grin. "I understand Spanish well enough to know you just said my Spanish is terrible."

Laughter echoed from offscreen.

"He said that you just spent two weeks here, and then a month in other Spanish-speaking countries, and your Spanish is *still* terrible," Clara translated.

"In my humble defense, we spent a week in Brazil, which is a Portuguese-speaking country," Edan said.

"Anyway," Clara said, casting an amused look in Edan's direction. "Not the point. We are briefly back in Guanajuato and then on our way to the UK, as you guys heard in Maddie's video announcement yesterday. Edan and I are heading up the new rebuilding teams, which are the new teams focused on rebuilding communities destroyed by scrabs. I'm sure you all remember our old team seven teammates Priya and Patrick, who will also be joining us on the rebuilding teams. Sadly, Laila is off to a fancy art school this fall, so she will not be there, but she did design all of the merchandise you can find for sale on our website. Also . . ." Clara leaned back, looking for something. "Where is he?"

"Hold on," Edan said, jumping up and running offscreen. He appeared a moment later, pushing someone into the chair beside Clara. Laurence looked at the camera and then at his sister.

"What are you doing?"

"We're live. Say hi to the internet." Clara waved.

Laurence grimaced at the camera and then halfheartedly waved.

"Your poor social media skills are genetic," Edan said from behind them.

Clara put a hand on Laurence's arm. "My brother, Laurence, will also be joining us in the UK. Don't let this face he's making fool you, he's actually very excited."

"This *is* actually my excited face," Laurence said, with a half smile.

"I know," she said, patting his shoulder. She pointed at the screen. "People are sending heart emojis. I think that means they like you."

Laurence turned red and bolted from the chair.

"We scared off Laurence," Clara said to the camera with a laugh. Edan walked out of frame. "And Edan, apparently. That's fine! I'll just finish this video myself!"

She turned back to the camera as Edan's laugh faded in the background.

"Anyway, we will all be part of the rebuilding teams," Clara said. "Maddie and Dorsey will be in Germany for at least the next few weeks, heading up the new combat teams, so if you're joining those, you will see them soon."

She leaned closer to the camera. "There's lots of info on the website, and you can chat with one of our people in New York if you have questions. I know that some of you out there may be wavering about doing this, so if you're looking for a push, I'm here to give you one. Join us. Even if it's scary, even if you don't think you have what it takes. Whether you're super eager to help or you just want to make a change in your life, we would love to have you."

Her fingers appeared close to the screen. "I'm going to have to figure out how to end this live video now. Oh wait, I see how to do it." She smiled. "OK, friends. I'm signing off. Think about what I said. I hope you'll join us. It might be the best decision you'll ever make."

Edan bounded into the frame behind Clara suddenly, leaning his chin on her shoulder. "I came because I was worried you didn't know how to end a live video and were just going to keep it going forever."

"I figured it out!" She pointed at the screen. "Right? I just press that."

"Yes. I never should have underestimated you."

She smiled at him, and then the camera. "No, you shouldn't have."

MUST-READ SCI-FI AND FANTASY BOOKS

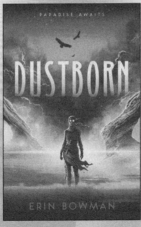